M000166974

THE SONGBIRD'S REFRAIN

Jillian Maria

Copyright © 2019 Jillian Maria

All rights reserved. No part of this book may be reproduced
or used in any manner whatsoever without the written
permission of the copyright owner, except for the use of
quotations in a book review.

First Printing, 2019

Print ISBN: 978-1-7338635-0-6

Edited by Bodie Dykstra. Book Cover Design by
ebooklaunch.com.

For information about purchasing and permissions,
contact Jillian Maria at byjillianmaria@gmail.com

byjillianmaria.com

This is a work of fiction. Names, characters, places, and
incidents either are the product of the author's imagination
or are used fictitiously. Any resemblance to actual persons,
living or dead, events, or locales is entirely coincidental.

For anyone who feels unseen, helpless, or like you can't possibly make a difference.

You *are* important. And you're more powerful than you know.

one.

"You aren't important" would probably never win the Most Optimistic Mantra award, but I found it comforting.

It worked like this: during fourth period, my teacher called me by the wrong name. After class, my academic advisor forgot about our appointment to go over college applications, so we had to reschedule. Then, on my way out the door, my phone buzzed. I checked it, hoping for news about the school's musical callbacks, but instead I got a spam email from a dating site that I was absolutely too young to be using.

After all that, a little teen angst seemed justified—or at least a *bit* of bemoaning this grand conspiracy against me.

Instead, I told myself, *You aren't important. None of this is a personal attack. Your teacher, advisor, and director aren't plotting Operation: Ruin Elizabeth's Day. They're just busy people with busy lives, and who are you? A high school senior with a decent*

1

GPA *and a hand that pretty much never goes up in class.*

You aren't important. Don't take it personally.

I rubbed at my shoulder, the fabric of my shirt gliding along the faded scar there. I glanced at the spam email again. At *least there are hot singles in my area who are dying to meet me.* I laughed, then looked around. The hallway was empty, and since my appointment got canceled, I had no reason to stick around. I hiked my backpack up higher on my shoulders and stepped outside.

The early October air nipped at my cheeks and nose. Shivering, I shoved my hands into my hoodie pocket. It was probably time to start riding the bus again, but I liked walking. Home wasn't far, and chilly air beat the clogged smell of hormones and gym socks any day.

I started walking, mentally listing the homework I had to do and the shows I wanted to watch after. It wasn't the best distraction from the missing callback, but I knew better than to dwell. *You aren't important,* I reminded myself, my hand snaking beneath my backpack's strap to rub at the faded scar on my shoulder again. I continued along the familiar route home on autopilot.

Until I saw the flier.

Even from a distance, seeing it tacked up on the brick wall made me stop immediately. It didn't look special—a bright blue eye, surrounded by peachy skin and gold text that I couldn't read from a distance, took up most of the space. But for some reason, looking at it made my insides curl like a tightly coiled spring.

It's looking back at me.

I knew, logically, that the eye was just ink and paper, but

2

it faced in my direction when not a single other eye did. No one seemed to even *wonder* what some scrawny teenager was doing stopped dead in the middle of an intersection while red numbers counted down a warning on the other side. They just moved around me, as unbothered as a stream flowing around a rock.

I rubbed numb fingers against my shoulder. I couldn't feel the concrete beneath my sneakers or the chill nipping at my cheeks. Hearing swallowed my other senses whole. Every voice, car, and footstep pounded in my ears, changing the shape of the breath in my lungs. No one caught my eye, no matter how frantically I looked.

I felt like a ghost. I could fade away, right there, and not a single person would notice.

My eyes drifted to the flier again. It felt like the only thing keeping me from disappearing into my own insignificance. I walked toward it, stealing every breath like a drowning woman swimming toward a life preserver in the middle of a choppy sea. It felt like it took far too long to reach the sidewalk.

I reached out until my fingertips brushed against the rough brick wall. The sounds of the city grew louder, threatening to sweep me away. My eyes scanned the dark gold script that arched over the thin blonde lashes like a tattoo on peachy skin.

Come see the extraordinary.

"Curious?"

The voice flung me back to my senses with all the grace of an airplane crash. I spun around to face a woman wearing workout clothes and a smirk.

Heavy lids drooped over her charcoal-colored eyes, and long brown hair clung close to high cheekbones dotted with several beauty marks. She looked cool and confident, like the twenty-somethings I saw on visits to college campuses. I felt very aware of how I must have looked next to her, with my overlarge school hoodie and untied high-tops.

Whatever had come over me when I looked at the flier was over. I didn't feel dazed or disassociated, just confused. I looked around, trying to confirm that it was *me* she meant to look at with that amused expression.

"I didn't mean to scare you." The humor in her voice suggested that she had very much meant to scare me. "I just couldn't help noticing you looking at our flier."

"Oh." I tried to think of something else to say. All I could come up with was *I hope that email about hot singles dying to meet me was telling the truth.* If I had any lingering doubts about being a lesbian, this woman could have crushed them without breaking a sweat—both metaphorically and literally, if her muscles were any indication. They were *very* visible in her light gray tank top, the kind with wide armholes showing off the bright orange sports bra underneath. *How isn't she cold in that?*

That wasn't even close to why I looked. *Eye contact, Elizabeth. Don't be a creep.* I swallowed hard. "Well, uh, yeah." *That was almost an actual sentence. Progress!* "I was walking home, you know, and I just—I saw it, and I got, I guess you could say—"

"Curious." Being cut off felt like more of a mercy than an insult. I was relieved that she managed to follow any of that.

My nerves loosened their grip on my tongue. "Yeah."

The woman leaned against the wall. The fabric of her tank top shifted, revealing defined abs through the low-hanging armhole. *Oh God, was I staring again? You were totally staring again. Get it together!*

I looked back up in time to see her lips curl into a sly grin. I tensed, sure she would call me out on gawking at her. Instead, she crossed her arms behind her head and flexed. At least I got to gawk in the general vicinity of her face this time—and I sort of got the sense that she wanted me to gawk. *Sure, uh-huh. Go ahead and justify it.*

"Well," she drawled, cutting off my mental scolding, "I'm glad you're curious. Not a lot of people look twice, to tell you the truth." She sounded almost wistful in a way that felt immediately familiar. *No way. You think this gorgeous woman feels as unnoticed as you do?* People probably looked at her all the time. I certainly couldn't stop.

She straightened in a fluid movement, like a darting snake, and held out a hand. "Bridget."

"Elizabeth."

I scrubbed my palm on my jeans. Judging by the look on Bridget's face when our palms met, it didn't do much good, but she didn't say anything. She just gave my hand a firm shake before releasing it.

I decided to ignore it, too. "So you're part of this . . . Um?"

It occurred to me that I still had no idea what the flier actually advertised. I turned back to it, a little wary. But the weird trance didn't return. *Maybe it's because Bridget is here?* I moved a little closer to read the sloping gold text. Above the eye, it said, *Come see the extraordinary*—the same words I read before.

Underneath the eye, it read 8:00 p.m., today's date, and an address I recognized as the old Filmore Building on 39th Street. *Is that place still open?* It certainly looked closed from the outside. I'd only been inside once, for a choir recital back in fifth grade, and it was pretty rundown even then.

Before I could ask, Bridget laughed, and the rough, sultry sound pretty much drove any other thought out of my head. *God, does she do that on purpose or is it just how she is?*

"Descriptive, isn't it?"

"Sure." I probably would've agreed if she told me the sky was purple. Warmth rushed to my cheeks. "I . . . I mean—"

She laughed, softer this time. It came across as kind instead of teasing. "I know what you mean, Elizabeth." Ridiculously, my heart fluttered a little at the sound of my name. She turned, shaking her head at the flier with a smile. "We're . . . unconventional." She wiggled her eyebrows for effect, like the dramatic pause wasn't enough. "We like to catch people off guard."

I could have figured that much out on my own. But I liked the way she said it, like it was an inside joke between us. I looked back at the flier, shifting my weight from one foot to the other. "So what is it? A show or something?"

"Or something," Bridget echoed, almost purring. "Maybe *and* something would be better."

I tried on a smile. "It sounds like you like being . . . unconventional." I mimicked her dramatic pause from before, and Bridget grinned. It made me feel weirdly mature.

"You could definitely make that argument." Her smile betrayed her solemn tone. I laughed, covering my mouth with my knuckles.

"What kind of show is it?"

Bridget paused for a long moment, tapping her chin. "Hard to explain," she finally said. "And I'm not being difficult here, I promise. You can't narrow down what we do to a single word or phrase. The Mistress finds things to suit *all* tastes."

"Oh God, this isn't one of those weird sex things, is it?"

For a second, I thought my cheeks would actually combust. Whatever momentum my not-entirely-socially-inept train had been gaining came to a screeching, fatal halt.

Seconds ticked by in silence. Bridget's eyes widened, her lips spreading in a grin. I had plenty of time to regret all my life choices before she started roaring in laughter.

If the sidewalk had decided to buckle beneath me and swallow me whole, I probably would've thanked it. By the time Bridget finally got her laughter under control, actual tears beaded in the corners of her eyes. She wiped at them, shaking her head. "Sorry, sorry. It's just . . . *No*, Elizabeth, this is not 'one of those weird sex things.' You're a little on the young side for me to be inviting you to something like that, aren't you?"

Any time now, sidewalk. I pressed a palm against my overheated cheek. If talking to her before made me feel cool and mature, now I felt like a kid who got caught trying on mommy's clothes. "I'm sorry! I just . . . *Wait.*" I took a moment, letting her words sink in. "Inviting me?"

"Why not?" Bridget reached up and plucked the flier from the wall. "You seem interested. We like it when people are interested." If her eyes really had been charcoal, her look could've sparked. "*I* like it when people are interested."

7

"Wow! I, uh . . ." I didn't know how to respond. *Why is she giving me that instead of letting me take a picture or something?* That would've made more sense—I assumed they wanted other people to see it, too. But I liked that she offered it to me. It made me feel special. Or, well, important.

Huh. Okay, starting to get the appeal now.

"Take it," Bridget said. "And come tonight, if you want. I'll be keeping an *eye* out for you. Heh, get it?" She wiggled the flier. The bright blue eye stared up at the sky.

But somehow, it still felt focused on me. Maybe it still had some of that hypnotic power after all, because it was in my hands before I even registered that I'd taken it.

I looked up. "Thank . . ."

But Bridget had disappeared, leaving me with only the flier in my hands.

It was a little like waking up from a dream. I blinked, suddenly aware of the sounds of the city, the passing people. The straps of my backpack dug into my aching shoulders. I checked my phone, shocked by just how long Bridget and I had talked. I crumpled the flier and shoved it into my hoodie pocket as I started for home. *I hope mom isn't worried.*

But mom wasn't worried. When I walked through the front door fifteen minutes later, she was sitting at the kitchen table, grading papers. She didn't look up from them as she greeted me.

"Hi, honey. How was school?"

"Good." I shifted my backpack. "Sorry I'm late. There was this . . . this, um . . ."

What was I supposed to say? *Hey, Mom, this super gorgeous woman offered me a flier to a show that I'm still not one-hundred* percent convinced isn't an orgy or something, and I'm actually seriously considering going because, uh, surprise! I'm super gay! That didn't really seem like the best way to come out.

Instead, I stopped talking.

"That's nice, honey," Mom said.

I walked away, trying to ignore the goosebumps shivering up my arms. All at once, my familiar kitchen, with its marble tabletops and cheesy black-and-white tiled floor, felt more like a movie set than my home.

She didn't look up at me. Not once. I walked into my bedroom, dropping my backpack at my desk and rubbing hard at my shoulder. Mom was *busy*. It wasn't personal.

You aren't important. Somehow, the mantra didn't comfort me like it usually did. *Maybe it only worked because you'd never actually felt important before.* I didn't realize how great it could feel when you were being more than tolerated—when you were being *enjoyed*.

I tried to focus on homework. But by the time Mom called me downstairs for dinner, I hadn't finished a single assignment.

During dinner, I tried starting up a conversation. My parents didn't ignore me. They didn't even act disinterested in what I had to say. But the topic just fizzled out, again and again. It was sort of like talking to an NPC in a video game, where you couldn't talk past a few scripted lines.

I excused myself as soon as I could and went back up to my room. As I did, I thought of a single phrase.

Come see the extraordinary.

I told myself I wasn't really considering going. Swapping out my baggy school hoodie for a nicer striped one, I thought

9

about the homework I had to do. I told myself that I had to wake up early tomorrow as I ran a brush through my dark brown bob, combing through the straight bangs across my forehead.

Elizabeth, you can't go running off into the night just because a cute girl asked you to.

But I was hardly thinking of Bridget at all. I was thinking of the homework I'd do tonight and the shows I'd watch when I finished that. And how I'd do the same thing tomorrow night and the night after that. When was the last time I actually left my house for something that wasn't school-related?

My room was comfortable, and it was mine. I liked spending time underneath the star-shaped string lights above my bed. My familiar pale walls and thick carpeting felt safe.

But people who went on adventures, people with igniting eyes like Bridget, didn't make decisions based on what felt safe. They made decisions based on what made them feel excited—what made them feel *seen*.

I grabbed the crumpled flier and smoothed it out. The blue eye was what made *me* feel seen.

I walked downstairs, pausing only to grab the heavy purse hanging off my desk chair.

Mom and Dad sat on the couch, watching TV. I paused at the entryway. "Uh, guys? I'm going out, okay?"

For one wild moment, I imagined them turning around and looking at me—*really* looking. Mom would ask me if I had finished my homework (I hadn't). Dad would ask me where I was going (an abandoned, probably dangerous building). They'd both ask when I'd be home (I had no idea).

They would forbid me from going, and that would be the end of it.

Did I want that to happen? Or did I fear it?

Neither of them turned away from the television screen. Dad gave a vague wave over his shoulder. "Okay, Lizzie." The familiar childhood nickname felt as jarring as my teacher calling me by the wrong name. "Have fun."

I watched them. Bathed in flickering blue light, they looked as insubstantial as the picture on the television screen—like I'd be able to click them out of existence with the push of a button.

I rubbed hard at my shoulder, telling myself I was being ridiculous. Still, I laced up my black high-tops a little faster than normal, eager to be out of a house that all at once felt too large and too small.

two.

I walked past the Filmore Building pretty often. It was on the way to my hairdresser and a corner store that sold snacks. I knew it as an old relic, two stories of crumbling gray walls and tall, dirty windows.

That wasn't what I saw when I turned onto 39th Street. Instead, I saw something surreal, plucked from a stage set.

Someone had covered the building with velvety black fabric. It draped from roof to pavement, gathering at the steps in a shrouded entrance. Circular paper lanterns hung in strings all along the front, alternating blue and green.

People lined up down the sidewalk, let in by two greeters standing at the entrance. As I walked past chattering couples and groups, self-consciousness wrapped itself lightly around my chest. *Is it weird to go to something like this by myself? I mean, I have no idea what "something like this" is.* I wasn't the only one. The two guys at the end of the line sounded just as curious as I took my place behind them.

"It's weird as hell," the first guy said. "What sort of act only stays in town for a night?"

"No idea," his friend replied, running a hand through his bright pink hair. "Maybe they'll explain inside."

The first guy grinned. A tongue piercing flashed when he talked. "Nah, no explanations for this artsy shit. Probably just some overpriced entry fee to see a coffee bean in a glass case or something."

As the pink-haired guy barked a laugh, my stomach dropped. I hadn't even thought about price! I looked through my purse, feeling past pens and empty packets of gum until I found a crumpled ten-dollar bill. I hoped that would be enough. If I took the time to go back home, I might miss the show altogether.

The line shuffled forward until I reached the edge of the black-draped Filmore Building. Every paper lantern strung up along the fabric had something written on it in dark red ink. I squinted at the blue lantern closest to me.

Katherine. The same name repeated over and over in a thin, slanting cursive, spiraling all over the surface. *Katherine. Katherine. Katherine.*

The line shuffled forward a bit. I read the green lantern next to it. *Sandra. Sandra. Sandra. Sandra.* It went on like that, every lantern with a different name in the same handwriting. *Ariel. Krystal. Renee. Joanne. Evangeline. Margot.*

The two greeters opened the curtains just enough to let people in, then closed them too quickly to reveal what was inside. On either side of the entrance, two lanterns hung, one blue and one green. As the two guys ahead of me entered, I stood on my toes to read them. The blue one said

Alice. And the green one—

Elizabeth. Elizabeth. Elizabeth. Elizabeth.

I forced down the shock that tried to well up in my throat, digging my fingertips into my shoulder. It was a common name. With a wall full of girl names, of *course* Elizabeth was going to show up at some point. I didn't have to get worked up about it. I didn't have to notice that the green lantern was really more of a greenish-brown—hazel, the exact same shade as my eyes . . .

"Enter."

An age-cracked woman's voice came from behind the curtains, jolting me out of my thoughts. The people at the entrance looked at me, prepared to let me in. Mumbling a quick apology, I walked through the thick fabric, catching a whiff of dust and something like incense. The curtains parted and dropped with an audible *thwump* behind me.

For a second, it felt like the velvety fabric had swallowed me whole. It surrounded me in a small tent-like structure. I blinked rapidly, trying to adjust to the dim light.

A lantern sat on the table in the center of the room. And behind that table sat a woman who stared at me with wide brown eyes.

For a long moment, all I could think to do was stare back. She looked to be in her mid-twenties, with long, pin-straight black hair and sharp features that cast wide shadows in the flickering light. A thin silver chain with a moon pendant hanging at the end stood out against the dark olive skin of her neck. It caught the light and sparkled above the midnight blue fabric of her peasant blouse.

But I kept going back to her *eyes.* They didn't leave my

face once, not even to blink. Only the rise and fall of her breath proved that she wasn't a statue.

I stood by the entrance. Seconds of silence ticked by before I finally coughed. "Um . . . Hi. Is this where I pay? Because I'm not sure . . ."

"Pay." Hearing the cracked old woman's voice fall from her lips shocked me. She spoke with a slight British accent, her tone soft. "No. I'd dare to say that you've paid enough." Her chest rose and fell. "Leave your name here with me. You will not need it moving forward."

Unease dripped down my spine, like the first drop of chilled rain. I told myself not to be ridiculous. "I'm Elizabeth."

"Is that so?" Her tone remained stoic, her face unchanged. "It is too early to tell if that will make a difference, I'm afraid."

"Um . . ." I pushed my hair away from my face. "What's your name?" I felt a little stupid as soon as the words left my mouth, but returning the question felt right.

"Curious." The woman blinked. "Madame Selene is the name I am given." She paused for a moment. Before I could think of something to fill the silence, she said, "You sing."

My breath caught in my throat. "Yeah . . . Yeah, I do. How did you—"

"Your heart," Madame Selene continued as if I hadn't spoken. "It sings as well. A song of longing. But for whom? The echo of a duet . . ." The silence between us seemed to gain weight. "It draws closer," she finally said. "There is someone with a heart to match your own."

All at once, the air in the room felt a little less oppressive.

15

It felt like being in a haunted house and noticing the wires that held up a ghost or the zipper on the back of a costume. *She might as well tell me I'm about to meet a tall, dark, and handsome stranger.* She was an actress—a good one—but that was all.

Part of me wanted to laugh, not at Madame Selene but at myself for getting so worked up. But that would've been rude. Instead, I played along. "Well, that's nice. Do you, um, have any idea when I'm going to meet her?"

Using the pronoun gave me an unexpected jolt of happiness. How often did I get to say stuff like that out loud? I realized I was gay a few years ago but hadn't quite decided how to come out. I couldn't really drop comments like that, not without worrying about it being weird. But this woman would be gone tomorrow.

Madame Selene looked away from me for the first time since I walked in. "It's time to go on."

She turned around fully, bringing my attention to a curtained exit on the tent-like wall behind her.

I didn't know what to expect beyond it. And honestly, it was kind of exciting. *This is what you came for, right? You wanted something different, and this is definitely different.*

"Right. Um, thanks?" I stood, giving an awkward wave. Madame Selene didn't react. I walked through the curtain and into another little room.

Something crunched under my feet. I looked down to see long white and little yellow-green feathers coating the floor. Mystified, I looked back up.

This room was lit much better than Madame Selene's. Instead of a tent-like structure, the fabric clung to actual walls. And on those walls were paintings.

If I had to guess, I'd have said that the same person painted all of them. One showed a woman with dark, freckled skin from the neck down. She wore an old-fashioned green dress under a brown corset. Another showed a pair of entwined hands painted in thick lines, one with pale ivory skin and the other a warm brown. Yet another showed a pair of blue and hazel eyes gazing into each other.

Feathers coated every inch of the floor, all the same white and yellow as the ones beneath my feet. Except for the center of the room. There, a bright red feather sat untouched and pristine.

A shiver rumbled up my spine, and my stomach churned. I clutched at the scar on my shoulder.

Red birds used to terrify me. They still made me sort of anxious, even though I'd been dealing with the phobia for years—ever since a red bird attacked me when I was a little kid. I rubbed hard at the scar the attack left, forcing myself to look at the feather. *It can't hurt you. You know that it can't.*

But this feather was unnaturally bright and almost the length of my forearm. Even though I knew from my research that birds as big and bright as I remembered didn't exist . . .

So it's fake. And even if it isn't, the bird that it came from isn't here. Getting scared is stupid. It wasn't like someone plucked the feather from the edges of my nightmares and plopped it down on the fabric-covered ground. I rubbed at my shoulder again, reminding myself that the universe didn't revolve around me. This particular exhibit wasn't created with the sole intention of freaking me out. *You aren't important.*

I walked past it, to the exit on the other side of the room. I glanced back once at the painting of the eyes. The red feather loomed in the corners of my vision, making the old scar on my shoulder tingle. I moved on.

As I pulled the curtains apart, I heard a woman's voice coming from inside—soft and breathy, almost trembling.

"I understand now. I won't ever fly."

I stepped into another "tent." Sheer gray fabric dangled from the ceiling in a canopy. Inside it, two women sat, clinging tightly to each other.

My first thought was that Bridget lied before and I had walked into something sexual. Even though the women wore layers upon layers of fabric similar to what hung from the ceiling, watching them felt shockingly intimate. They clung to each other desperately, seeming to breathe in sync. Their lips hovered near each other but didn't touch. Instead, one of them—in a voice a bit lower than the first—spoke.

"I don't have the strength to wonder why." The two leaned into each other, foreheads brushing. Their lips still didn't meet.

I hovered near the entrance. Even though this was clearly a performance, I felt like I had walked in on something private. I didn't want to give away my presence. Instead, I watched as they pulled away, lips hovering less than an inch apart as they traded lines.

"I've longed for women and for men."

"I've started and stopped and started again."

"If they refused, I've moved along . . ."

"And if they did not, it did not last long."

"I've known heartache in all its forms."

"I've known melancholy and forlorn."

"But nothing compares to the pain that's revealed."

"From loving a woman who cannot be real."

The two leaned forward again. There was something in the poem, or maybe just in the desperate delivery, that left me with the same dry-mouthed feeling I sometimes got after listening to a beautiful song. Something in my chest fluttered, and I hurried to the next section before they could start another poem. They didn't glance in my direction when I moved—they just kept clinging to each other.

The next room was different from all of them. Instead of billowing like a tent or standing straight like walls, the fabric hung in many glowing flaps. Lights beneath flickered in strange patterns.

I walked over and opened one. It revealed a small television screen playing a fuzzy, silent, black-and-white video. The picture was so distorted I couldn't really tell what the video showed, but it looked like a small girl dancing in a tutu and lumpy tights and sleeves. The video looped after maybe ten seconds. I watched the girl trip and fall a few times before I dropped the flap and opened the one next to it.

This one revealed a young woman swimming in a tank of water, flinging herself up in the air, and diving clumsily back down. She seemed to be wearing a lumpy bodysuit, odd shapes dangling awkwardly from her form. But the video was still too fuzzy for me to figure out exactly what it was.

The next screen showed an older woman with a hunched, crooked back. She seemed to be sewing, hands shaking almost too hard to function. And she wore that same lumpy outfit that the rest of them wore.

Another showed a girl around my age. She was painting on a stage. Her outfit was even more misshapen—she looked like a pillow missing half its stuffing. She even seemed to be wearing lumpy gloves, which made holding the paintbrush difficult. I watched her fumble and almost drop it, leaving a sloppy line along the canvas that disappeared as the video looped.

No matter how many flaps I opened, they all followed the same basic format. *And I thought the rest of the exhibits didn't make sense.* Out of all of them, this one was by far the weirdest. Maybe because the video quality was too poor for me to actually figure out what was going on.

I opened five or six more flaps before deciding that I'd seen enough. I walked to the only part of the fabric that wasn't glowing—the exit to the next room—and stepped through into darkness and the sound of voices.

All around me, whispers echoed too quietly for me to make out what they were saying. I couldn't see my hand when I waved it in front of my face. I stood still, worried about bumping into something.

I turned around, figuring I'd open the flap from the video room and get some light from there. But even with my arm stretched as far as it would go, my hand only grasped at air. *Did I really take that big of a step when I walked in?* Something like seasickness swayed behind my eyes. I stumbled forward a few steps, hands grasping instinctively at the empty air.

The whispers grew a bit louder, and I could make out a handful of words. I also noticed a staticky drone underneath them as the volume grew.

"It's time—"

"Yes, yes, almost—"

"Do you think—"

"This time, she'll—"

"I hope—"

"*Shhhhhh!*"

At the sound of the hissing warning, every voice fell silent. Seconds seemed to swell into minutes. My heart pounded like it did during the build-up to a jump scare in a movie. When nothing happened, I took a few cautious steps into the dark. The silence sat hard against my skin, and finally I had to break it before it crushed me.

"Hello?"

As if in response, a woman started weeping.

An invisible hand grabbed my heart and squeezed. The weeping sounded closer, more immediate than the piped-in whispers. I stumbled forward into the darkness, trying to find the source. The sound grew louder.

My own eyes started watering in response. *Keep it together. What is with you? Someone's in trouble. Crying with her won't help.* "Hello? Are you alright?" The voice kept on sobbing. "It's . . . Hey, it's alright. Just . . ." The sobbing became even louder as I walked closer. The fist around my heart squeezed hard enough to crack.

My fingers brushed fabric. I grasped at it gently, expecting a shoulder or an arm. But it wasn't a person at all. It was the draped fabric that led out of the dark room. Her sobbing came from the other side.

"What's wrong? Are you hurt?" I clutched at the fabric but didn't quite walk through, waiting for a response instead.

The woman took a shuddering breath, her sobs winding

21

down to a wavering voice. "I'm sorry. I understand everything now. I'm *so* sorry."

I stepped through the curtains, the beginning of a question on my lips.

Sound and light hit me in a wave, practically knocking me over. Instead of a single sobbing voice, a crowd of people chattered. As my eyes adjusted, I saw them walking around and sitting in neat rows of fold-out chairs.

There was no crying woman—only a final black-draped room far larger than any of the ones that came before it. The black fabric gathered and ended at an empty stage.

three.

I stood at the back of the theater, looking around to confirm what I already knew—the woman wasn't here. I rubbed at my shoulder. *It was just an act. Part of the show.* But the thought felt hollow, like the promise of no pain from a doctor holding a needle.

A man in a black vest stepped in front of me. When I made eye contact, he gestured at me to follow him.

"Um . . ." I looked around. Across the room, an older man in an identical vest guided another person to their seat. *Oh.* "Right. Yeah, okay."

I let him lead me. I expected him to put me near the back, since the front rows already looked pretty packed. But the usher led me right up to the stage, motioning to a single empty seat in the center of the front row.

"Oh. Um, they aren't saving that seat for anyone, you don't think?" I eyed the people sitting to either side of the empty seat. The usher shook his head and gestured at the seat again. I gave in. "Okay . . . Thank you."

I awkwardly made my way to the seat. The people on either side of me chattered away in a conversational hum. They didn't seem to have a problem with me sitting there—or anything else. *They definitely didn't hear that woman crying. What's going on?*

I couldn't find answers in the muffled conversations around me. Or on the stage, a raised platform shrouded by thick black curtains.

I rubbed at my shoulder, taking a steadying breath. *Alright, Elizabeth. You know you can exaggerate things sometimes. Just think of how long red birds scared you. You're doing the same thing with this crying woman—imagining it as more than it is. The woman is an actress. You're being dramatic.*

By the time the lights dimmed, I almost believed that.

Two crew members pushed a target with a painted bull's-eye onto one side. From the other side, a figure strode in. I recognized her, even though she wore dramatic red eyeshadow and had her hair pulled up to reveal peekaboo strands of red, yellow, and orange.

Bridget stood in front of the audience, wearing a strappy sports bra and matching black shorts. *And I thought her abs were impressive before.* Heat rushed to my face.

"Hello, everyone!" Her eyes scanned the front row, and I swore they landed on me. "As *some* of you might know, my name is Bridget. And let me guess. You're probably expecting me to stand up here, give you some spiel, right? Tell you what this show is and what it means. *Well,* I'm not going to do that."

Two crew members with matching black T-shirts and

porcelain doll faces walked onstage. A girl came from the right, carrying a lit torch, and a boy came from the left, dragging a large rolling case a bit taller than he was.

Bridget spread her arms, fingers splayed. "I think explanations are *boring*. All I want to do is make you feel something. Happiness. Sadness . . ." The boy twin pushed the case toward Bridget. She pulled it in and flicked the clasp on the front. It fell open to reveal a wide range of knives, swords, and—

Whoa. Is that an axe?

Bridget looked up and wiggled her eyebrows. "Or fear."

She used a light, teasing tone, earning a giggle from the audience. But the giggle sounded a little nervous. Bridget's eyes, as cold and sharp as the weapons next to her, flashed beneath the stage lights.

"So, no," she continued, "I'm not here to lecture you. I'm just here to see how you feel when I do . . . *this*."

She spun in a single fluid motion, grabbing the axe and letting it fly. The audience gasped—the throw looked so uncalculated, so careless. I thought she'd have to miss, that the axe would go flying backstage or maybe hit one of the crew members.

Instead, it buried itself right in the center of the painted bull's-eye. The audience sounded almost relieved when they clapped.

Bridget grinned. "*Psh!* You guys haven't seen anything yet."

The girl twin held up her torch. The boy took a short sword from the case and touched it to the flames. The blade immediately lit up, impossibly orange and bright, but neither twin flinched even as several audience members did. The boy handed the blade to Bridget and repeated the process with a knife.

Bridget began to juggle them, teeth bared in a grin. A low, dramatic tune started up.

The twins lit another weapon and threw it in. Bridget caught it effortlessly, her hands never once faltering. By the time the case stood empty, Bridget juggled all of them in an arc so wide I started worrying they would brush the ceiling. *All this fabric has to be a fire hazard, right?*

But *Bridget* didn't seem worried. Grinning effortlessly, she tossed one of the flaming knives at the target. It landed right above the axe, flames spluttering harmlessly before going out. She continued, throwing a sword, a knife, a dagger. They spiraled around the axe with perfect accuracy.

When Bridget only had a few knives left, the girl twin added the torch into the mix. Bridget threw the rest of her weapons at the target quickly, then tossed the torch high into the air. It just barely missed the ceiling, flipping a few times before landing handle-down right in Bridget's hands.

Before the audience could even lift their hands to clap at this, she turned to us, pressed the torch to her lips, and roared with all the fierceness of a dragon.

Flames shot out from the torch in a great, blinding gust. Screams rang out all around me, not quite loud enough to block out the sound of Bridget's laughter. I flinched back, screaming as the heat washed over me, bracing against the pain—

Except the pain didn't come.

"Awww, what's wrong?"

I looked around, expecting lingering flames and burning bodies. But the fire Bridget roared over the audience had disappeared. Everything was fine. *I* was fine. I didn't have a single mark on me, and neither did anyone else. They all looked as confused as I felt, though.

Still patting instinctively at my arms, I turned back to Bridget. She grinned down at me—or at least it felt like it was at me—while holding the torch in one hand. "Like I said, I like to make people feel things, because half the time, it seems like people are walking around asleep. No excitement, no intrigue—no freedom from their own dull routines. They're all caged, and they have no one to blame but themselves."

I remembered the epiphany I had while looking at the flier. I knew exactly what Bridget meant.

"The next time you feel that way," Bridget continued, "remember me. Remember the girl who let you dance in the flames without getting burned."

She gave a final bow and left the stage to loud applause.

Several crew members joined the twins onstage, working quickly. While some cleared away the target and weapons from Bridget's act, others brought in two ladders. They climbed to the top and messed with the fabric hanging from the ceiling. Like magic, several strips of bright red silk dropped, dangling almost to the floor.

While they did that, two people in black leotards came onstage.

They seemed to both be in their early twenties, but that was where the similarities ended. Her pale skin seemed bright and blinding under the stage lights, while his dark skin glowed warm beneath them. Her dyed blonde hair fell past her shoulders in straight, jagged layers; his dark, natural curls didn't even brush his ears. She looked out at the audience with teeth bared in a bold grin; he gazed out with a sweet, almost shy smile. Even their black leotards seemed to oppose each other—his was modest and sleeveless while hers had long, solid dark sleeves but sheer fabric almost everywhere else.

The girl waved. "Hello, everyone! I'm Violet, and this is Mark. Are you guys having a good time tonight?" Good-natured applause echoed through the auditorium. "Awesome." She glanced over her shoulder as the crew members walked offstage, carrying the ladders with them. "Looks like we're all set! You ready, Mark?"

Mark nodded. Dramatic, sweeping music started up, and the two bowed to each other. Then they moved perfectly in unison, twirling away from each other, toward the red fabric. They both gripped separate strips, and somehow, those strips lifted them up into the air.

The strips of silk glided across the fabric-covered ceiling in a way that just didn't seem possible. Mark and Violet spun, creating an intricate dance where they complemented each other but didn't touch. They swung in matching arcs and jumped from one strip to the other. The silky strands curled together and then parted before the figures on the ends could meet. At one point, Violet hung upside down with her feet locked in the fabric while Mark swooped below her, reaching up so their fingertips could graze.

Finally, as the music reached a crescendo, they met. They crashed together gracefully and twirled. The red fabric surrounded them, hiding them from view as the song ended.

The audience clapped slowly, almost hesitantly, like they were waiting for something. I kept expecting Mark and Violet to emerge from the fabric, but they didn't. The stage remained still and silent.

People started to whisper, and I shared their worries. The move had looked calculated, but what if it wasn't? Were they stuck in there?

Then I heard the music playing almost too quietly to be heard.

I strained forward in my seat, trying to hear. It slowly grew louder, audience members taking notice one by one. I heard an unfamiliar instrument that sounded only a little like a violin.

As the audience fell silent, it got even louder. I didn't recognize the gentle, lilting tune, but it set off something warm and familiar in my stomach anyway, the way all good songs seemed to. I almost felt lyrics perched inside my throat, like they longed for me to sing them. The melody soared above our heads, then landed gently, like a bird touching down on soft grass.

And then, right as the tune paused, the red fabric dropped.

Violet and Mark were gone. The red fabric danced across the stage, twisting into a shape that was vaguely human. It shifted, and with a graceful whisper, it *became* human.

Like the gods in myths, breathing life into a statue, the silk became a woman in a red dress.

Even standing still, she seemed full of life and movement. Auburn hair spilled over her shoulder like a waterfall, one bare foot pointed and ready to twirl. Her brown skin soaked up the stage lights, like sunlight sparkling against half-buried gold. She stood with her face pointed toward the light and her eyes closed, showing only full lips and a slightly pointed nose.

She captivated everyone in the audience, regardless of gender or sexuality. I didn't feel attracted to her, exactly. The way she commanded attention went beyond attraction and into something I couldn't even begin to define.

The music began again. She opened her eyes and began to dance.

Usually, when people danced, they followed the music. But when she danced, the music followed her. With every twirl, with every glance, with every wave of her hand, with every flare of her dress, the tune swelled and ebbed and submitted to her will. And so did everyone watching her. Every member of the audience sat in captivated, stunned silence.

The woman on stage lifted her hands. Stage lights twirled around her as she continued to dance, reds and greens and blues that entwined and separated in an intricate duel. When the song hit its final, low note, the red light swallowed the rest, covering the entire stage except for the bright, colorless spotlight that surrounded the woman.

I knew who she was before she even opened her mouth. How could she be anyone but the leader Bridget had mentioned?

"I am the Mistress." Her voice, low and sultry, carried easily. She scanned the room with dark eyes set high on her face and lined elegantly with gold. "I began this show many years ago because I value art in all of its forms. Since then, our exhibits have grown and performers have come and gone. But nothing is more special to me than our final act."

She paused. The silence felt like a tangible, physical thing, her voice a knife that cut through it.

"Our final act," she continued. "A final work of art. She's different from anything you've ever seen before, but do not let that frighten you away, because art is about finding beauty in the strangest, most frightening of places. If you listen to her tale, I'm sure you'll find that this is true."

She turned, nodding at someone offstage before striding out of sight in the opposite direction.

Two crew members walked across the stage, pulling a large birdcage on a wheeled platform. Bell-shaped with thin gold bars, it stood taller than them by quite a bit. A large pile of white feathers lay inside, rattling softly back and forth as the cage moved. It stopped in the center of the stage, but the feathers still seemed to pulse. It almost looked like they were breathing.

The mass sat up. It opened its eyes. My heart strained against its own cage, pressing hard against my ribs.

It *was* breathing. It was a *person*.

Blue eyes peered out of the mass of white—the exact shape and shade as the eye on the flier.

four.

few people gasped, but I couldn't make a sound. My breath had turned to ice in my throat.

The feathered woman sat on the floor of the birdcage, slumped like she could hardly hold herself up. Those bright sky-blue eyes scanned the front row. When they landed on me, she trembled, face contorting into a pained frown. I felt the most insane urge to reach out, to comfort her. I sat on my hands instead.

"Once upon a time," she began in a forced, rough voice, like she had to physically choke the words out, "there was a princess who lived high up in a tower, locked away from the rest of the world."

She closed her eyes. Her low, sweet-toned voice trembled for a moment. When it did, I recognized it. She was the woman I heard sobbing in the dark room. *Of course.*

The audience stayed silent as she continued. "She was lonely, but not for long. She gained a friend—a beautiful person with the ability to turn into a bird." She paused for a moment, opening her eyes and glancing down at her feathered body. "A bird that could fly."

Listening to her speak was *so* much more powerful than looking at a picture of her eye from across a crowded intersection. I didn't just feel seen—I felt *understood*, down to my bones, in a way that I couldn't logic myself out of.

The feathered woman wrapped her arms around herself, bowing her head. But her voice still came out clear. "The two could not be more different. The princess was trapped, unable to ever leave her room. Her friend was free to fly wherever they pleased. And yet, every day, when the princess woke up, she would find her friend sitting at her window."

The story should have been a happy one. But the feathered woman looked like she was about to cry. My own throat ached in response.

"The two fell in love," she continued in a low, trembling voice. "And one day, the princess asked her lover, 'Why? Why do you love me?' Her lover responded, 'What do you mean?'"

Her voice changed subtly as she spoke the characters' lines, bringing them to life.

"The princess said, 'You could love any person that you so choose. You could love no one and touch the sun. And yet you return to me, again and again. Why?'"

The feathers around her eyes shifted as she scanned the front row again. When she spoke next, her voice was almost too quiet for me to hear. I strained forward in my seat.

"Her lover responded with the warmth of a thousand suns in their voice. 'My darling,' they said."

Her eyes landed on me. This time, she did not flinch away. The soft accent that she had used for the lover's voice faded away, and there was only her.

"'I don't want to be a bird if I cannot choose who flies beside me.'"

Her eyes held mine, drawing me in just like the printed eye on the flier had. But this time was different. She *actually* saw me. My breath shifted to keep pace with the trembling of her feathers.

I didn't know how long it took for her to finally break the silence. But when she did, her voice rang hollow, like words of comfort over a coffin. "And so the two lived happily ever after."

The audience's applause sounded too loud as the Mistress swept onstage. She reached out to caress the golden bar of the birdcage. Tears welled up in the feathered woman's eyes as she flinched backward.

"Thank you for coming," the Mistress said. "Goodnight."

Stage lights glinted off her bared teeth for a moment before dimming. Right before everything went dark, I heard the feathered woman sob.

I leaped to my feet, sure that others would, too. They had to realize that something was wrong. Maybe some of them *had* even heard her crying in the dark room, and they'd know that she needed help.

Others did stand, but only to clap. The house lights went up, revealing drawn curtains and an empty stage. I tried to find at least one person who looked as disturbed as I felt. But no matter where I turned, there were only cheerful smiles and eyes that skated over me, like I didn't even exist.

Cool night air chilled my shoulders, sending my hair into my face. The ushers had pulled open a curtain-draped exit along the left wall. As people filed toward it, their conversations washed over me in a wave.

"That was cool!"

"I didn't really get it."

"The story was sort of lame . . ."

"Holy shit, that dance, though!"

"Incredible!"

"Anticlimactic, I guess?"

"Nothing to write home about, you know?"

No one noticed that feathered girl, the way she flinched back, the way she cried—the same way that no one ever noticed me.

I took a deep breath, chilled air pouring into my stomach. Her eyes made me feel seen. And now, I was the only one to see her. Didn't that mean something? Didn't it have to?

No, Elizabeth. It doesn't mean anything. You don't know her. You owe her nothing. The rational part of me tried to argue, but it sounded distant and weak. My hands hung limp at my sides. The sound of her sobbing haunted me—I kept replaying the fear I had seen on her face, right before the lights went down.

It didn't matter if I owed her anything or not. I didn't want her to feel scared, like no one was there for her.

I looked over to the exit. The ushers focused on the leaving guests, nodding polite goodbyes. They didn't even glance in my direction as I inched toward the stage. *Of course they aren't looking. You aren't important.* I could have laughed as I pulled myself onstage, slipping behind the thick curtains.

They enveloped me, then swallowed me whole.

I couldn't find the stage when I moved forward. I couldn't find my way off when I moved back. Instead, I stumbled through what felt like yards of thick, bunched-up velvet arranged in the same narrow rows as a hall of mirrors. It felt like a more claustrophobic version of the maze of exhibits.

Velvet-choked air clawed down my throat, clogging my nose with the stale scent of mothballs. The space between the fabric and my skin seemed to get smaller, and so did the space between my heart and my ribs. *How is this much fabric even possible? How did they pull it all over the stage?* I wasn't even trying to find the woman anymore—I would have settled for finding my way out.

Then the sound of her crying started up again.

Just like in the dark room, the sound of her voice guided me. "Hello?" A desperate edge clung to my voice.

"No . . . Please . . ." I'd never heard anyone sound so broken. During her story, her voice wavered, but there was still something sweet and melodic underneath. Now she sounded hoarse and listless.

I pushed forward. Finally, I stumbled through the velvet and into a wide, black-coated room. The feathered woman lay in the center, curled up on the fabric-coated floor and sobbing.

I went to her, cautious, dropping to my knees when I reached her. "Hey . . ."

She didn't react. I moved to touch her, then stopped. Up close, I could see how the feathers dug into her skin like the roots of a tree. They pulsed in an almost sickly way, reminding me of the way open wounds felt. I drew my hand away, revulsion shuddering up my spine.

I looked around, half-wishing for someone to materialize, to help her. But we were alone. I was all she had right now.

"What . . . What can I do?" I spoke a bit louder, and she reacted this time, making a sort of choked sound. She shook her head rapidly, curling in tighter on herself and bowing her head.

"N-Need . . ." She finally choked out. I leaned down, trying to see her expression.

I reached out, then stopped again. Even if I ignored how disgusted they made me feel, those feathers looked painful. Would touching them hurt her? I didn't know. I didn't know anything. I leaned forward a little farther. "What do you need? I want to help!"

Finally, she looked up at me. Her eyes widened, and she clutched at both of my hands. The feathers radiated a sickening, feverish warmth, feeling every bit as disturbing as they looked. I forced myself not to pull away. I couldn't do that to her.

"Y-You," she sobbed. "I can't . . . It's . . ."

She gagged, like the words she wanted to say choked her. I leaned forward, squeezing her hands. Watching her sob was like watching a glass fall and knowing that I couldn't catch it before it shattered. Panic snatched at my breath.

"Hey . . . It's alright! It's alright!" It *wasn't* alright. Even the air around us sat wrong, heavy against my shoulders. It *smelled*, reminding me of the nursing home my grandma lived in during the last few months of her life. But the smell wasn't antiseptic or any kind of medicine. I didn't know *what* it was.

It's the smell of death, Elizabeth.

The thought startled me. It sounded like me, but it didn't *feel* like me. I looked around, half-expecting someone to be whispering in my ear.

The feathered woman drew in a shallow breath, her sobs shuddering to a halt. The silence that replaced them made my ears ache. I opened my mouth to speak, but she interrupted me before I could.

"It will start for you now, won't it?" She breathed out a trembling sigh. "I remember. God, I'm so . . ."

She made another wretched gagging sound, doubling over. Before I could think to grab her, she went limp, slumping ungracefully into my lap.

"H-Hey!" I turned her over, nausea coiling in my stomach. Some part of me knew what had happened even before seeing her closed eyes and still face. She moved like a rag doll, the sick pulsing of her feathers gone, the feverish body heat already fading.

She's dead. The strange voice that sounded like mine echoed in my head, pouring down my throat like cement.

"No . . . No, this can't . . ." I shook her gently. I couldn't comprehend this. Dying people didn't speak so clearly. They didn't cry so loudly. There had to be something, some transition between living and not. I missed something—I must have.

My hands fluttered around her like anxious birds, even though I didn't know what to try. CPR, maybe, even though I'd only ever seen that done on TV. But before I could do anything, the black fabric rustled. A low, throaty chuckle echoed, filling the space around us. I clutched the feathered woman's body closer on reflex. Something in the back of my mind noted mournfully that her feathers were already cold, colder than they should have been after only a few seconds. *This doesn't make any sense. It's a nightmare. It has to be.*

The laughter grew louder, stopped echoing, and became *present*. The fabric shifted, and the Mistress stepped forward.

On stage, she had been captivating, the very picture of grace and beauty. Up close, she still captivated attention, but in a different way. She radiated danger like the air before a hurricane.

She glided forward, too quick for me to even think of running. I hadn't even moved the feathered woman's body to the floor before she was in front of me.

The Mistress laughed, low and sinister. "So gentle with her! You needn't bother, you know."

She didn't try to reach out or grab me. That would have been almost easier to handle. Instead, she fixed me with her gaze. Up close, I could see that the outer edges of her irises weren't circular but diamond-shaped, filed to points. Brown faded to red just around her pupil. My stomach churned in disgust.

The Mistress gave an impossibly knowing grin. Then she spoke in the strangest voice I'd ever heard. It echoed with the force of a shout but hit my ears at the volume of a whisper.

"*On your knees.*"

My legs unhinged, and I landed hard, almost falling flat on my face. *What–*

The Mistress laughed, scattering my thoughts like they were a startled flock of birds. "Good," she said, her voice returning to normal. Then, in that echoing tone from before, she said, "*Stay down.*"

I tried to rebel against the command, but my mind seemed disconnected from my body. It felt like a nightmare, no logic or control. But I could smell stale velvet and death. I could feel the ache of the landing in my knees. *This isn't a dream.*

The Mistress circled me, her gaze crawling across my skin like an insect. "You're . . . quite the unimpressive one, aren't you? More so than most." She gestured to the prone body of the woman at my feet. "But maybe I'm being unfair. After all, the doves are always so much more captivating. You have a tough act to follow, if you will."

The teasing lilt of her voice reminded me of Bridget, but I didn't feel like a co-conspirator this time. I felt like the butt of a very dangerous joke.

"What are you talking about?" My voice squeaked, shrill and fearful.

The Mistress smirked. "Oh, I *do* love it when they're fresh." She cocked her head to the side. "We don't have the time to talk now. I have so much to get ready. It's time for you to *sleep.*"

The whisper-shout of her command echoed dizzily in my mind. The fabric rushed past me in a blur as I fell forward, vision already fading.

My hands landed on the cooling pile of feathers that had once been the blue-eyed woman, and I was gone.

five.

First, I felt sheets beneath me. Then warm fingers laced through my own. I heard calm, even breathing beside me, and I knew who it was. *Wait until I wake up and tell her about the strange dream I had, where we were strangers and she was a dove locked in a cage . . .*

Except none of that was right. There was no one beside me, and I wasn't on a bed. I opened my eyes.

Wherever I was, it was too dark to see. I wasn't lying comfortably on sheets but sprawled awkwardly across a cold metal floor. Something prickly poked at my legs, which were half-numb and curled beneath me.

My entire body felt itchy and *wrong*, like something else had taken control while I slept. Or *someone* else.

The Mistress.

Memories came flooding back. I tried scrambling to my feet, but they felt heavy and awkward after being stuck beneath me. I went clumsily to the floor again, but my movement must have triggered something. Soft lights started to glow all around me.

The lights glowed in blue and green paper lanterns. I recognized them as the same ones that were strung up along the front of the Filmore Building, only now they seemed to be glowing inside the feathered girl's birdcage. The thin gold bars, close enough to touch, cut through my view of the lanterns in front of me.

And a little farther back, they also cut through my view of the ones behind me.

And the ones to my sides.

The lanterns are outside the cage. I'm inside it.

The realization climbed up my throat like bile. I looked around, hoping for a different explanation, but none came. Above my head, the bars closed in a dome too high for me to reach. I sat on a gold circle of metal that was wider than I was tall and littered with long white feathers.

I heard a high, whimpering noise. A few seconds later, I realized it was coming from me.

The glowing lights stretched farther and farther away from me, revealing a black-draped space maybe twice the size of my house and four times as packed full of things. I recognized some of them, like the target to my left and a painting from the exhibit to my right. But there were other things, things I didn't recognize: a bookcase, a plush-looking armchair, a small wooden table with an ornately carved base. In the very back of the room, large, shadowy cocoons hung from the ceiling, several feet off the ground.

A pile of clothing sat on the ground a few feet away from the cage. A shudder crawled nauseatingly up my spine. My *hoodie is in that pile. My jeans, too.* My high-tops lay scattered to the side, one of them still laced with the sock inside.

I looked down, trembling and unable to stop. I wore a thin white dress and nothing else. I looked back at the pile of clothes and located my bra peeking out from beneath my hoodie. My eyes stung like they wanted to cry, and my throat ached like it wanted to scream, but I couldn't figure out how to unlock either.

Had I only been awake seconds, or had I been sitting there for minutes, piecing things together? I wasn't sure. Like the bookshelf off to the side, the inside of my brain felt like someone had taken its contents and thumbed through them with dirty fingers. Everything felt out of order.

I wobbled to my bare feet carefully, half-expecting to shatter into pieces if I moved too fast. I had to cling to the thin gold bars of the cage for support, the gaps only slightly bigger than my grasping knuckles.

Something like a sigh echoed through the space, even though my lips were pressed tightly together. The shadowy cocoons began to sway slightly. I squinted at them, stomach churning. *There, dangling out of the one on the left—is that an arm?*

"Finally stirring, are we?"

My heart leaped to my throat, and my already shaky truce with my legs came to an abrupt end. I tumbled to the floor, clinging to the bars to keep from falling flat on my face. I looked around for the source of the voice and found it almost instantly.

The Mistress grinned at me from the other side of the bars, off to the right. Behind her, Bridget strode in through black curtains. I caught a glimpse of the light beyond them before they dropped closed again.

Bridget made a dismissive noise in the back of her throat, face harsh in the dim glow of the lanterns. "*Finally.*"

My heart pounded against my ribs, as if cracking those could be the key to shattering the bars of the cage. I had seen how terrifying the Mistress could be up close, but the cruel glint in Bridget's eyes was completely new.

"What is this? Some kind of joke or something?" I wanted to sound angry, indignant. Instead, I sounded like a child arguing against their bedtime.

"Or something," Bridget purred, sickeningly familiar. "Maybe *and* something would be better."

I remembered loving how daring the glint in her eyes had seemed before. Now, the way she looked at me made me think of the way she looked at the target before throwing knives at it.

"Bridget . . ." I trailed off, hating the wavering tone of my voice. And what could I say? I hardly knew how to *feel.*

"*Bridget,*" she mocked in a strident tone. "Oh my God! One conversation and suddenly you think we're besties or something? What, you think I'm gonna take you shopping? Braid your hair? Play spin the bottle with you?"

She couldn't have been a further cry from the confident but friendly woman who had handed me the flier. "This . . . This isn't you." I immediately realized exactly how dumb I sounded. I had met her *once.* How was I supposed to know who she was?

The mocking gleam in Bridget's eye echoed my self-scolding. "Idiot." The word came out sharp, like a slap. "I'm whatever I want to be. The charmer. The nightmare. The *flame.*" She lunged for the bars like a snake. With a loud *clang*, sparks flew from her hands. I flinched back, covering my face and crying out.

"That's enough, Bridget."

The Mistress's voice hardly rose above a whisper, but it startled me as much as a shout. Bridget backed off immediately, her expression rearranging into something polite and respectful.

"Of course, Mistress."

The Mistress strode forward on silent, bare feet. A silky black dressing gown billowed around her legs like a storm cloud. She reached up, tapping a long red fingernail against the bar of the cage. My stomach curled itself into a hard knot.

"What is this?" My words came out in a rush, almost a sob. "Why are you doing this? Why am I here? Why did you *take* my *clothes?*"

The Mistress seemed amused by the last question, red lips quirking up. "One of my employees redressed you." She raised a single, well-groomed eyebrow. "Don't fear, little bird. Redress you is all they did. They are quite respectful, unless instructed otherwise."

Something about this made Bridget snicker, but the sound seemed to come from a million miles away. The fact that someone replaced my clothes while I slept made me feel violated, yes, but what happened to my body felt minor compared to what happened to my *mind.*

She told me to sleep. She said "sleep" and it was that easy, like she flipped a switch, and what else can she do? I still feel her. The

45

inside of my skull feels like a smudged windowpane–

The Mistress's amused voice interrupted my racing thoughts. "You seem as though you have a lot to ponder, little bird. I wouldn't want to interrupt that, would I? I just have a few questions before I leave you to your own devices. So, what kind of bird are you?"

Her words felt like something out of a nightmare, nonsensical but horrifying. "I-I don't–"

Something that might have been annoyance flashed across her features. "I don't think you want to make me ask you again, little bird." She grinned. "Not using *that* voice." She dragged a fingernail slowly up the bar, her insinuating tone tracking a similar path along the inside of my skull.

"Don't." My skin prickled with goosebumps so hard I thought they might break open. "Please, I'll tell you whatever you want. I just don't know what you're *talking* about."

Bridget let out a short bark of laughter. "*God,* this one's slow." She rolled her eyes, casting a conspiratorial gaze at the Mistress. When the other woman gave her half of a grin, she lit up like a fireworks display. She turned back to me with renewed energy. "Come on, don't keep the woman waiting! What do you do? Writer? Dancer? Mime? Living statue?"

Desperation forced the answer out before magic could. "I'm a singer. I sing." I had never felt less like singing in my life, but it was the only thing that seemed to fit.

Something cut through the amusement in the Mistress's pointed irises. It flickered for a second—there and then gone. "A songbird, hm? It's been far too long since we've had one of those."

"Please, just . . . just let me go home." I knew that the

words wouldn't make a difference, but not saying them felt too hopeless.

The Mistress smiled, knowing and superior. "This is your home now. It's where you've always belonged, little songbird. And while that is what you'll be known as from now on, I *will* need you to give me your name. Names have power, you see, especially when given by their owner. Will you tell it to me easily, or shall I force it out of you?"

"*Don't do it,*" a voice seemed to whisper in the back of my head. But I didn't have a choice. The Mistress could force me to do anything.

"My name is Elizabeth."

All humor fell out of the Mistress's face in a wave. She threw herself at my cage, teeth bared in a snarl. I had no doubt that Bridget could be dangerous, but when she leaped at the bars, it startled me. When the Mistress did it, I expected her to strike me dead where I sat.

"Liar!" she screeched, like a bird of prey. "Liar, you liar, *tell the truth!*"

She spoke in that commanding tone, forcing the words from my throat in a wail. "I am! I am! My name is Elizabeth!"

"Mistress?" Even Bridget sounded a bit frightened. "It doesn't mean anything, right? I thought—"

The Mistress cut her off, slowly stepping away from the bars. "It *doesn't.*" She took a breath, rage calming into cool contempt. "Of course it's nothing, my dear." Her tone made it sound like *Bridget* was the one whose anger had frightened five years off my life. "It's a common name."

"Right! Super common," Bridget echoed, too eager.

The Mistress turned back to me. "I don't care what your

47

name is, little songbird. It doesn't matter. Your fate will be the same as all the others, either way." She smirked, cool and collected, as if that shrieking, angry woman had never existed. "You're going to die in that cage."

She said it in a normal tone, but it felt as impossible to disagree with as that other, whisper-shouting voice. By the time I found my words, she was already striding toward the exit with Bridget in her wake.

I spoke without thinking. "You can't do this!"

The Mistress paused, glancing over her shoulder almost idly. "Oh? And who will notice you're gone?"

The certainty in her tone made me feel very small. But people didn't just disappear with no one noticing, not even people like me. "My parents will notice! My teachers, my classmates! I have a life!"

The Mistress laughed. "Do you, now? Well, it was easy for me to erase you from it. No one remembers you anymore, little songbird. I saw to it. It was almost too easy, you know. You are singularly *unimportant*."

My breath caught in my throat. It didn't feel like a lie. How could it, when I often told myself the exact same thing? The Mistress turned my morbid truce with my own insecurities into a weapon.

Her eyes gleamed knowingly. "Or maybe I'm lying." Her pointed irises captured mine. "Maybe I killed them all, little songbird. Did you think of that? Your parents, your teachers, your classmates—even vague acquaintances you didn't know you knew. Maybe I simply murdered all of them. It doesn't matter. It doesn't make a difference to you either way, because you're never going to see any of them again."

My breath stuck like glue in my throat. *Please don't let me cry.* The thought was almost childish. *She's taken every bit of dignity I have. Please don't let her have that, too.* "Why?" My voice wavered, on the edge of breaking. "Why are you doing this? What did I ever do to you?"

The Mistress's smile somehow managed to grow even colder. "You finally ask the question that matters. You'll understand soon enough."

And with that, she swept from the room. Bridget followed, leaving me alone.

Except I *wasn't* alone. As the curtains closed, two familiar voices called out softly from the back of the room.

"It will begin again . . ."

"Once she rewrites the end."

They were the women from before—the ones who recited poetry while holding each other. I scanned the room, trying to find them. "Hello?" I felt desperation, a longing for answers squeezing my chest.

They didn't speak again. But the hand—it *was* a hand—dangling from the shadowy cocoon in the back opened and closed in what might have been a wave. I recognized the wrappings as the gauzy gray fabric that surrounded them during the exhibit.

Oh God, they're in there. My breath hitched. *She's storing them in there like a bunch of old coats tucked away for the summer and—and—*

And she's doing the exact same thing to me.

Finally, the tears came, fast and hot. I hung my head and sobbed, hands curling into fists around the white feathers scattered across the floor of the cage.

six.

I screamed for help until my throat went raw. I tugged at the padlocked door until my shoulders ached. I tried to twist and contort my hands through the bars of the cage until the skin of my knuckles turned red and rough.

Nothing did any good, but I couldn't just sit still. I paced the edge of the cage, my thoughts going in the same circles as my feet.

There has to be a way out.

Are you kidding yourself? This isn't like those cartoons you watch. You can't bend metal bars like a superhero, and there isn't someone coming to save you. This is it.

I have to do something.

Like what?

I don't know. Throw myself at the bars of the cage?

It's too heavy to knock over, and even if it wasn't, would being in a sideways cage be any better than being in an upright one? Face it: you're trapped here.

But that can't be right. There has to be a way out . . .

My head started to swim, either from dizziness or my thoughts. I sat down on the cold metal floor, pulling my knees up to my chest.

I scratched at my shoulder—then my arms, my neck, my collarbone. I scratched until I left irritated marks all over my skin. It itched like someone had stripped it off and put it back on just a bit wrong.

Something moved in the corner of my eye—the entrance to the room. I scrambled to the center of the cage as the curtains shifted. Light flooded the room, half blinding me. A silhouette walked in and let the curtains drop closed behind them.

I blinked away the spots in my vision to see Mark, one of the dancers from the main show. He stood at the edge of the room, looking in my direction without making eye contact. His arms clung tightly to a soft-looking bundle, holding it to his chest.

"You're awake. I heard. And . . . yeah." He spoke so soft I had to lean forward a little to hear.

Silence sat heavy between us. I really had no idea what to say to him, what to do. My confusion about his nervous energy wiped my racing thoughts blank. So I just said nothing. After a few tense seconds, he eventually walked forward.

"I'm sorry? You're confused. I brought you this." He showed me the bundle in his arms—a thin pillow wrapped in several blankets. He slipped them through the bars one by one, the pillow just barely fitting through.

Every time his hands brushed against the metal, he

flinched slightly, like he expected the bars to open up and swallow him whole.

"Don't worry," he said as he pushed the blankets through. "She says it's okay for the—for you. To have these, I mean. You'll have to take them out later. When you—well, when you're moved. But I'll come back. To push them through again." He spoke in a nervous staccato, voice wavering and catching on random syllables. It reminded me a little bit of how I sounded when I had to give speeches in class.

I kept waiting for him to turn cruel and teasing. He worked for the Mistress, after all, and he didn't seem surprised to see me in here. But he didn't seem *happy*, either. It didn't make any sense, and part of me thought it had to be some sort of trap. But the nervous tremor in his hands and his voice didn't feel fake.

I had to say something, if only to test the waters. "Thank you." I pulled the blankets through. They were soft, but they still made my skin itch. "It's . . . um, Mark, right?"

His eyes flicked up to my face, then back down. "Yeah."

"Hi, Mark. I . . ." I trailed off, remembering how the Mistress reacted to my name. I didn't want another reaction like that, but telling him my name felt important. I knew it was common, but it was still *mine*. It was part of my identity, part of what made me more than just a victim.

Keeping all that in mind, I spoke.

"I'm Elizabeth."

Mark's eyes widened, his breath leaving him in a loud *whoosh*. He took a step back, toward the exit.

I spoke without thinking, wanting to get the words out before he bolted. "Does that mean something to you? The—

She—People. People are acting weird about it."

"It's nothing. Lots of people, you know. They have that name. It's—I have to go." Abruptly, he turned away and started to walk—almost run—toward the curtains.

"Wait!" The lanterns flickered a little. Mark stopped. I pushed on, hardly daring to breathe between words. "I'm sorry if my name, um, scared you. I didn't mean for it to. You're right. You're . . . it doesn't mean anything."

He didn't turn around to face me, but he didn't leave, either. I kept going, desperate to keep him, desperate to talk to someone who actually *listened* and reacted to what I said with something other than contempt. Someone who could, possibly, give me answers. I needed something, *anything* other than confused hopelessness and terror.

"Forget my name if you have to, okay? It's not important." *You're not important,* my mind echoed. It had never been easier to ignore—I had bigger things to deal with than a lack of self-esteem. "What's important is that I'm . . . I'm only seventeen, Mark. Just a senior in high school. I want to go to college, figure out my major, figure out my career. I want to get a degree. I want to move to a new city and meet new people. I-I want to visit Disney World, just once."

I couldn't tell for sure, but I thought Mark's shoulders trembled. I hoped that meant I was getting through to him. At least striking a nerve.

"There's a lot I haven't done, you know? And I want to. *Please*, Mark, let me out of this cage. I won't tell anyone about this. I won't get anyone in trouble. I'll—"

"I can't." Mark turned to face me. Guilt and defeat danced across his features as he tugged his sleeves over his hands. "I'm sorry. Really. But I can't."

I didn't have any tears left in me. His words just filled my stomach with a hollow, nauseous emptiness, like the yawning chasm beneath a crumbling cliff edge. "She'd hurt you if you did, wouldn't she?"

I didn't have to say who *she* was. He didn't have to answer. We both already knew.

Sighing, I wrapped one of the thin blankets around my shoulders. It irritated my itchy skin even more, but I wanted the pressure. "If you can't let me out, could you at least bring me some food? Or water, maybe?"

The pity lurking around the corners of Mark's expression flooded his face. Having that look trained on me almost made me uncomfortable, but I still preferred it to how the Mistress and Bridget treated me.

"Do you *feel* hungry? Thirsty?"

I didn't, actually. I'd only asked because I didn't know when I'd have another opportunity to. But once he mentioned it, I realized how strange it was. My stiff muscles made me think that I had slept for a while. I should've at least woken up with a dry mouth. But even though I felt wrong and uncomfortable on a number of levels, I wasn't hungry or thirsty at all.

Mark nodded like my expression had answered the question for me. "I *could*. Bring you food and water, I mean. But you don't need it. And it's better if I don't. You don't exactly get bathroom breaks. You know?"

A shudder worked its way up my spine. I ran my fingernails up and down my arms. "So, what? Am I just supposed to starve to death in here? Is *that* what she wants?"

54

Mark shook his head. "No. Do you know how long you were asleep?"

The question seemed to come out of nowhere. Even if it echoed my earlier thoughts, it didn't answer my concerns. "I . . . I don't. Why do you ask?"

Mark looked around, brows drawn together. I couldn't figure out if he wanted to make sure we were alone or if he wished someone else would come and tell me instead. When no one appeared, he sighed.

"You've been asleep for two weeks. If you were gonna— you'd already be dead. You know, if that was gonna happen."

Maybe this shouldn't have shocked me, considering what I'd seen and felt the Mistress do. But surprise still managed to steal the breath from my lungs, leaving my voice a hoarse whisper. "How? How am I alive?"

Mark's eyes widened. His shoulders tensed. His gaze flicked toward the exit, and panic clutched at my heart with icy fingers. I didn't want him to leave. Not just because I wanted answers, either. Mark offered me kindness—or he seemed to. I wasn't ready to go back to loneliness, to fear, to waiting for the Mistress or Bridget or someone not so kind.

"*Please*, Mark." My voice wavered and broke.

Silence stretched between us for what felt like an eternity. Finally, Mark sighed, hanging his head.

"It's magic, Elizabeth."

The silence in the wake of his words seemed very loud. I froze, not breathing—even my heart seemed to stop beating. I opened my mouth to tell him he was crazy, that magic didn't exist. Then I closed it, because how could I deny it? How could I say magic wasn't real when the Mistress had strung up my brain like a puppet, forcing me to bend to her will?

I couldn't deny it. But I couldn't *believe* it, either. Part of my mind continued insisting that I'd misheard, that there was a reasonable explanation for all of this.

"What?"

"Magic." Mark's grave voice wavered on odd syllables. "*Her* magic. Magic keeps you alive. Magic makes *all* of this possible. She's powerful. So powerful." Awe and fear swirled across his face like paint on a palette. "I can't really explain it. I'm sorry. But you'll see."

I opened my mouth, then closed it. Shock left my tongue numb and dead in my mouth.

He sighed, giving me an apologetic look. "It's a lot. I know. I need to—you should get some rest. Sorry." He turned away.

"What? Wait!"

This time, he didn't break stride. He just walked out of the room.

I stared at the curtained exit for a long time, half-wishing he'd walk back through or that something else would happen. I couldn't stand sitting here with my terror and confusion, with my maddeningly crawling skin.

The places where I'd itched particularly hard prickled. My shoulder especially twinged like something was crawling beneath my skin and trying to force its way out. It felt just as wrong as the inside of my mind after the Mistress had messed with it.

The thought hit me like a bucket of cold water to my face. Did the Mistress mess with my body along with my mind?

I looked down. White feathers were scattered across the floor of the cage.

"No."

The flier had shown peachy skin surrounding the blue eye.

"*No.*"

The eye belonged to the feathered woman. That eye belonged to her, which meant that the skin had to belong to her, too.

She hadn't always looked like that.

"No . . . No, no, no." I ran my fingertips along the faded scar on my shoulder. Something poked out from the tissue there.

Even though part of me didn't want to, I craned my neck to look.

For a second, I couldn't process what I was seeing. In spite of everything, my mind just refused to believe it. I thought I was getting sick, that pus leaked out of the scar where I had scratched it.

But that wasn't it. Of *course* that wasn't it.

I heard the helpless little giggles a full five seconds before I realized they were coming out of my mouth. I clutched myself, desperately trying to stop the trembling that consumed every inch of my body. But I couldn't stop. I couldn't *breathe.* As I tasted salt water on my tongue, I realized that hysterical laughter and sobbing sounded and felt pretty much the same.

Little yellow-green feathers grew around the scar on my shoulder. And all over my arms—on my elbows, my wrists, and the sides of my fingers—my skin rippled and bulged in awkward, itchy lumps.

More feathers were waiting to sprout.

seven.

his has to be a dream.

The thought had no real conviction. I couldn't feel the metal floor of the cage in a dream. I couldn't taste my own fear and tears in a dream. And my subconscious was definitely not messed up enough to give me the feathers tenting beneath my skin and threatening to burst forth.

But I couldn't believe I wouldn't wake up in my own bed to the sound of my alarm. I couldn't believe I wouldn't start my day as usual—showering, singing along to whatever playlist fit the morning's mood, realizing I'd have to hurry to get to school on time when I got carried away, waving goodbye to Mom and Dad as I rushed out the door.

The thought put a lump in my throat, but I'd pretty thoroughly cried myself out earlier. I curled up between the blankets Mark left me, closing my eyes and hoping against hope that when I woke up, it would be in my own home.

The moonlight landed soft upon the trees, setting the leaves alight with silver warmth.

It took everything in me not to turn around. A foolish, romantic notion perhaps, but I could all too easily picture what Alice must have looked like behind me. Her elegant features would be tight with concentration, wisps of black hair falling over her forehead. I adored her no matter what she looked like, but I adored her most of all when she forgot herself, became lost in her art.

Alas, she asked me to look out the window for this, and I had never been able to deny Alice anything.

"The painting is done."

I turned around.

Alice beamed at me, spots of rosy pink set high on her pale cheeks. Paint freckled the soft white fabric of her blouse, which hung off her shoulders, and at some point, she had loosened the ties of her bodice—they didn't wear them in her region, I knew, so perhaps she found them uncomfortable. It might have been distracting, but her smile was so dear that it demanded all my attention.

"Would you like to see?" she asked, her blue eyes sparkling.

I nodded, walking across the room to her. What I saw on the easel made my heart stutter and sing in my chest.

Alice had painted me in lover's strokes, through eyes that saw me far kinder than I saw myself. The painted moonlight against my brown skin accentuated the freckles across my face, making them appear attractive instead of childish. Lush dark curls framed my face like a halo. There was something refined and beautiful in the arch of my back, the full curve of my skirts.

And there, in the hazel diamonds of my eyes, sat a look of utter peace, something I rarely felt.

I looked down at Alice. Her eyes were full of love. I felt myself falling into them, as I so often did, bright blue fading to something slightly darker right at the pointed tips of her irises.

"I love it," I said, and leaned down to press my lips to hers.

"I'm glad."

The voice of Alice—of that woman—echoed, then became younger. And I became myself.

My head swam like I had just stepped off the world's fastest rollercoaster. I felt very aware that, just a second ago, I had been someone entirely different—someone with freckled skin and curls, someone with pointed irises like the Mistress. It was a dream. It had to be. And so was this . . . whatever this was.

I floated, bodiless, in an unfamiliar bedroom. Outside the window, I could see warm afternoon light and distant mountains. The walls were pale pink, covered in sketches and pictures cut out from magazines. A desk sat in one corner. A guitar on a stand and a violin in a case leaned against a wall, with sheet music in a neat stack nearby. A twin bed with a plush comforter faced the door.

And lying on her stomach on that bed was a girl.

She seemed to be close to my age. She had her brown hair thrown into a messy topknot and she wore a soft-looking sweater with a skirt. She lay upside down on the bed, with her stockinged feet kicked up over the pillows. Lying nearby her head at the foot of the bed was a fat gray cat with a slightly squished face. The girl read to it in a silly, melodramatic voice.

"Madeline realized that Dahlia was close—close enough to touch. She could smell the scent of her perfume, something floral and surprisingly sweet. Everything about Dahlia was surprisingly sweet." She giggled, reaching out to scratch the cat on the top of its head. "Like you, Smush! My little grumpy-face."

Turning back to her book, she continued reading. Her eyes

scanned the page. They were blue, but unlike the two women in the dream from before, her irises were shaped normally.

"Madeline looked up to Dahlia's face, almost afraid of what she would see there. But once she looked into those beautiful violet eyes, she couldn't look away.

"'I'm very glad,' Dahlia said again, her voice husky and quiet.

"For once, Madeline didn't think. She simply closed the distance between them, pressing their lips together." The girl buried her face in her arms, giggling. "Finally! Smush, aren't you excited?" She poked the cat's cheek. The cat let out a quiet mew. "I know, right?" Giggling, she pushed herself up and smoothed out her book again.

But when she opened her mouth to keep reading, all I could hear was a metal ticking noise.

The scene in the girl's bedroom faded, and so did the sense of weightlessness and floating. Only the sound of the metal ticking remained. I groaned, hating how heavy and wrong my limbs felt.

The light metal sound stopped. Someone laughed, the sound crawling down my spine on thin spider legs. *The Mistress.*

"Good morning, little songbird!"

Dread as heavy as concrete filled my stomach, and I opened my eyes. Bridget stood right at the bars, knife held against the metal—the source of the ticking. The Mistress stood a few paces behind, wearing a smug smile.

Part of me wished, almost childishly, that I could just go back to sleep. That moonlit room with Alice or the unfamiliar bedroom would've been far better than this. Maybe some of my thoughts showed on my face, because Bridget laughed, twirling her knife between her fingers.

62

The Mistress only smiled. "Sit up, little songbird. I want to take a look at you."

I shuddered. As much as I hated all of this, I hated the thought of her using that whisper-shout on me even more. So I sat up, letting the blankets fall away from my body.

Bridget raised an eyebrow, head whipping from the Mistress and back to me. "Whoa! You outdid yourself, Mistress. This one sprouted really fast."

Sprouted. The word ached like a physical illness. I looked down at myself.

The bumps along my arms, my elbows, my wrists—they had all turned to feathers poking through my skin. The ones along my upper arms were the same yellow-green as the ones on my shoulder, but the ones at my elbows and wrists were gray. I held up my shaking hands. A few darker gray feathers were just starting to poke out along the sides of my fingers.

New bumps prickled along my knees and ankles. A few more bumps spotted my collarbone. The feathers around my scar were full length now, a little bit longer than my fingers.

My stomach churned hollowly as I ran my fingers along my face. When I felt little bumps along my jawline, I whimpered.

Bridget laughed again. "Aw, little songbird, you should be happy! You get to make your debut early. Way better than just sitting here!"

I didn't understand her. I didn't *want* to understand her. I turned to the Mistress. Her eyes, the diamond shape that I couldn't even escape in my dreams, sparkled with a cold sort of glee.

"*Move.*" Her voice echoed. I flinched, waiting for my body

to obey her against my will. But instead, my blankets and pillow lifted off the ground. "*Here.*" They floated through the bars of the cage, then dropped at the Mistress's feet. Her eyes flicked up. "*Move.*" The paper lanterns strung around the top of my cage spread out, hovering in the air instead.

Bridget watched the Mistress, eyes shining. "Oh! Can I call them?"

The Mistress looked down at her, smiling with a cold kind of fondness. "Of course, my dear."

With a grin, Bridget snapped her fingers, raising her voice. "This one's ready!"

As if they had been waiting, several crew members swept in. Most of them went deeper into the storage space, but two walked toward me. I recognized them as the twins who helped Bridget set up her act. The girl circled around to the back of my cage while the boy gripped the front bars. Together, they pushed me toward the back of the room, where the cocoons hung.

"W-Wait!" I didn't want to stay in the storage room, but I didn't want to go on to whatever they had planned for me next, either. Bridget's words echoed mockingly in my head. *What did she mean by my debut?* The answer danced out of my reach, kept away by fear.

My cage rattled past props and clothes and things I didn't recognize. My eyes skated across a broken violin on the ground, a pile of old sheets, empty tubes of paint. I kept searching, like I expected to find something that could magically help me.

Two crew members, a woman with silver hair and a man with broad shoulders, worked to lower the gauzy fabric cocoons from the ceiling. Behind them, at the very back of the room, another curtained exit sat along the wall. The fabric swayed slightly, and I could hear distant cars and wind.

The twins didn't pause. They just pushed me straight through.

Autumn wind bit at my cheeks. We'd exited onto a small, unfamiliar city street. In front of me stood a building covered in black fabric. It looked exactly like the Filmore Building, without the paper lanterns.

My stomach swooped like I was in free fall. Bridget's words, combined with their earlier questioning, suddenly made a disturbing amount of sense. *They're going to make me sing.* Stage fright was probably a stupid thing to feel, considering everything else that had happened, but I still felt it crawling up my spine on thin, shivery legs.

"Are you surprised, little songbird?"

A yelp clawed its way from my throat as I spun around. The Mistress and Bridget had followed us out. Behind them sat an unassuming trailer.

I blinked. The trailer looked too short and narrow to hold the storage room inside of it, but I could clearly see black fabric spilling out of the back. As I watched, the poetry women stepped out, gauzy veils covering their faces. More crew members followed, carrying props and paintings. From around the front, Mark and Violet came, Madame Selene trailing idly behind.

"Hey, the Mistress asked you a question! What an impolite birdy you are!"

Bridget's harsh, rasping voice grabbed my attention. I

opened my mouth, afraid that the Mistress would use that awful voice on me if I didn't respond. "I-I . . ." The word scratched against my throat.

Bridget laughed. "Doesn't sound much like a songbird to me!"

The Mistress only smiled, her eyes cool with contempt. "You *are* surprised. Surely you didn't think we were letting you stay here for free, did you? You have to work for such accommodating room and board!"

Her gaze seemed to have actual weight, pressing down hard on my chest. All I could do was stare back at her, feeling my heart hammer against my ribs.

Finally, she laughed, spinning around to walk into the fabric-covered building.

Bridget paused just long enough to leer at me. "Break a wing, little songbird!" Then she followed after the Mistress, cackling.

I watched them go. I was so wrapped up in them I didn't even notice the crew members until they jerked my cage forward. I fell on my hands and knees with a yelp.

The twins pushed me, their faces as blank as mannequins. I had only a moment to watch as other crew members started to haul out the string of paper lanterns before they pulled me into the building.

Madame Selene's section had already been set up. She sat at her table, staring straight ahead, looking like a doll waiting to be wound up.

The twins left me there, in the flickering lantern light, and went out. Crew members passed by, dragging props or pieces of props, but none of them even turned to glance in my direction. *You aren't important.* I shivered, turning to face Madame Selene.

"Why did they leave me here?" I didn't know why I was asking. I just needed someone to acknowledge me.

Madame Selene turned to me with a stoic, unreadable expression. She paused, as if waiting for the room to empty before speaking. "Not every question has an answer, songbird."

"What do you mean?"

"You ask for a reason where reason does not exist." Her eyes narrowed ever so slightly. "At least in this regard. The bird is left in my domain until it is time for her to be moved. It is simply the way things are done."

I wrapped my arms around myself. Overly warm to the touch, the feathers growing along my arms seemed to pulse beneath my palms. I shuddered.

"This is *terrible*." My voice wavered and broke. It somehow managed to feel like a dramatic exaggeration and an understatement all at once.

Madame Selene cocked her head to the side, just slightly. "The threads of your fate are more frayed than the rest." Her words came out even slower than usual, deliberate. "Perhaps you may find comfort in that."

Before I could ask what that meant, the silver-haired crew member and the one with broad shoulders came and started to push me away. But as we left Madame Selene's room, her voice followed us.

"Or perhaps not."

eight.

When we reached the auditorium, other crew members were setting up chairs and rolling Bridget's target onto the stage. The crew members in charge of moving me ignored them, instead simply dragging my cage up and then off to a cramped, curtained area stage right.

The Mistress stood inside near the stage, wearing a smug grin. Bridget, standing dutifully beside her, twiddled her fingers at me as I rolled in. "Welcome, little songbirdie!"

The black-draped pocket felt far too small. I scooted to the center of the cage, wary of any reaching arms. I saw Mark and Violet in the very corner, but they focused on each other. Mark, in fact, seemed to be purposefully not looking at me. Violet leaned against his side, murmuring gently to him.

I opened my mouth to call out to him, then closed it. *He's obviously avoiding me. What good would talking to him do?*

Bridget's laughter hit my nervous ears like drills. "This birdie's gonna be fun. I can tell."

I turned back to them. The Mistress gave me a cool, amused look. "Well, we'll see, won't we?" She leaned forward. Her face stopped just short of the cage bars, and she spoke in that familiar whisper-shout. "*When you get on stage, sing.*"

The words vibrated beneath my skin, settling uncomfortably against my vocal cords. I pressed my fingertips to my neck, stomach lurching when they touched a cluster of new feathers bunched in the hollow of my throat. They felt warmer to the touch than the rest, almost feverish.

Disgust every bit as powerful and skin-crawling as magic shuddered through me.

The Mistress smiled and stepped back. "It's time to begin." And with no further explanation, she leaned forward and started a quiet conversation with Bridget. In the corner, Violet raised her voice just slightly, and Mark added his own words to the mix.

Other voices joined them, too many for the number of people backstage. I strained to hear what they were saying.

"Dude, weird. Do you hear . . ."

"Voices, can you make . . ."

"Can't really tell . . ."

"Wonder what all . . ."

I remembered hearing the feathered woman's voice in the dark room, remembered her responding to me. The voices belonged to the show's guests. *Can they hear the Mistress and Bridget, Violet and Mark? Could they hear me if I spoke?*

"Hello? Can you hear me?" My voice trembled a bit. Mark

glanced over in my direction for just a second before dragging his eyes back to Violet. Although it was hard to see in the shadows, I thought he laced his fingers through hers.

"Um . . . yeah?" A girl's voice called back, distant but clear.

Panic rose like a fist in my throat, threatening to choke me. But I couldn't let it, not if I had any chance of getting through to someone. I opened my mouth, shouting as loud as I could.

"Help me!"

The exact second I spoke, the Mistress let out a deep, inhuman laugh. It seemed to shake the fabric walls around us. Bridget roared along with her, but even that paled in comparison.

Distant screams and laughter mingled together.

"Oh my God, what even *was* that?"

"Stupid jump scare. Should've seen it coming . . ."

I listened to them fade away as the girl and her friends walked out of the dark room.

They think it's an act. Like a haunted house. The knowledge sat heavy on my shoulders, like an evil presence. The Mistress smiled at me, all smug self-assurance.

She *wanted* me to scream, I realized. It was part of her game. She wanted me to reach for freedom so she could rip it away from me. She wanted to break me, shatter me until I was as empty as the glassy-eyed crew members acted.

"*Has she?*" The words seemed to be coming from inside my head, but I didn't recognize them as my own thoughts. It sounded the same as the voice that identified the stench of death hanging around the feathered woman.

"*Has she broken you?*" it asked.

I didn't know how to answer that question. But I didn't try calling out again.

Listening to the people walk through was a special kind of torture. They might have helped me, if they knew. But there was nothing I could do to call out to them without the Mistress interfering.

I thought of that voice, the strange whisper-shout I couldn't disobey. For a moment, I wished I could steal it, could bend the room to *my* bidding. The thought made my stomach curl in on itself. Was it because I was jealous of the Mistress or because I felt sick at the thought of becoming anything like her? I felt both of those things pretty thoroughly, and I didn't know which one of them made me more upset.

As more and more people passed through the dark room, the sounds beyond the stage grew louder. Nerves mixed with the existential terror and dread that had become my life. I'd sung in front of groups during choir, but that was different. My voice was just one of many there, easy to miss if it shook.

The lights dimmed, and Bridget skipped onstage. She went through her act, exactly like she had the night I went. The same shocked gasps and screams sounded when she blew fire at the audience, except the flames never touched them, I saw now. They stopped at the very edge of the stage and curled against an invisible wall. Magic seemed to be the only reasonable explanation.

Loud applause accompanied Bridget as she strutted offstage. The twins went to the wings on the other side.

Violet and Mark went out next. I watched from backstage as they danced and intertwined. Even Mark seemed fearless to me as he performed, not freezing beneath the gaze of the audience.

The music rose to a crescendo, and they wrapped themselves up in the fabric, just like they did during the performance I saw. The Mistress muttered something, and they appeared backstage with a soft popping noise. *Magic, again.* Violet leaned against the fabric-draped wall and looked up, crossing her arms over her chest. Mark sat cross-legged on the floor and looked at his lap.

The music started up, low and as beautiful as ever. The Mistress's act was about to begin.

I looked to her. She already had her gaze trained on me. Even in the dim light, her eyes seemed to sparkle with the cruel humor of a bully playing a joke. As the music grew louder and louder, I couldn't look away from her, even though I wanted to. *She's got me under her spell. She can put anyone under her spell without even trying.* Hopelessness tugged at my heart.

She reached up slowly, grinning, and snapped her fingers. She vanished, reappearing in a flurry of red fabric onstage.

In stories, people became less beautiful when you knew how awful they were. This wasn't the case with the Mistress. Her dance was just as captivating as it had been the first time, her movements just as graceful and alluring.

She finished her dance. The audience applauded loudly.

"I am the Mistress." She held her head high, eyes scanning the audience. "I began this show many years ago because I value art in all of its forms. Since then, our exhibits have grown and performers have come and gone. But nothing is more special to me than our final act."

I recognized this speech. I remembered her giving it word for word when she introduced the feathered woman.

"Our final act," she continued. "A final work of art. She's different from anything you've ever seen before, but do not let that frighten you away, because art is about finding beauty in the strangest, most frightening of places. If you listen to her song, I'm sure you'll find that this is true."

The Mistress turned to me, nodded, and strode off in the opposite direction.

The cage began to move. I gasped, looking around. The silver-haired woman and broad-shouldered man pushed me forward. I rolled onto the stage slowly, like a convict on death row being led to their execution.

It's too bright! After being in the dim wings, the stage lights were blinding. Their heat seemed to actually have weight.

And so did the gaze of the audience.

I squinted out at them. The dark shadows of their silhouettes seemed to multiply. How had it gotten so big? The auditorium hadn't looked nearly large enough to hold all these people. It felt like the weight of thousands of eyes were trained on me, waiting for me to do something.

Sometimes I daydreamed about singing in front of people, but never like this. This wasn't a dream—it was a nightmare.

Confused murmurs and awkward shifting echoed through the crowd. From the far side of the stage, I could *feel* the Mistress's amusement, her contempt. I felt like a bug frying to death under a magnifying glass held by a sadistic kid.

I took a breath. It came out against my will in a croaking sort of song. "A-Aaahhh . . ."

The Mistress's magic. She commanded me to sing once I got on stage. I could feel the magic seizing my vocal cords, forcing me to sing something—*anything*. But she hadn't commanded me to sing anything in particular. And she hadn't commanded me to be good.

Sing for help! Tell them you're trapped here! The thought flitted across my mind, but I rejected it instantly. If I saw a girl onstage, covered in feathers and singing about how much she wanted to be set free, I'd assume it was an act.

I had to sing. The tension in my throat from the magic began to ache, and I just wanted to get this over with, just wanted to be off this stage and away from the searing lights, the eyes. In a blind panic, I opened my mouth and sang: "Twinkle, twinkle, little star . . ."

Laughter echoed through the audience. It started out scattered but quickly grew louder. I couldn't blame them—I sounded ridiculous singing a children's song in a cracked, awkward voice. I finished as quickly as I could. By the end of my song, most of the audience was laughing at me.

The Mistress's magic let go of my throat when I finished.

I couldn't feel much relief from that. Maybe it was ridiculous to feel humiliated, considering everything else that was going on. But the laughter that rolled over me reminded me of why I had once considered *you aren't important* to be a comforting mantra. I never wanted people to look at me like *this* again.

I bowed my head and squeezed my eyes shut, willing this to be over.

"Thank you for coming." The Mistress's voice sounded pleased. "Goodnight."

The floor rattled beneath the wheels of my cage. I buried my face in my hands as I heard Bridget's laughter and the sounds of exiting guests. I didn't look up until I felt the stale air of the storage room pressed against my skin.

Crew members walked wordlessly through the space, dragging props back to their rightful places. The poetry women stood right in front of my cage, clinging to each other.

Their gauzy veils hung around their necks, giving me a clear view of their faces for the first time. One had wavy black hair and dark skin. But it was the other one, an Asian woman with round cheeks, that caught my attention.

Everything from her warm brown eyes to the slight widow's peak at the top of her head reminded me achingly of my mom.

Homesickness welled up in me and exited my throat in a sob. I didn't want any of this. I wanted a life that was no longer mine. I wanted a mom who probably didn't know I existed anymore.

"H-Hey."

I looked up. Mark approached my cage hesitantly, holding my blankets and pillow. Behind him, crew members led the poetry women to the back of the room.

I wiped at my eyes. "Are you here to laugh at me, too?" I wanted it to come out bitter and a little angry, but I just sounded whiny and tear-choked.

Mark flinched, and despite everything, I still managed to feel guilty. "Sorry," I mumbled.

"No." He pushed the blankets through. "It should be me. I should—you know." He sighed.

I pulled the blankets through the rest of the way, into my lap. "Mark, what is this about? Why bother putting me through all that?"

Discomfort twisted the expression on his face. "The show needs a bird."

"Okay." That didn't really answer any of my questions, actually, but I decided to come at it from another angle. "But, like, she can command me to do anything, right? She could have told me to sing a certain song in a certain way. But instead it was like she was . . . I don't know. Setting me up for failure or something." I paused, the thought sinking in. "*Was* she setting me up for failure?"

She let me scream backstage because she wanted me to see how powerless I was. What if letting me fail did the same thing?

"*Has she broken you?*" The voice echoed again in my mind. Even if I could answer it, what would I say, with tears streaming down my cheeks and clogging up my throat?

"I—I can't. Elizabeth, I can't." Mark's voice came out even more jagged and awkward than usual. "These things. You ask too many questions. If she thinks I—she'll—*she'll*—" A note of hysteria crept into his voice.

I held my hands up, palms out. "Mark, it's okay." *Am I seriously the one comforting him?* "I won't tell her I know anything. What could I possibly get out of that?"

He stayed tense, but his voice came out a bit steadier. "I hate this. I feel like I'm a part of it. You shouldn't want to talk to me."

I wrapped my fingers around the bars of the cage. "Well, Mark, so far, talking to you has been the least terrifying part of all of this. So . . ."

He looked away. His chest rose and fell in a shaky sigh. "I'll come back tomorrow."

"Alright." Silence hung thick in the air between us, like the gauzy fabric of the poetry women's cocoons. I watched as they rose into the air for a moment, then looked back down. "Goodnight, Mark."

"Goodnight, Elizabeth."

He left, and with nothing else to do, I curled up on the blankets he'd left, drifting off.

"Dear songbird!"

Alice's voice sounded at my back, a happy trill. I spun around to see her holding out a crown of flowers, just close enough to brush the tip of my nose.

She laughed, perhaps because of the startled expression on my face. The sound of it sent a little thrill through me, immediately followed—as it always was—by a sense of guilt. Alice was not mine. Alice would never think of me in the way I occasionally thought of her, in passing.

As if to confirm this, she dropped the flower crown on top of my head. It bounced gently against my curls before settling. Alice giggled. "Adorable," she said, tapping the tip of her finger against my nose. She looked so pleased with herself that I had to smile, even though something in me did not care for the way she treated me like a child.

She'd never see me as anything more than a child.

Alice's giggling echoed, became younger. And then a voice sounded: "Smush, stop!"

The scene shifted. I was myself again, back in the bedroom of the girl with the topknot. But instead of lying on her bed, she sat at the desk in the corner. Her cat stood on top of it, chewing on the end of her pencil.

"Hi, hello, I was using that!"

Giggling, she held the cat to her chest and made some truly ridiculous kissy faces at it. Smush let out a low mewl and tried to squirm away. In other circumstances, the completely unamused expression on its flat face might have made me laugh. If I had a body to laugh with.

Shaking her head, the girl let the cat to the ground. "Sure, now you want your space." Smiling, she grabbed her pencil and went back to what she was doing.

I wonder if I can see . . . As soon as the thought crossed my mind, I was floating next to her.

The girl jumped and looked around, eyes wide and startled. The urge to apologize welled up in me before I realized that I wasn't technically here. And she wasn't technically here, either. This was all just some random dream, right?

I looked down at the page. The girl had sketched a profile view of a girl with a bob cut and a flower crown. And even though I knew this was just a dream, the thought flashed across my mind anyway:

That sketch looks a lot like me.

nine.

The dream faded, and I opened my eyes. But the memories lingered.

Seeing the kind-of sketch of me was weird, sure, but the first dream raised way more questions. I must have been that woman from the painting again. I felt the flower crown settle against my—*her* curls. But in the last dream, she and Alice had pretty obviously been a couple. That didn't seem to be the case in this one. What was that about?

Are you seriously trying to rationalize your dreams right now? Is that your priority? My hand went to my shoulder. Instead of meeting skin, my fingers met the sickly warmth of the feathers growing there. My stomach gave a seasick lurch. The thoughts were right. I had bigger things to worry about.

At least they were my *real* thoughts this time, and not those weird ones that seemed to come from somewhere else. I already had more than enough to deal with without adding a literal voice in my head to the mix.

I looked down at myself, even though part of me didn't want to. More feathers had sprung up in little clusters all over my body. A couple along the side of one knee. A thin line on my collarbone. My dress itched along my ribs and hips, and when I looked, I saw new bumps there.

They didn't hurt—not really. They reminded me a little of the way a tooth with a cavity felt wrong even when it didn't hurt. And looking at myself felt uncomfortable, like looking at a stranger.

The fabric-covered entrance near me shifted. I tensed, waiting for the Mistress or Bridget to walk through. But it was just Mark, here like he promised.

"Hey." He hovered by the entrance, shuffling his feet. "Um. Sorry. Did you still want . . . ?"

I sighed, sitting up. "Yeah. Yeah, I guess I do." I didn't really know what to talk about, honestly. But talking to him sounded better than sitting here alone, speculating about the imaginary people in my dreams, and watching the feathers break through my skin.

Mark nodded. "I get it. Some of the others felt that way, too. The girls before you, I mean. The ones who wanted to talk. Hang on."

He disappeared into the depths of the storage room for a moment. There was a clanging noise, and then he came back, dragging a folding chair behind him. He brought it up to the front of the cage, closer than the chair by the bookshelf.

"There." He set up the chair and sat down on it. "So, what did you want to talk about?"

I pulled some of the blankets into my lap, wrapping my

arms around them. What could I possibly say? I couldn't ask him to let me out, and telling him about the dreams or the voice in my head just felt weird. I looked down at the floor of the cage, plucked a white feather stuck to the blankets. "Um . . . The woman who came before me. The one with the white feathers. Did you know her name?"

Mark sighed. "Yeah. It was Elle."

Elle. Something warm and relieved bloomed in my chest. There wasn't much I could do for the feathered woman who died right in front of me, but at least now I could think of her by her name.

I held the blankets to my chest. "You mentioned . . . girls before me."

Mark startled, then nodded.

"How many?"

To be honest, part of me didn't want to know the answer. But a larger part of me *had* to know.

Mark shrugged, shoving his hands into his pockets and looking away. "I don't know. It's been going on for a while. Longer than I've been around, and I joined when I was just— well, it's been years, anyways."

The air around me turned thick, and I had to work to pull it into my lungs. *Years? The Mistress has been kidnapping girls for years?* "How, um . . ." I forced a deep breath. "How long does she keep them?"

At first, he didn't answer. In the silent, stagnant air, even the sounds of Mark fidgeting with his sweater sounded loud.

Finally, he spoke, a nervous tremble in his voice. "As long as they last. A couple of months, usually. One lasted half a year, but that's the longest. That I've seen, anyways."

I tried to do the math in my head. It felt like too many girls to be going missing with no one to make the connection. It wasn't like the show was a secret—it had fliers and people came to see it. But then again, I remembered what the Mistress said. "Does she really . . . erase us from the world?"

Something stricken and frightened swallowed Mark's expression. It took years off him, made him look twelve instead of twenty-something.

"We shouldn't talk about that. *Her*." His voice trembled harder, almost ragged. "It's a bad idea."

"*She can't hear.*" I almost jumped at the sound of the voice. It definitely was not my thought this time. "*He's just being paranoid.*" I didn't know how much I could believe a literal voice in my head, but I knew it didn't matter. I wanted Mark to stick around. I rushed to reassure him.

"Alright, that's fine. Can you . . . tell me about Elle, then? I'd like to know what she was like, if that's okay."

Mark frowned, his gaze turning distant and thoughtful. "I don't know. She slept a lot? And didn't talk. When she was awake, I mean. I don't really—I don't force them to talk. Not if they don't want to. I'm sorry."

I sighed a little, pulling the pillow into my lap and resting my chin on it. "I guess that you wouldn't *really* know what she was like. Being in this cage, it . . . it's like . . ."

Finding the words to explain everything I'd felt since waking up in this cage seemed impossible. And even if I could, my throat felt too tight to push them out.

The life I lived before all of this felt like it belonged to someone else. And there was a voice—not a literal voice, but just my plain old thoughts and insecurities—that nagged at me. *Was there anything about your past self worth saving? Can you think of a single person who would miss you?*

"Elizabeth?" Mark's soft voice held a note of alarm. "Are you okay?"

I tried to answer him, but the breath caught in my throat and came out in a shuddering wheeze. I closed my eyes, shaking my head.

It didn't take too long to get under control, though. I managed to not burst into random tears or anything like that. When I looked up, Mark nodded, his face equal parts pity and understanding. "Do you want to—to talk about it?"

I sighed. "It's just, um . . . I guess I'm feeling almost disgusted with myself? Because, like, all of my problems and the things I complained about before seem so minor now. I could've solved so much by just putting in a little effort, putting myself out there. And maybe then, I wouldn't even be here. I wouldn't be in this position at all."

I knew it was irrational as soon as I said it, but the certainty still sat heavy in my chest.

Mark nodded slowly. "I get it." His tone made me wonder if he had similar thoughts telling him he wasn't important.

"Is that why you talk to the ones who want to talk, Mark?"

He looked down at his fidgeting hands. "I can imagine how you feel. Trapped. And the kinds of thoughts that come up when you—" He cut himself off abruptly, pulling in a deep breath. "You don't deserve this, Elizabeth. You know that, right?"

I didn't realize how much I needed to hear those words until he said them, because a part of me believed that this must have happened for a reason. I must have done something to deserve this. After all, I went to the show. I wanted an adventure, something different. *Be careful what you wish for.* It sounded like a joke, just like *you aren't important*, right up until you realized it wasn't funny.

I liked to think of myself as pretty self-aware. But my insecurities still knew how to disguise themselves as humor.

"Thanks, Mark," I said.

"No one deserves this," he went on, gaining speed. "Not you or Elle. Or any of the girls who came before you. Or any of the ones—"

"Mark."

A curt but soft female voice cut him off. Violet stood at the curtained doorway, wearing a leather jacket and ripped jeans. She stared at the ceiling with her arms crossed over her chest.

Some of the ever-present anxiety in Mark's brown eyes softened. "Oh. Time for the show already?"

"Yup." Violet popped her lips around the end of the word. "You done?"

Her scowl and the way she pointedly refused to look in my direction prickled at me. Sure, much worse things had happened to me just recently, but I didn't like the tension in her shoulders, the way she treated me like an inconvenience.

I decided to at least try to talk to her. I didn't think she was dangerous, not with the way Mark acted. "Uh . . . hi, I'm—"

"Save it."

I wasn't sure what I was expecting, but having the blonde girl cut me off in a sharp voice wasn't it. I turned to Mark,

84

who just stared at the tips of his sneakers, his hands deep in his hoodie pocket.

I turned back to Violet again. She was still scowling, still not looking at me. She glared at the wall instead.

"Um, excuse me, I—"

"I said to save it." Violet ran a hand through her straight, bleached hair, chipped black nail polish barely visible on the tips of her fingernails. "I don't need to know your name. What's the fucking point? I can't do anything to help you. You've gotta know that. So why bother pretending like you give a shit about me or Mark?"

"Vi," Mark said softly.

Some of the annoyance in her expression dampened, but not *all* of it. "*Ugh.* I'll be waiting in our room." She looked at Mark. Her expression softened, and her tone turned gentle. "Do what you have to do. Then come get ready. Okay?"

Mark ducked his head a little, nodding. "Yeah. I'll see you soon."

She turned on her heels and walked out, leaving me and Mark alone.

Silence stretched between us for a moment. Finally, realizing Mark wouldn't be the one to break it, I coughed. "So, uh, that was . . ."

"Weird, I know. Sorry." Mark rubbed the back of his neck. "It's probably better if you don't talk to her. She's . . ." He trailed off, making a vague, unhelpful hand gesture. "It's not personal. I promise."

"What is it, then?" Something petulant crept into my tone. I heard it but couldn't help it. "It's not like I'm here by choice."

Mark sighed, fidgeting with the gray sleeves of his sweater. "It's—It's complicated. She doesn't like to think about it. You, I mean. Or the girls like you. We can't help them, you know? There's nothing we can do. And she feels bad—she *does*. Really. She's a good person." He looked down at his hands. "A *great* person. She doesn't like seeing people hurting. So she just ignores it."

"It, um, doesn't look like this is all that fun for you, either. But you're nice to me."

"Yeah. Well." Mark tucked his hands into his sleeves, balling the edges in his fists. "It's like she says. Kindness only does so much. Sometimes it doesn't do *enough*. We both know. Sometimes it's better to just stay away."

He spoke so firmly. It made me wonder if he was echoing Violet's thoughts or stating his own.

"You do help me, though. Talking to you helps." At the very least, it made me feel a little less alone.

He nodded, like he expected this. "I'll come back, then. Whenever I can."

I fidgeted with the white hem of my dress. He was right. This little kindness *wasn't* enough. But it seemed to be all that he was willing to give me. For now, at least, I had to take what I could get.

"Thank you, Mark."

He nodded, then stood there, fidgeting. He opened his mouth to say something but closed it instead. And then he walked away.

A few minutes later, the silent, glassy-eyed crew came in, preparing for the show. The Mistress didn't accompany

86

them. Instead, they took the paper lanterns away from the cage themselves and waited for me to push the blankets and pillow through. I didn't even consider keeping them.

I didn't need the Mistress in the same room as me to know there would be consequences for disobeying her. And I wasn't ready to face them.

"*Has she broken you?*"

Not for the first time, I found myself unable to answer that question.

ten.

I actually sang somewhat well this time. I couldn't really be happy about it, since I still wasn't singing by choice. But listening to the polite applause of the audience felt a little better than listening to their confused laughter.

The Mistress didn't seem upset that I'd done okay. She seemed as smug as ever as she bid the audience goodnight and the crew members dragged me back to the storage room.

Mark came to return my blankets and pillow but didn't stay. "Violet's waiting," he'd explained.

So, left alone, I lay on the floor of my cage. The chill of the metal just barely reached me through the blankets.

I held a hand above my head, studying the tiny feathers that had sprouted along the sides of my fingers. I tried to imagine my whole arm covered, my whole body covered, until I didn't even look human anymore. A shudder crawled its way up my spine.

I remembered how worn and broken Elle had looked. I

didn't want to imagine myself in that same position, but what could I do? The Mistress had taken everything from me.

"*Has she?*"

The voice sounded clearer than ever. I drew the blankets to my chest, whispering into the quiet of the room.

"Hello? Is someone there?"

No answer. I shivered despite the warmth of the blankets. I didn't know what frightened me more: the idea of being haunted by some bodiless being or the idea of going mad behind these bars. Because I didn't want to think about it, and because I didn't really have an answer to the voice's question, I just closed my eyes.

Slowly, I drifted off into sleep.

The sound of the violin, high and sweet, reached me from the next room.

I paused in my cleaning to listen, closing my eyes and allowing the music to sweep me away. Of all the benefits of having Alice in the house, this was second only to her pleasant demeanor. I could sing, but a lone voice didn't have the same sweetness as an instrument.

Something light and gentle fluttered in my chest. I began to hum along.

The scene shifted, and I shifted back into myself. But the music stayed.

The girl with the topknot stood off to the side, playing her violin. She closed her eyes, only occasionally glancing to the sheet music on the stand in front of her. She knew this song already—loved it, judging by the look on her face. She looked the same way I felt when I sang a song I really liked.

For a moment, I felt just like that curly-haired woman felt when she listened to Alice play. Light and fluttery, like I wanted to hum along.

I woke up with the girl's violin still echoing in my ears.

A pang of disappointment ached in my chest. The dreams of Alice and the curly-haired woman were unfamiliar but sweet. The dreams of the girl with the topknot were familiar and comforting. Being awake, in my cage and in my body, was none of those things.

I sat up, looking over myself. Even more yellow-green feathers now dotted my upper arms, along with gray ones on my lower arms and knuckles. Warm feathers pressed against my skin beneath my dress, along my hips and ribs. Bumps dotted my thighs and itched along my sides.

I could feel the feathers that hadn't grown yet, too, like beads of sweat that dripped along the insides of my bones. Part of me just wanted to curl up, to close my eyes a little longer, to hide from reality until I became a lifeless pile, just like Elle must have done.

"Has she broken you?" the voice echoed again. And in spite of everything, I didn't want to answer it with a definite yes.

So I opened my eyes, and I stood. I paced the edges of my cage, trying to will some muscle back into my tired legs.

I wondered if the dreams were my subconscious's way of helping me escape all this, giving me a place where I felt loved and safe. But that didn't feel right. After all, I wasn't always loved—sometimes, when I was the curly-haired woman, Alice and I weren't together.

And wasn't it weird to dream of the exact same people three nights in a row? Normally, I hardly ever remembered my dreams.

What, do you think the dreams are magic? The thought—my thought, for sure this time—wanted to come off as teasing, like the idea was ridiculous. But it wasn't ridiculous. An evil witch kidnapped and cursed me. Magic surrounded me on all sides. Was it really so weird to think that these dreams were magic, too?

Of course, if they were magic, that meant they were from the Mistress. And that meant nothing good could come from them.

"That's not true."

I stopped pacing and looked around, like I expected someone to be there on the other side of the bars. But the soft glow of the paper lanterns revealed nothing but an empty storage room.

Hearing voices is probably the least of my worries, but it still creeps me out. I sighed, giving up on walking for the time being. I went back to the blankets in the center of the cage.

Mark didn't come to visit me. It made sense that he couldn't come every day, I guessed. But it still disappointed me when the curtained entrance rustled only to reveal the crew members getting ready for the show.

Being dragged out of the storage room almost felt routine, even though it had only been a few days. Maybe it was because of the way no one even looked at me. Bridget stood off to the side, polishing a knife. Mark and Violet made their way to the entrance of the black-draped building. Smiling, the Mistress watched the poetry women cling to each other.

You aren't important. I shuddered.

Just like the first few shows, the crew members left me

with Madame Selene. She fixed her glassy gaze on me.

"Do you recognize the plumage?"

"Uh, sorry?" I hadn't honestly expected her to speak.

She inclined her head ever so slightly toward me. "The pattern growing under your skin, songbird."

Her words sunk in. I looked down at the feathers coating my body and nodded. "I look like a green finch." The answer came easily. I had a bit of an obsession with birds back in middle school. I think I just wanted to prove to myself that the red bird from my nightmares didn't exist—or that it wasn't as terrifying as I remembered it, at least. Whatever the reason, I knew exactly what I was turning into. "A songbird."

The irony was not lost on me. I wondered if the Mistress had planned it. Then again, she didn't seem to know that I sang until I told her.

Madame Selene nodded, her expression as unreadable as ever. "More suited to you than some others."

"Are you going to tell me what that means, or . . . ?" I couldn't help the edge that crept into my voice. Fear and exhaustion frayed my nerves.

Madame Selene didn't seem particularly offended. She continued staring in that way she did, where I couldn't be sure that she was really seeing me. "The meaning . . . No, I cannot grasp that for you. I can hardly grasp the concrete, the here and now."

I frowned at her. "Because you're a fortune teller?"

Madame Selene breathed in and out. "The future is not linear, songbird. It frays into a million fragments of possibilities. And in your case . . ."

I opened my mouth, then closed it. Something in the

intensity of her expression kept me from interrupting.

Eventually, she continued. "Most birds have only a few potential paths, and all threads lead to the same end. With you, things are much too frayed."

My heart thumped hard against my ribs. *Is she saying I don't have to die here?* It sounded like that, but I couldn't be sure. I couldn't even be sure that she could really see the future, although it wasn't too hard to believe. If I could believe that magic was real, I could believe anything.

"What can I do? What can I do to get out of here?"

I felt stupid as soon as I asked. There was nothing I could do; surely Madame Selene would tell me that. I could only hope that someone else came along to save me. I didn't know how to get free. I didn't even know *why* I was here to begin with. *Would that even make any difference?*

The voice chimed in, startling me. "*Yes. It has to.*"

"The answers are inside your mind already," Madame Selene said.

I rubbed hard at my shoulder, wanting to believe but not quite daring to. "The voice! Is it real? Am I going crazy?"

Madame Selene shook her head. "The echoes of that forgotten song . . . cannot give you the answers you seek. At least, not as you are now. Your ears are not equipped to hear them."

"Is, um . . . Is there a way for me to hear it, then? Who is it?" I didn't know if I could trust the voice or if it was even real. I didn't know if I could trust Madame Selene, either, for that matter. But since they were my only options, I at least had to give it a try.

Besides, while I couldn't be positive about Madame

Selene, the voice felt good. It asked me if the Mistress had broken me like it wanted the answer to be no. It was with me from the very beginning, warning me against the stench of death as I watched Elle fade.

Madame Selene shook her head. "You ask the wrong questions, songbird."

"Well, what are the right ones?"

Madame Selene only stared. I groaned, pressing my palms against my cheeks. The feathers itched. "I don't know why I expected an answer from that." I didn't know if she couldn't help it or if she was just playing some sort of joke on me. Either way, frustration bit at my insides.

Beggars can't be choosers. That had been one of my mom's favorite phrases, and I thought of it—and her—with a pang. I knew she was right, but I still felt a childish urge to throw my hands in the air and give up. Or at least complain a little more before trying again.

Madame Selene looked more mystified than anything by my annoyance. "You already asked the right question. I, in turn, gave an answer. An answer is no less an answer just because you did not hear it."

"I've heard everything you're saying! I asked how to get myself free, and you said that the answer is already in my mind. So you must have been talking about the voice . . . Wait." I paused, thinking carefully over her words. "*Were* you talking about the voice?"

Madame Selene shook her head—left once, right once, and then back to center. "It is a rogue player. Not meant to be brought in. She will do everything in her power to silence it, if she finds out. No, you cannot start with that."

I didn't ask who "she" was. I didn't need to. Even Madame Selene's solemn voice turned quiet, almost reverent, when talking about the Mistress.

"But she's going to try and stop me no matter what I do, right?" I couldn't imagine the Mistress just letting me go if I did things right, like the villain in a video game.

"She will not stop you from gathering information." Madame Selene folded her hands together. "In fact, she anticipates it. She's given you the tools to learn the truth."

My breath stuttered in my chest. "The dreams. They *do* come from the Mistress?" The voice had told me they didn't. Between it and Madame Selene, who was I supposed to trust?

Except that wasn't quite right. The voice said *that's not true*, but not after I thought the dreams came from the Mistress. It told me that after I thought nothing good could come out of them.

Before I could open my mouth to ask, the crew members came in and wheeled me away.

I sang on autopilot—the theme song to my favorite show, just the first song that came to mind. Maybe I even sounded okay. It didn't matter. My mind stayed a million miles away, even as the Mistress swept onto the stage, the show ended, and the crew members dragged me back to the storage room. I thanked Mark for bringing the pillows and blankets back without even really seeing him. I just kept turning Madame Selene's words over and over in my mind, like pieces of a puzzle that wouldn't quite make a picture.

My heart felt like it was trying to break through my ribs, the same way I wanted to break through the cage bars. I didn't know which dreams to pay attention to. The dreams of Alice? The ones where I hovered near the girl with the topknot? Both? Neither?

I guess there's only one way to try and find out. I pulled the blankets over myself, hoping I'd be able to get some rest.

I thought it would be like the night before a big exam or the night before the musical audition. I'd toss and turn, practically begging for sleep, but it wouldn't come. I wanted it so bad that I'd cheat myself out of it somehow.

That didn't happen. Exhaustion washed over my bones as soon as I rested my head on the pillow. Sleep found me almost immediately, pulling me with warm hands into the dark.

eleven.

The moon hung full and bright in the sky, like a lantern. My sister and I had a tradition on nights like these. Whenever possible, we walked beneath the moonlight, gathering wildflowers. Of course, she could not always be called upon, busy as she was. But I made my way to her room all the same, inhaling the scent of aged wood and the ghost of incense.

I wondered if Alice would be in her room, too. It seemed likely. My sister was not one to wait in such matters, and she had no reason to. The thought sent a small pang through me. But why should it have? My sister's lovers were nothing new. She took them in, had them for as long as she and they cared for, and then sent them on their way. Alice was no different.

Alice was no different. The flutters in my heart when I looked at her were a childish daydream. Jealousy, perhaps, at my sister's ability to so effortlessly charm such gorgeous people.

I knocked on her door, resolving to put such petty thoughts out of my head. "Big sister?"

"You may come in."

That voice did not belong to my sister. So Alice did stay in her room. The sound of her voice sent a small thrill through me, something beyond my control and utterly unfair. This was unacceptable. I had not breathed a word to either of them about my feelings. I had no intention of changing that tonight.

I would invite both of them out, if only to prove to myself that I was not beholden to some jealousy-fueled crush.

I opened the door to find Alice alone. Her pale skin glowed in the moonlight, hair plaited in a thick, loose braid that fell over her bare shoulder.

The rest of her was bare, too.

I backed away, covering my eyes with my hands. As if that would do anything to remove the vision of her, the softness of her waist and—

"I'm sorry! I didn't realize . . . I just . . . I was looking for—"

"I heard." Alice spoke in a light, easy tone. If she had been my sister, I would have been sure she was mocking me. But that didn't fit Alice at all. In the months since coming, she had been nothing but kind to me. "Your sister is not here right now. May I do anything to help you?"

The sound of her voice grew closer. I peered through my fingers to see if she had put on a robe. It took only the slightest of glances to see that she had not. I covered my eyes again.

It took a considerable amount of willpower to keep them closed, however. Alice had the sort of beauty that rent the heart and stole the breath straight from your lungs. How did my sister even stand in her presence without going blind? How did she dare touch that skin, caress that cheek? If I were in my sister's shoes, I would simply faint dead away.

I supposed that was why I was not in my sister's shoes.

From somewhere slightly farther away, I heard Alice laugh. The sound was soft, almost musical. "You can open your eyes now."

I peered through my fingers, hoping it would be for the last time. Relief washed over me when I saw that Alice had donned a simple nightgown. It was thin but certainly better than before.

She looked at me with a fondness that made something warm and comforting bloom in my stomach. "I'm sorry if I made you uncomfortable. To be quite honest, I sometimes forget that your region has such . . ." She made a vague hand gesture, smiling. "Such concerns."

"Well . . ." I did not know how to respond, frankly. Alice was kind, but not naive. She had to understand why it was inappropriate for me to see my sister's lover in such a state.

Still, she crossed the room gracefully, nightgown slipping to reveal a single bare shoulder. Was she even aware of it? I was. Quite acutely.

"In my region, this means nothing." She spoke in a soft voice, but her bright blue eyes sparkled with good cheer. "The human body is just that—a body. It keeps us alive, but nothing more. Why do we hide it away? What is so private about flesh and bone? It is our hearts—our souls—that need protection. And those are much harder to share without consent."

The sound of her voice was nearly hypnotic. I could have listened to it for hours, watching her lips shape the words. Her lips . . .

My thoughts turned traitorous again. I uttered the first thing that came to mind. "And besides, you're loyal to my sister."

Some of the light in Alice's eyes dimmed. Of course, that was the exact wrong thing to say. She probably hadn't even begun to think of it like that until I brought it up.

99

"Besides, I'm loyal to your sister," she echoed.

I swore that melancholy colored her voice. Something that almost sounded like resignation. But surely I only heard what I wanted to hear. The thought made me feel quite disgusted with myself. Was I so selfish that I wanted Alice to be unhappy? I refused. I would not begrudge someone as gentle and kind as Alice her happiness. I would not allow my feelings to complicate matters, to make her feel even an ounce of pity or guilt.

"What did you need her for?"

Alice's voice snapped me back to the present—and reminded me that I came to my sister's room for a reason, not just to indulge in such pitiful, pining thoughts. "I was intending to invite my sister out on a walk. It is our tradition on nights like these. We collect wildflowers together."

An excited smile overtook Alice's features. She wore her emotions without reserve. My sister smiled at men while cursing them under her breath, and I would sooner cut off my own hand than let someone see me in tears. But Alice never seemed to hold such deception or fear. There was no doubt in my mind that the excitement on her face was genuine.

"Indeed? I'd come with you, if you'd have me."

My heart lurched in my chest, my pulse fluttering through my veins like a song. Everything in me wanted to say yes. I wanted to walk beneath the moonlight with her. I wanted to bathe in its silver glow with Alice at my side. I wanted to offer her flowers, to reach for her hand.

But Alice was so sweet, so trusting of me. She didn't even move to dress in anything other than that flimsy nightgown. And if anyone were to see the two of us, beneath the stars together—if word were to travel back to my sister, who always seemed to know everyone and everything . . .

No. I could not let that happen.

"Perhaps that is not the wisest decision, Alice . . ."

The concern on her face was as easy to read as the excitement. It hurt my heart to see it, sadness and worry all mixed together. Not that there was really any cause for worry. Such news would upset my sister, surely, but she was ultimately a fair woman. She would not make assumptions or harm me over a rumor.

"Do you not enjoy my company?"

The hurt in Alice's voice nearly broke me. "No! Or yes . . . Yes, of course I enjoy your company. It is just . . ."

"What?" The confusion in her voice sent a pang of guilt through me, which was the root of my worry, I supposed. I did not think my sister would be angry with me; I merely knew that she should have been, because I longed for Alice to break her heart and come running to me, to let me enfold her in my arms.

I was, without a doubt, the most despicable kind of person.

I chose my words with care, not allowing any bitterness or regret to seep into my tone. I could not–would not–be as open with my emotions as dear Alice. "You are my sister's lover, Alice. It isn't appropriate. If we were seen out together, alone, people would think . . ."

Alice's bright, musical laugh shocked me. "People think all manner of strange things. Just imagine what they'd think if they peered through the window when you walked in, little songbird."

She meant it as only a friendly tease, I knew. But it stung–that the words were friendly, platonic. A curt, harsh voice burst from my mouth without my permission. "Must you use that name?"

For a moment, I swore that Alice flinched. I stepped backward, shaking my head, upraised palms facing her. "I'm sorry, Alice." The last thing I wanted to do in this world was cause her any sort of pain. "I did not mean—"

"It is my fault, surely." Alice's voice remained steady, which was a bit of a relief. I did not think she was able to hide hurt any more than her other emotions. "I did not realize that the nickname bothered you so. I've heard your sister use it for you so often . . ."

I suppressed a childish urge to run for the door, keeping my tone as even as possible. "It does not bother me when she uses it."

Alice stepped forward, the nightgown slipping farther down her shoulder. And even though I didn't want to make her upset, some barrier within me had unlocked.

I felt the words tumbling out of me unbidden. "My sister has used that nickname for me since I was a child, because she sees me as a child, even now that we are grown. But I don't want you to see me in that way, Alice! I don't want you to see me as merely your lover's pure, innocent sister, one who wouldn't be affected by your gazes, your fond words, you answering the door without your nightgown and—"

One look at her stopped my words cold. I forced myself to turn away from her, both wanting and not wanting to. Part of me felt like running for the door, but I feared that moving could cause me to shatter.

"Wait." Alice's voice came out even quieter than usual, halting. "You mean that your feelings for me are . . ."

I forced myself to take a deep breath. "I know you never meant for this to happen, Alice. You couldn't have known. Everything you've done, every kindness you've shown me . . . I know it was just that: a kindness. Because you are kind, Alice. You're so wonderfully, unbelievably you. And I cannot blame you for—"

"You—"

102

"—for being who you are or for loving my sister. I never asked you to choose between us, and even if I did, I know that it wouldn't be a choice at all."

"That—"

"My sister is radiant and wonderful. I'm just the little songbird she allows to stay with her—"

"Please."

The warm touch of her hand on my arm cut me off far more effectively than her words. I turned to see tears rolling down her cheeks. My heart shattered and fell to the floor in a pile of glass.

"I have been unfair to you." She looked down until I could only see the uppermost point of her iris. "Dreadfully unfair. I apologize."

I wanted to hold her close to me. I wanted to run screaming from the house so she never had to look upon me again. I did neither and simply stood before her.

"I thought my actions . . . I thought you only saw me as a friend. If I had known—"

"I understand, Alice. It's not your—"

"You do not understand!"

Had Alice ever spoken above a soft tone before? I would have startled back were she not still clutching my arm.

She was still clutching my arm.

"I have had . . . What I mean to say is, I have never seen you as a child. Quite the opposite. My actions, they weren't . . . I thought it would be safe, that you would never see me as anything other than your sister's . . . that you wouldn't . . . I never expected you to fall for me, as well. I didn't expect my actions to affect you as they did. I'm so sorry. This is my fault. I've manipulated you."

The words "as well" rang in my ears, as loudly as a bell tower. "Alice, you've fallen for me?"

Alice wrapped her arms around herself. "Not at first. Not every kind thing I've done for you was motivated by . . . well. Please, please don't believe that. There were simply moments—the day I picked you flowers, when I kissed you on the cheek, answering the door just now—they were my way of indulging in these feelings, I suppose. I meant for it to be innocent. But I was wrong, you understand. I was so wrong—"

"Alice, I—"

"You really are a songbird. A beautiful bird who deserves to fly far, far away from here someday, and I—"

I never guessed that Alice had this side to her, that her thoughts could become just as self-loathing as my own. I needed to stop her, needed to cut her off before she said something so terrible about herself that my heart shattered.

I stepped forward. There was a moment of Alice's surprised breath on my cheek, and then I pressed my lips to hers. I told myself it would only be for a moment, and then we'd pull away, we'd talk this through, and we'd . . .

We didn't.

How many times had I imagined kissing Alice? I imagined her lips soft against mine, gentle like butterfly wings, elegant and graceful just like her. But kissing her was nothing like that. Our lips crashed against each other, rough and desperate. Our teeth knocked against each other and our breath came out in ugly gasps and I was fairly certain there was spit running down my chin. None of that mattered. The kiss was still far better than anything in my fantasies. The kiss was real.

"Wait . . ."

I forced myself to pull away at her words, breathing heavily. Her eyes widened in surprise. But what else could I have done? Who wouldn't stop when asked to do so?

My heart pounded heavy and solid against my ribs. I waited for her to say, "But I love your sister" or "How could you do that?"

Instead, she said, "You deserve far better than I. You deserve flight, songbird."

Something in me broke. How could Alice feel so worthless? Had my sister not told her how incredible, how radiant, how amazing she was?

Perhaps she didn't deserve her, if this was the case.

"I don't want to be a bird if I cannot choose who flies beside me." I caressed her cheek, her skin soft against my palm. Her blue eyes, as clear and bright as the sky, bore into mine. She did not pull away. "Alice, I choose you. If you'll have me, I choose you."

Alice moved toward me this time. Her hands traveled up my sides, gripping my waist. I never imagined this. I never imagined the trails of fire her fingertips could leave, even over cloth. I never imagined how one touch of her lips would make me hungry for more. As we drew together once again, I realized it was too late to turn away, too late to do anything but give in to what we both wanted.

And even if it weren't, I wouldn't want us to.

twelve.

I woke up gasping, still feeling Alice's phantom fingers untying the lacing at the top of my dress.

Except it *wasn't* my dress. The dress belonged to the curly-haired woman with the hazel eyes, not me. Those thoughts weren't mine, even though my heart still pounded with the force of her emotions. I sat up, a shiver crawling down my spine. *Get it together, Elizabeth.* My entire body trembled, probably because of the sweat turning cold all over my skin.

I let out a low, shaky breath. I hadn't even had *my* first kiss yet. I definitely wasn't prepared to live through someone else's so vividly, especially since the memory of Alice's skin against mine told me that things had gone much further.

Madame Selene said the dreams would have answers, but what was the question? What were they trying to tell me? That I was very, very gay? *I already figured that out for myself a while ago, thanks.*

It felt weird. Alice looked like a grown woman. And the curly-haired woman looked like an adult, too, so it probably wasn't that weird for them. But it had been weird for me.

I lay back down, staring at the domed ceiling of the cage above me. I wanted to guess at what it all meant, what these strange women had to do with me being locked up in here, but guessing was *all* I could do. No matter what wild theories I could come up with, I didn't have anything concrete. And I didn't want to go up against the Mistress with something as flimsy as a guess.

You don't want to go up against the Mistress with anything. It's crazy to even try. You know that, don't you? My chest ached with a hopeless sort of weight. I didn't want to give up, but I didn't have any idea where to go from here.

I closed my eyes, and eventually, combing over and over the same thoughts exhausted me. I dozed back off.

I floated in the back of an unfamiliar classroom.

The class seemed ridiculously small to me, hardly a dozen girls sitting in desks. They wore matching plaid skirts and blouses, all listening with varying degrees of attention to the teacher at the front of the room.

The girl with the topknot sat at a desk by the windows. She didn't seem to be listening to the teacher at all. She had her eyes locked on the drifting clouds over the mountains in the distance. A dreamy little smile grew across her lips.

The bell rang. The girl jumped, letting out a nervous-sounding giggle.

"Oh, hey, I missed the homework. Could anyone . . . ?" She looked around, but her classmates were all chattering while they gathered their things. None of them seemed to hear her. She held

out a hand as if to tap a nearby girl's shoulder . . . then drew it to her chest, her cheeks flushing. The other girl walked away without even noticing her.

Sighing, the girl with the topknot gathered her books and walked out of the classroom.

I woke up again with one thought: *you aren't important.*

The girl reminded me a lot of myself—or who I used to be, anyway. Maybe I couldn't make that judgment based on one dream, but it seemed right. She didn't look confused or hurt when the other girls ignored her. She looked resigned, like she had gotten used to it.

Were *these* the dreams to pay attention to? Was there something about *this* girl that could help me? I couldn't see how.

I sighed, going to rub away a headache forming at my temples. My fingertips met feathers instead of skin. With shaking hands, I felt more growing along the tops of my cheeks. I wondered if they were gray like the ones that coated my arms or yellow-green like the ones that draped over my shoulders, dotted my thighs, and grew in lines along my hips, just beginning to change the shape of my dress.

My stomach lurched, shock stealing my breath. It should have stopped startling me, but I hated feeling new clusters of feathers. It felt like I was being stolen, inch by inch.

I thought about Elle. I hadn't even recognized her as human. My body wasn't nearly as bad as hers—you could still see some of my skin, and my face must have looked somewhat like my own. I at least still had hair framing my face, even if it felt limp, greasy, and unwashed.

But my body *felt* wrong. The Mistress twisted it into

something beyond my recognition without my consent. Just looking at it made me feel violated.

The curtains at the entrance shifted. I looked up, automatically tensing. But it was just Mark.

"Oh." I relaxed just a little, curling my fists into the blankets. "You came back."

"Yeah." He rubbed the back of his neck. "I said I would."

"Right."

The pauses between our sentences seemed overly long, weighed down with all the words we weren't saying. I knew I had to pick my words carefully. Talking about the Mistress sent him into a panic. But what else was I supposed to talk to him about? The Mistress and her show had become my entire life.

I ventured a comment on the show, hoping that much was allowed. "Um. So do you and Violet rehearse a lot? That dance looks hard."

Mark's eyes widened in surprise, not fear. "Oh. No. I mean, not really. The Mistress, she kind of—she helps things along, I guess."

Figures. I ran my fingers through my hair. "Oh. Um, what do you do, then, when you're not here?"

Mark shrugged. "Violet and I watch a lot of old movies. Play video games. Sometimes we even do dance and stuff. Not because we have to. Just for fun."

The answer struck me as wrong, even though I didn't think he was lying. It just seemed way too *normal.* "So you're not . . . kept somewhere? Like . . ." I gestured to the gauzy fabric cocoons that held the poetry women.

"Oh! Oh, no. Violet and I have a room. The rest of the

109

trailer—it's pretty normal? Not like this."

A list of questions thick enough to choke on clung to the back of my throat. But I saw the way Mark's eye darted around. I saw the tension in his face as he chewed the inside of his cheek, the way he gripped the edges of his sleeves hard enough to make the muscles in his arms tremble.

He would leave if I asked the wrong thing. I didn't want that.

So I asked something safer. "Um, what sorts of movies do you guys watch?"

Some of the tension in Mark's body drained as he talked to me about cheesy horror movies, first-person shooters, the ways he filled his time. I wondered if I could at least try to mention the show again, just to see how he'd react.

"How do you guys afford this stuff? Do you get, like, a paycheck?"

Mark tensed again, but he answered. "Uh, not really. But we can ask for stuff. The Mistress's never said no. Even got Violet a truck when she asked for one. We sometimes use it to go to the movies and stuff. When we have the time. As long as we're back in time for the show, it's fine."

I tried to imagine that. The way he talked about it, the Mistress almost seemed *generous*. But that didn't seem to fit her at all. She didn't strike me as the kind of person who gave. Just the kind of person who took.

"*She doesn't care for money.*" The voice spoke up, sure and grave. "*She has power.*"

I didn't know for sure whether to trust the voice, but this much rang true. Locking someone in a cage wasn't the only way to have power over them, after all. You could make them dependent on you, too.

A shiver crawled up my spine, and I wrapped my arms around myself. Mark opened his mouth, probably to ask what was wrong. But before either of us could talk, Violet walked in.

"Time," she said. Tension sat in the narrow gap between her dark eyebrows. She reminded me of a snake, ready to strike if I spoke.

I didn't. I knew it wouldn't do any good.

"Alright." Mark stood, brushing off his jeans. He glanced at me. "I'll see you later?"

"Yeah." I waved. Having Violet in the room made me feel tremendously awkward. "See you."

He left, and I had a few moments to myself to gather my thoughts.

At least I knew a little bit about how things worked around here: about the trailer and about how the Mistress treated the rest of the performers—or Mark and Violet, at least. Probably Bridget, too. I didn't know about the rest of the people, the crew members and Madame Selene. I didn't think I'd even heard any of the crew members speak, so I had no idea what they were like. Their matching glassy eyes and slack expressions made them seem more like dolls than real people.

Maybe I could ask Mark about them next time, if I asked about them the right way.

Thinking about it like that made me feel kind of gross. I didn't want to manipulate Mark or treat him like something I could use. He was the only kind person here. I didn't want to treat him poorly.

The voice piped up then, in a tone so cold that I actually shivered. *"Kindness will be no comfort when you're dead."*

The curtains rustled, and the blank-faced crew members walked in. But the chill lingered.

Bridget sneered at me when they brought me outside. "How's the little songbird doing?"

Her eyes twinkled with a kind of cruel joy, like she was already looking forward to making fun of my answer. Remembering how she had treated me before, the way she had laughed *with* me instead of *at* me, made me feel disgusted and used. *My standards must be really low.*

"Leave me alone." I curled in on myself. Part of me just wanted the crew members to come wheel me to Madame Selene's room. She could be confusing, but at least she didn't seem to actively enjoy seeing me here.

Bridget laughed. "God, you broke quickly, huh? At least some of the other birds tried screaming for help by now. Not that help ever came. And if it did?" Bridget puffed out her chest proudly. She flicked her wrist, and a silver knife appeared out of thin air. She brandished it, grinning. "I took care of it."

The high, jagged sound of her laughter bounced off the buildings around us. Part of me wanted to say that she was lying. I'd never really seen her be violent. Maybe she was just trying to scare me as some sort of sick game.

But somehow, I didn't think that was it. After all, her role model was the Mistress, and the Mistress was evil.

But not evil to her, maybe. She gives Mark and Violet whatever they want, doesn't she? Maybe it was about having power over them, but Bridget didn't seem to mind.

"The Mistress is the one who taught you that trick with the knife, right?" I scooted to the center of the cage, out of the reach of grasping hands—although that wouldn't do much good if the knife could fit through the cage bars. "Is that why you stay here? Why are you so loyal to her?"

Bridget smirked at me, all cool amusement. It looked like the sort of expression the Mistress would wear. I wondered if she was faking as easily as she faked her friendly smile. Maybe she was just trying on her idol's expression.

"She gave me a new life. She gave me *freedom*." She laughed, brandishing her knife. "Just don't go asking her for the same thing! I don't think she'll be as kind to you."

Before I could ask anything more, the crew members wheeled me away.

I didn't think it would do any good, anyway. Maybe I could get information from Mark, if I said the right thing. But I didn't think I'd get anywhere by quizzing Bridget about her relationship with the Mistress or her ideas of freedom.

Instead, I turned my thoughts to my own.

thirteen.

Over the next couple of weeks, I sang on stage every night.

I never grew to like the shows, but at least being wheeled to and from them gave me a slight break from the monotony of the fabric-draped room. Boredom wasn't the right word to describe how I passed the hours, but staring at the same props until my eyes dried out got old. Mark didn't come to visit every day, and without the shows to mark the time, I was pretty sure I'd go crazy.

On stage, I sang whatever song came to mind—songs from the radio, from musicals, from the old CDs my parents used to play. Sometimes I remembered all the lyrics. Sometimes I forgot. Sometimes I sang well. Sometimes I didn't. Sometimes the audience clapped for me. Sometimes the curtains closed on uncomfortable coughing and silence.

It didn't matter. The Mistress always watched me from the shadows, and I could always feel her smug satisfaction. It burrowed under my skin, pulsing in my throat where her command lingered.

After the show, I slept. And with sleep came the dreams. Usually I'd have one of Alice, followed by the girl with the topknot, but sometimes I just saw one or the other. I liked the dreams of the girl a bit better. The ones of Alice were fascinating, but living through the curly-haired woman's emotions often made me wake up *more* exhausted.

My dreams of the girl, on the other hand, weren't particularly interesting. I watched her while she read or sat in class. Sometimes I'd catch her playing violin—she was really good at that. But at least I got to think my own thoughts in those dreams.

Also, I liked watching her. Something about her felt comforting, familiar. Her life wasn't exactly the same as the one I had before. Her school was different, she lived in an apartment, and she liked different things. But it was close, and I missed home a little less when I was with her.

But once I woke up, I spent most of my day thinking of the Alice dreams. If anything had the answers that Madame Selene hinted at, I thought it would be those.

The dreams of Alice told a story, even if I saw it out of order. One night, Alice handed me a flower, and I mentally scolded myself for thinking that her gaze lingered on me when she had my sister. In the next, we swore our undying love to each other in whispers beneath the overbright moon.

I always woke up from the ones before the confession with my heart aching. I didn't love Alice, not really. And she didn't love me. She loved the diamond-eyed woman with lively curls and sharp features.

How were we connected? We had to be in some way; the nickname and the eye color would have been clues even if I didn't dream through her eyes. Did we have a psychic link or something? Did she exist right now in some other world? Was it the world the Mistress came from?

I didn't know, but I had plenty of time to think about it.

Thinking could only do so much, though, especially when it felt like I was running around in circles, like the mental version of a hamster on a wheel. When I couldn't do that anymore, I did my best to pass the time. I counted every paper lantern and memorized every name scrawled on them. I looked at the pile of old clothes and made up stories about who had once owned them. I squinted at the bookshelf on the far wall and tried to make out the titles there.

Sometimes, Mark came to see me. I didn't really get much more information out of him. Whenever I tried broaching the topic of the Mistress, he'd clam up and stop coming around for a few days. And because having him there was better than not having him there, I stuck to safe topics.

The voice, which had begun piping up more, didn't like him. "*He really isn't going to do a single thing to help you,*" it snapped one day as he followed Violet out.

He's probably scared of the Mistress, too, I reasoned back at it. I wasn't sure if it could hear my thoughts—it rarely responded—but talking out loud to it would've felt weird. *And it's not like he can leave. He has no money. The Mistress has him trapped, too.*

"*Just not in a cage.*" The voice surprised me by actually replying. And I couldn't really argue with it.

But Mark wasn't the only one I talked to regularly. Before

116

the shows, I almost always talked to Madame Selene, as well.

Madame Selene was both easier and more difficult to talk to than Mark. I didn't have to worry about scaring her off—nothing seemed to scare her. But she also had a hard time putting words together, and I didn't always know what she meant. Sometimes, she could hardly talk at all. She just stared off into space, going almost as glassy-eyed as the crew members.

My conversations with Mark and Madame Selene kept my days from looking too similar. So did the dreams and the quality of the show. But there was one thing about my imprisonment that remained constant.

The feathers still grew.

They grew until they covered my arms completely with a thick coat, all the way down to the tips of my fingers. My legs followed along just a few paces behind until they became more feather than skin. They sprouted along my stomach and my back. They prickled beneath my bangs and itched their way across my chest.

And then, one day, I woke up to a thick chunk of hair lying on my pillow.

My hand shook as I felt around my skull. My fingertips met a patch of feathers to the left of where my hair parted, farther to the back. They stuck out straight in a thick clump, just a little smaller than the size of my fist.

How long before I stop looking human? With feathers covering my cheeks and forehead in awkward clumps, it felt like only a matter of time. My head ached with the hollow-boned feeling that new feathers brought. Their heat radiated against my scalp to the point where beads of sweat surrounded the clump, dripping through my hair.

Mark didn't come that day. I wasn't sure what I would have said to him if he had.

When the crew members rolled me into Madame Selene's exhibit, she looked to me and sighed. "The time for you to unlock your potential is running thin."

Even though I suspected it, the words still hit me like a physical blow. "What can you tell me?" I knew as soon as I spoke that it was the wrong thing to ask. Madame Selene did better with direct questions, but I needed time to gather my thoughts.

I needed *time*.

"It is difficult to say." Madame Selene blinked slowly, lacing her fingers together. "The less likely the thread is, the more frayed it becomes. I cannot read a message printed onto scraps." Her tanned complexion paled to gray just slightly, like the very effort of trying made her feel sick.

"So, what can I do?" Silence hung in the air between us. I wasn't really asking Madame Selene, anyway. I was asking myself, because I knew that no matter how much I pushed and prodded, Madame Selene couldn't give me what I wanted. I wanted answers, neatly wrapped.

I didn't play video games often before all of this, but when I did, I always told myself I'd do it alone, without cheating. I never did. When things got too hard, I'd always cave in and look up online how to beat it.

I wanted to do the same thing here, but this was one puzzle I had to put together myself.

How could I even hope to do that? The pieces I uncovered made countless different pictures. And it wasn't like I could use trial and error to figure out which one was right. It would only take one wrong move to mess up everything. If the Mistress knew that I had hope, she'd do whatever she could to crush it.

I sighed, leaning against the bars. "Hope" didn't come close to how I felt in that moment. *No matter what I do, the Mistress is going to overpower me. What does it even matter?*

Madame Selene's fingertips brushed my shoulder. I jerked away on instinct—I hadn't even heard her come toward me. She let me move, but her fingers reached through the bars as far as they could.

"If you give up hope, then the thread is already broken." Her voice sounded especially shaky. It always trembled, in an aged sort of way, but now she sounded like she was on the verge of tears.

I'd never seen her like this. Even though she'd never been cruel to me, she always seemed a little detached. I never really got the sense that she cared or that she wanted me out of this cage.

I reached out to her. She gently curled her fingers around my feather-covered hands as best as she could. All at once, I thought of my parents holding my hands as I crossed the street—Mom on one side, Dad on the other. I didn't remember the context, but I remembered being very little, feeling safe and *loved*.

I couldn't remember the last time someone made me feel that way.

I loved my mom and dad. I missed them both, sometimes so much that it felt like my chest would tear itself apart. But I missed them because of where I was now, not because of what I had before. I missed not being in a cage more than I missed my home. I missed not seeing the Mistress more than I missed seeing Mom and Dad.

When I left for the show that night, I remembered thinking that they looked like ghosts in the light of the television screen. Now *I* was the ghost, and I couldn't think of a single way that my parents' lives would change. At some point over the years, the hand-holding and the hugs had stopped.

I looked at Madame Selene's fingers wrapped around my own feather-covered ones. "Maybe if someone had done this more often, I wouldn't have come here." My voice wavered on the edge of tears, full of stupid self-pity. I knew it was pointless to try and blame what had happened on a cruel universe. The universe wasn't conspiring against me. *You aren't important.*

But still, some things just bothered me. It had been so easy for Bridget to lure me in. She made me feel *special*. She made me feel *important*. But would she have made me feel that way if I had anything else to do with my time or anyone else to share it with?

"The threads of the past have already unspooled." Madame Selene's words were gentle, like she knew they weren't the words I wanted to hear. She squeezed my hands ever so gently. "No amount of wondering will be able to wind them back."

I sighed, hanging my head so my forehead pressed against the cool metal bars. "I know. I can't change anything. It's just . . . This is all so insane. I can't believe I'm supposed to fight the Mistress with . . . what? My dreams?"

"No." Madame Selene's voice wavered slightly. "The dreams are not your ammunition, songbird. They are a gift."

I looked up and frowned, feathers shifting awkwardly between my furrowed brows. "But you said those dreams were from the Mistress. How could anything from her be a gift?"

Madame Selene's fingers turned clammy under mine. An intense concentration crept beneath her usual stoic expression. "A gift is no less a gift just because the intention behind it is cruel." The words came out slow, faltering. "The Mistress's punishment—watching that tale—can be used to your advantage."

Punishment. That made sense. It hurt to be so close to Alice and then wake up alone.

Madame Selene didn't seem finished. I stayed quiet, not wanting to distract her. Finally, she continued. "But . . . the true gift . . . comes from another. From a rogue player. One cut from the weave with a knife, long before. But not completely. No . . . the essence . . . remains . . ."

Her face contorted suddenly, and she jerked away. I called out, banging my hands against the cage in an automatic attempt to reach her.

She trembled for a moment, then staggered to her seat. She looked spent, and I knew I wasn't getting anything more out of her. Still, I clutched at the cage bars, desperate for just a little bit of hope. "Is there still a chance for me? Is there still a future where I don't die in this cage?"

Madame Selene nodded, just once.

The crew members came to wheel me away. I couldn't do anything but watch as Madame Selene fixed her gaze on the entrance and waited for the first guests to come through.

fourteen.

I couldn't get to sleep that night.

Usually I'd be occupied by thoughts of my performance, especially when I did poorly. But even though my voice shook and wavered through that night's song, the awkward silence of the crowd wasn't the thing keeping me up.

I couldn't get Madame Selene's words out of my head. I kept trying to figure out what she meant by the "true" gift, the one that had apparently come from someone other than the Mistress. Someone who wasn't supposed to be here at all.

Someone who *wasn't* here at all, maybe.

Someone like the voice?

It sort of made sense, although I might have been able to logic anyone into the role. It wasn't like Madame Selene had given me a whole lot to go on. But the voice had *something* to do with all of this. Assuming I wasn't just going insane, why else would I be hearing it? Madame Selene had called it a rogue player, and that seemed like a good description. It felt totally out of my control.

But what did the voice have to do with the dreams the Mistress gave me? Unless it didn't have anything to do with *those* dreams. I had two kinds, after all. And if I assumed that the ones of Alice and the curly-haired woman were from the Mistress, did that mean that the ones of the normal girl with the topknot came from the voice?

I couldn't be sure, but it was the closest thing I had to a lead. I took a deep breath, curling on my side and hugging one of the blankets close to me. *Well, voice? If the dreams of that girl are coming from you, give me something I can work with.*

The voice didn't answer, at least not in words. But something happened, something that calmed my racing thoughts and smoothed my twitching nerves. It felt almost like a kinder, slower version of the Mistress's first spell, the one that put me to sleep—except this gave me the choice to either follow it or stay awake.

I closed my eyes.

The girl played her guitar.

This was new. I assumed that she played, since the guitar sat in her room, but I'd only ever seen her play the violin.

She didn't seem to be as good at the guitar. She plucked along slowly, sitting in front of her computer, pausing and unpausing what looked like a tutorial video. I assumed she just started playing without the same professional instruction that she obviously had on violin.

I wondered what made her pick it up.

Even with everything going on in the waking world, listening to her play made me smile—or it would have, if I had a body to smile with in these dreams—because I recognize the song she plucked out. It was the theme song to one of my favorite cartoons. She must have been a fan, too.

Someone knocked on the door. The girl stopped playing. "Yeah?"

An older woman's voice sounded from the other side of the door, muffled but understandable. "It's time for dinner, Alice."

The shock woke me right up. Alice. Her name is Alice. It couldn't be a coincidence. There was no way. Alice wasn't a common name, and besides, their eye colors were the same.

Just like me and the woman I was in those dreams.

"Sweet dreams, little songbird?"

I jumped, clutching the blankets to my chest. The Mistress sat on the chair near the bookshelf, smirking. She held a glass of red wine in one hand.

Thoughts of dreams and Alices flew from my head, birds scattering toward freedom. This felt very wrong. It was the middle of the night—I definitely didn't sleep that long—and the Mistress sat alone. Had I ever actually seen her by herself? Not since Elle. The memory made the breath turn thick in my throat.

"W-What . . . ?" I couldn't find my voice. Something reflected in those diamond-shaped irises, something frightening. In Alice, the odd shape looked beautiful and ethereal. In the curly-haired woman, it looked lively and warm. But in the Mistress, with her cruel grin and the red tinge around her pupils, they just looked inhuman.

"You're staring." The Mistress smiled. "I don't blame you. You all look at my eyes like that. 'You' meaning the birds, naturally. No one else in their right mind gets close enough.

125

The rest watch me dance—they watch me onstage. Distant, untouchable. They love me there. But offstage? There is nowhere I can go away from this show. I'm just as trapped as you are." Her eyes roamed up and down the gold bars of my cage, and she let out a harsh, humorless bark of a laugh. "Well. *Almost* as trapped."

I didn't say anything. I *couldn't* say anything. Her eyes kept drawing me back. They reflected too much of the light, giving her all the flat warmth of a mannequin.

"The truth is, I'm *bored*." She heaved a sigh. It rattled through the air like wind through a graveyard. "Bringing in the fortune teller helped for a little while. As did the poets. And the rest of the main act are not without their charms—especially Bridget. But at the end of the day?"

She looked down at her wine with a thoughtfulness that felt almost mocking. My pulse hammered against my ears.

"When the doves are here," she finally continued, "things are *much* more interesting. They're entertaining to visit, at least. But you little green finches?" She let out a small scoff, her lips curling upward. "There's nothing I can do but watch you suffer. And even *that* gets old after a century or so."

Alarm stole the air from my lungs, like a bird of prey snatching a fish. *Century? Did she say century?* Maybe the fact that she was immortal shouldn't have surprised me, but the idea still made my skin crawl.

"Bridget thinks you're unintelligent." She stood, trailing one fingertip along the edge of the bookshelf. "But I don't think that's true. You know things, don't you, little songbird? *More* than the others."

I understood, in that moment, why Madame Selene had

sounded so urgent. In my mind's eye, I saw those threads she talked about. I saw the Mistress's hands grasping a pair of scissors, preparing to cut. I opened my mouth to tell her she was wrong, that I didn't know anything—

But then the voice cut in, quiet. "*Don't do that, Elizabeth. She'll hear the lie in your voice right now. She's looking for it. Your best chance is to stay silent.*" It spoke with such *confidence*. I pressed my lips together.

This made the Mistress laugh. "Well, I'll give you one thing, little songbird. You do know when to . . . How is it said? *Sit* down and *shut* up." She shook her head, teeth bared in a mockery of a grin. "Admirable qualities. Not every bird had them, you know. Some of them *never* stopped twittering."

I had to physically stop myself from letting out a sigh of relief.

"Oh, but there *is* something about you, isn't there?" The Mistress's airy tone felt phony and forced, like lines delivered by a bad actress. "Something more. There's a . . . color about you, something the other birds never had. And there's the way you look at people. You've got a certain . . . curiosity? Or something to that effect. Sometimes, you still look like you're trying to figure things out. I'd say you had a touch of precognition, but . . . no, that isn't for *you*."

Her expression turned from airy to angry in the time it took to blink. My heart stuttered against my ribs.

"No wonder," she mumbled to herself, dark as a storm cloud. "What a self-fulfilling prophecy it all turned out to be."

The glow of the paper lanterns dimmed, like even the

lights wanted to shrink away from the Mistress's anger. The shadows grew across her face in long drips, pooling at her feet. And even though the lantern lights didn't flicker, I swore the shadows started to move.

I wanted to say something—*anything*—to cut through that heavy air. But the voice had told me to stay silent, and it didn't seem like it had any more instructions. Besides, the fear of saying the wrong thing grasped at my throat, every bit as powerfully as one of the Mistress's commands.

The Mistress didn't seem annoyed or angered by my silence, but she didn't have her usual smug superiority, either. She just seemed slightly unhinged, like she had borrowed Bridget's impulsivity for the night but kept the power she had to back it up. *God, she has so* much *power.*

Her lips curved up into what would have been a smirk if her eyes hadn't still been flat and unamused. "I could kill you right now, you know." She stepped toward me, bare feet slow and purposeful against black fabric. "It would be a shame to break my perfect streak . . . but it would be something different, after all of these years. To kill you outright instead of letting the magic do it slowly. Maybe it would entertain me, even."

She stopped in front of my cage. Her face held the sort of flat bloodlust that belonged on an animal's face, not a person's. "Why, just look. Look at how easy it is."

I shook my head, everything in me screaming out against this. The Mistress laughed, a sound completely devoid of warmth. I flinched backward on instinct just as she spoke in that whisper-shout. "*Don't move.*"

She froze me right in the middle of my flinch, my arms

halfway up to my face and my shoulders just beginning to hunch forward. It shouldn't have been physically possible to hold. In the few long seconds that the Mistress regarded me, my muscles started to ache and my body couldn't even tremble to release the tension.

The Mistress stayed in my line of sight. She still smiled that cold, lifeless smile, but something started to flicker in her gaze. Behind the animal bloodlust sat a refined, matured version of the sort of glee sadistic kids got from ripping the wings off flies.

"*Don't blink.*" She spoke in that same whisper-shout.

Was I able to blink before? I hadn't noticed, but now all I could think about was how dry my eyes were. I couldn't do anything to fix them. My vision started to blur, the shapes of the various props warping and lurching forward.

A small, strangled noise escaped my locked throat. The Mistress shook a finger, one eyebrow raised. "We can't have that, now can we?"

The words sounded like a mockery of her usual smug, collected tone. Breathy and high, with spots of color on her cheeks, she reminded me uncomfortably of how Alice looked in some of my more vivid dreams.

"*Don't breathe.*"

My breath cut off with a strangled gasp.

Everything in me turned to chaos. My body couldn't find a reason why I couldn't move or blink or breathe when just a few moments ago I could do all of those things. I imagined red lights flashing, sirens blaring. And above it all was a thought—the only conscious thought I could have in the panic. *This is how I die.*

The Mistress towered above me. She looked into her wine glass and swirled it. She brought it to her lips so slowly that it felt like I should have died five times over by the time she lowered it. She seemed larger, warped, like how ants under a magnifying glass probably saw their tormentor.

Darkness fuzzed around the edges of my vision, then spread. And then, distant but still resonating with that strange power, came the Mistress's voice.

"Very well. *That's enough.*"

I collapsed to the floor in a mess of spasming nerves and scrambled brainwaves. I heard something: a harsh rattle like a rusty hinge. I didn't recognize it as coming from me until the third or fourth breath. My heart thundered in my temples and throbbed in every feather, so loud it almost formed words: *I could have died. I could have died. I could have died.*

Until that moment, my impending death hadn't felt real. I knew the Mistress planned to kill me. I saw Elle die. I heard about all the girls who came before her. I felt the feathers that broke through my skin. But even in a situation that dire, my death had always felt like something hypothetical.

It didn't feel hypothetical now.

From where I sprawled on the floor, I looked up at the Mistress. She stared down at me in cold amusement. Did victims of serial killers see a similar expression if they got a chance to glimpse their attackers? I didn't think so. The Mistress didn't look like even the most awful humans.

"There." The satisfaction in her voice was unmistakable. "That odd color is gone now. Everything is as it should be."

Without a single explanation, she turned and walked out

of the room.

The lanterns grew brighter again. I sat up slowly, still trembling. I moved to press a hand to my throat, my limbs feeling shaky and weak. *Did that really just happen? Did she almost kill me . . . and let me go?* But my hand didn't meet the small patch of feathers at the hollow of my throat, like I expected. They met more.

Feathers now circled my neck in a thick collar, like a noose.

fifteen.

Every rustle of the fabric made me jump.

I didn't think the Mistress planned to come back. Whatever she wanted from me, she had gotten it. But even though logic told me I was safe—for now—the fear remained. I knew that any moment she might swoop in like a bird of prey to finish the job.

The hours passed. I wished that Mark would come visit or something. Anything to keep me from sitting here, waiting for the worst to happen. But when the curtains finally parted, they just revealed the crew members preparing to bring me to the show.

The Mistress stood outside when I was wheeled out, but she didn't even turn to glance in my direction. She walked into the black-draped building with her usual poise and grace. Whatever happened last night was really over.

Had it been a mistake? She'd told me a *lot*, like the fact that she had been at this for a century. And there was also that thing about precognition. I didn't think I had that, but I couldn't shake the feeling that it meant something.

Or maybe not. Maybe this was all part of it—the next step in her ultimate plan to break my spirit and mind along with my feathered body.

I couldn't be sure. Not until I had more information. And the way I was going, I couldn't get information from dreams. I kept learning things, like the girl's—*Alice's*—name, but I didn't have the time to put everything together. I couldn't figure out the connection between her and the other Alice, not for sure and not on my own.

When the crew wheeled me onstage, I performed through numb lips, my mind a million miles away, forgetting the lyrics to the song and cutting off early. I couldn't even tell if the audience applauded me because I sang decently or just to be polite.

After the show, Mark came in to hand me my blankets and pillow back like he always did. We had fallen into a routine. A simple "thank you" and "good night" were all we exchanged. I was usually too eager to get to my dreams, where Alice or—well, the other Alice—waited for me.

But tonight, I spoke. "Hey, Mark. Could you, um, stay?" His eyes widened. Before he could say anything, I hurried on. "Please, just for a little bit. It's just . . . all of these dreams, everything. I'm *really* freaked out. If I have to be alone with my own thoughts, I . . ."

Did pity color Mark's expression? Or was that guilt? I thought it was probably a mix of both. If the way his breathing sometimes shortened and his expression turned panicked was any indication, he knew a little bit about thoughts being haunting.

Using something like that against him made me feel a little guilty. I didn't like being manipulative, but I didn't like anything about this situation. I needed answers.

"I can stay. For a little bit." He paused for a long moment, plucking at his sleeves. "Do you—want to talk about it?"

I let out a long, shaky breath. I had a goal but no plan. I had no idea where to even start. "It's just, um . . . It's like I said. About the dreams. I know you don't like to talk about them, but they're always one of two things."

Mark made an odd face. I couldn't figure out what it meant, so I let it pass without comment.

Instead, I continued. "In most of them, I'm not even myself. I sound like me, but I look like a stranger and I *feel* like a totally different person. I'm thinking all these thoughts, and none of them make any sense. None of them are mine. And the emotions—everything—it's all so vivid. I'm even more tired when I wake up."

Mark was nodding. I didn't think he even realized he was doing it.

I decided to test my luck. "Madame Selene told me that the Mistress gave me these dreams. Do you know why?"

Mark's chest hitched, his breath coming in on a harsh gasp. The words fell out of me in a desperate rush.

"Please, please understand—I'm not trying to get you in trouble. I'm just losing my mind in here, Mark. I'm dreaming of living a life that isn't mine, of loving a woman who doesn't exist or who used to exist or who exists . . . somewhere else. I don't know. I don't *know*, and that's what's driving me crazy."

I wasn't even lying, really.

Mark fidgeted with his sleeves, looking down. "You'll find out eventually. The rest of them—they put the pieces together. In the end, I think. When then ne—when the end comes."

The truth seemed close enough to touch. My voice shook. "Mark, listen. I'm already dying. I know that." The new feathers around my throat ached. I told myself that the next words out of my mouth were a necessary lie. "I know there's nothing I can do to change that. I just want to know why."

For a long moment, I thought Mark would run. It would be all over then. But instead, he sat on the ground in front of me, drawing his knees up to his chest.

"So long. It's been going on for so long." His spoke in a rush, almost too quietly to hear. "Longer than I've been here. And I've been here for—God, almost ten years. I've seen so many girls. So many girls . . ." His voice broke.

I took in a deep breath and let it out slow. When I told him what I thought he wanted to hear, it didn't feel like a lie. "I forgive you, Mark. I don't think you're a bad person, really. I think you're just . . ."

"Surviving." Mark ran a hand over his buzzcut curls, sighing. "That's what Violet says. She says that's all any of us can hope for." He glanced up at me and winced.

Yeah, not the best choice of words. But I tried to use it to my advantage. "I have a hope, too, Mark. If I can't hope to survive, I can at least stay . . . I don't know. Sane? If you help me." I paused, bracing myself. "Please, just . . . tell me about the girls in my dreams. Why do their eyes look like the Mistress's? Where do they come from?"

"I—I . . ." Mark sighed, shaking his head. "I don't know the answer to that." My heart dropped into my stomach, only to fly back up when he continued. "I only know that they're not from here. This world, I mean."

"Aliens?" They didn't seem totally human, but the idea of another planet felt a little far-fetched.

Mark shook his head. "Not exactly." He couldn't look me in the eyes. He fidgeted with his sleeves instead. "The way I understand it—and I *don't* understand it, not really—is that they lived in a kind of alternate dimension. A world almost like ours. It had people like us—almost. Except for the eyes and the magic."

My heart thundered in my chest. "The Mistress came from there, didn't she?" I phrased it more like a statement than a question, but Mark nodded anyway. I pressed on. "Did she, um, know those women? *Does* she know those women?"

I felt guilty for the savage joy that welled up in me when I saw the defeat on Mark's face. He tucked his hands into his sleeves. "It happened a hundred years ago, she said. She was a powerful witch, and she talked a lot with witches from other . . . regions, is how she put it. One day, a witch from far away came to visit. The Mistress let her stay in her home." He sighed. "Her name was Alice. She was beautiful. And she and the Mistress hit it off. They started dating, I guess. That's the best word for it."

What remained of my skin crawled. "But then Alice fell for her sister instead, right?"

Mark hung his head. "I told you that you'd figure it out."

I scooted forward, clutching the bars of my cage with

feathered fingers. "Keep going. *Please*. The Mistress must have found out, right?"

Mark sighed. "Alice and the Mistress's sister told her. They felt too guilty. They decided to come clean." He shook his head, speaking in a flat voice that turned the insides of my bones to ice. "Their mistake."

Something in the pit of my stomach trembled. I had a pretty good idea of what came next, but I had to ask. "What happened?"

"The Mistress killed them." Mark's voice trembled. "Both of them."

I shivered. It wouldn't have been an easy death. I imagined Alice, the woman I felt such love for in my dreams, gasping for air like I did last night. She didn't deserve that. And neither did the poor woman who loved her. *No one* deserved that.

Mark shook his head. He didn't seem surprised by my reaction. "I'm sorry, Elizabeth."

Part of me didn't want to keep going, but I needed to know as much as possible. "That wasn't the end, right? She came here . . . to do what?"

Mark looked down at his lap. "She—the Mistress, I mean—decided that dying wasn't enough. She wanted them to suffer more. She trapped their souls, kept them from moving on. Then she came to our world with them and started taking people for her act."

I couldn't quite wrap my head around that part. "Why? Why an act?"

Mark gave a small shrug. "She never told us that. But . . ." He looked at me, not quite meeting my eyes. "I *do* know that

137

the people here—the ones she took, I mean—she took on a whim. This show isn't about them. It's about you."

My mouth went dry. "Me?"

"Well, not you exactly." Mark gestured a bit with his hands as he spoke. "It's about the cycle. I don't know all the details. I just know that a girl with blue eyes gets kidnapped. She grows white feathers. She has the dreams about what happened—from Alice's point of view. And then, right before she dies—"

"A girl with hazel eyes shows up," I finished for him. My voice sounded distant. "A girl like me."

"Yes." Mark rubbed at his eyes, looking like a tired child. "It all goes back to those two."

I took a deep breath. "So you're telling me . . . what? Was I the Mistress's sister in a past life or something?"

Mark frowned a little. "I don't know. I don't think so. She takes girls of all ages. Most of you are here for less than a year. There are probably a bunch of future victims alive right now. Including ones with green feathers. I do think the Mistress chooses them ahead of time. Bridget always seems to know where to go to invite them."

My temples began to throb. I decided I'd come back to that—I didn't want him to feel like I was pumping him for information to use against the Mistress. "What about the other people in the act? You said the Mistress just takes them at random?"

"I guess so." Mark rubbed the back of his neck. "Most of them were here before me. Except—" Instead of finishing his sentence, he looked over his shoulder, up at the gauzy cocoons.

"The poetry women," I finished for him.

He nodded. "Another girl wrote the poems about a year ago. A green finch, like you. Rochelle. She would recite them on stage every night. The Mistress had her write a bunch down. A few months later, she took them." He gestured at the cocoons. "I don't know why. If I had to guess, I'd say that maybe the Mistress got jealous. They were pretty obviously, you know, a couple. I guess they still are, but—but they're different now." He pulled on his sleeves so hard I thought he might tear them off. "I don't think they can kiss anymore."

My heart ached for them when I looked up at the cocoons. "And the others?"

"Most of them are just husks. The stagehands, I mean." Mark sighed. "That's why they don't talk. Or age, I'm pretty sure. They're sort of like dolls. But I know they used to be people. Madame Selene's not like them, but—you know. Her mind isn't exactly in great shape, either."

A chill trembled through me even with the room's stuffy, stale air. I almost didn't want to ask the next question. "What about you and Violet and Bridget? Why are you guys . . . ?" *Normal* was how I wanted to finish that sentence, but it didn't quite fit. *I don't really think there's anything normal about Bridget.* But judging from the guarded expression on Mark's face, he knew what I meant.

"Well, I don't know about Bridget. I don't really talk to her. She scares me a little, honestly. And Violet and I . . ." He swallowed, loud enough to hear.

"It's okay, Mark." I tried to encourage him as gently as I could.

"We . . ." He paused for a long moment. Then he spoke in a rush. "We weren't stolen by the Mistress at all. We joined by choice."

I stared at him as the seconds ticked by in silence. A thousand words tried to claw their way up my throat, but I could only manage to choke out one of them. "Why?"

"You have to understand." He stared at me, wide-eyed. "You *have* to. We didn't know at first. What this all was, I mean. We were just kids. I was thirteen, and—and neither of us had it great at home. Violet, especially. It was bad. My parents, they—they hit me, but Violet's—you know. Whatever you're thinking, they probably did worse." His hands curled into loose fists, trembling a little.

Nausea coiled in my stomach. "That . . . That sounds awful, Mark." I hoped he could hear how sincerely I meant that. "I'm so sorry." *I'd probably do anything to escape something like that, too.*

Mark's eyes fixed on the wall behind me, like he was seeing something else. "We were each other's one good thing." He spoke with more certainty than I'd ever heard from him before. "And when she saw the show? She loved everything about it. Decided to pack her bags and beg to join. Asked me to come with. And how could I say no?"

"You couldn't." I kept my voice low, quiet. "When did you find out? About . . ."

I trailed off, but Mark knew what I meant. "The Mistress told us almost right away. I guess she was bragging, or—or she thought maybe we'd get scared off."

"But that didn't happen," I prompted gently.

Mark shook his head. "Violet—it's hard to explain. She

140

liked it. Not the cruelty, just—just being with someone like that. With someone who could crush anyone in her way." He wrapped his arms around himself, looking up at me with pleading eyes. "She wasn't like she is now. You know? She was just a kid. And she was *so* scared all the time. I couldn't protect her. And I thought maybe *she* could. So I guess—I guess I sort of liked it, too."

I thought about that. I felt unnoticed in my own home, but I never felt afraid. At least the people who hurt me now were strangers, not my family. "I get it, I think."

Mark slumped, relaxing muscles I hadn't even realized he'd tensed. Maybe he'd expected me to scream at him. "Yeah. Sometimes I think we should leave. But this is our life. We don't have anywhere to go. And Violet, she loves performing. She's not like me. She's good at not thinking about anything else. And I could never leave her."

"You love her." I didn't phrase it as a question. I tried to imagine having someone I'd do anything for, someone I'd throw away all my morals for, just for a chance to stand by her side.

Someone I'd give up flight for.

Someone that I loved the way I loved Alice in my dreams.

"Mark, can I tell you a secret?"

He looked up at me, surprise coloring his features. "Of course."

"You know how I mentioned having other kinds of dreams?" I waited for him to nod before continuing. "They're of this girl. She's around my age, I think. She goes to a private school. She plays violin really well, and she's learning guitar, too. She has this chubby gray cat named

Smush. And she has bright, *bright* blue eyes. I think . . . she's supposed to be the next girl the Mistress takes."

The realization came to me as I spoke. I probably would have figured it out the night before, if the Mistress hadn't come in and terrified me.

"I dreamed her name last night," I continued. "It's Alice."

Mark sucked in a sharp breath. "I don't understand." He seemed to be talking to himself more than to me. "I figured it had to be a coincidence. Elizabeth's a common name, you know? But Alice, too?"

I remembered how angry the Mistress had been when I gave her my name. "The Mistress's sister was named Elizabeth. Is that what you're saying?"

Mark fidgeted with the edges of his sleeves, the answer written across his face before he even spoke. "Yeah. Her name was Elizabeth, too." He shook his head, sighing. "It's probably nothing. A coincidence. And this other Alice—can you say for sure that she's real?"

"No." It was true, in a sense. But even though I couldn't prove it, I knew she existed. A girl named Alice was out there, living in a city near the mountains, and every day we were getting closer to her. And she had no idea. She had no idea that her life was about to be stolen in a humiliating, painful way.

I can't let that happen. The thought was sudden and fierce, but I didn't think it came from the voice. I didn't want that to happen. Alice seemed nice, and she didn't deserve this.

Besides, in order for her to become the Mistress's next victim, I would die. Horror rolled through me like frost beneath my skin.

"I think I've told you everything I know." Mark's voice startled me from my thoughts. "Does it feel better? Knowing?"

I curled my fingers around the bars of the cage, nodding. "It does, Mark. Really. *Thank* you."

Mark stood slowly. "I should go now. Violet doesn't like sleeping alone."

"Of course." Knowing what I knew now, I felt a small pang at that. But I thought it would be better not to comment on it. Instead, I just watched him as he went to the exit.

"Goodnight, Mark."

"Goodnight, Elizabeth."

sixteen.

I hardly slept that night. I replayed Mark's words in my mind until the inside of my skull buzzed.

At last, I had all the puzzle pieces. Right now, they fit snugly into a picture of the Mistress's making. But was there a way for me to rearrange them and make a new picture?

I lay on my blankets. I dozed but only caught glimpses of dreams before startling back awake. A forest. A bedroom. A city. A school. The Alice from the past, fixing the glossy black braid that hung heavy over her bare shoulder. The Alice from the present, twisting her brown hair into a messy bun.

The first Elizabeth, staring pensively at her lively curls and freckles in a mirror.

I got so used to thinking her thoughts, to living in her skin. I hadn't ever really taken the time to consider who she was as a *person* outside of her love for Alice. Now I did.

She was the Mistress's *sister*. She lived in the Mistress's world, a world of pointed irises and magic.

Magic.

My heart stuttered, then slammed into my throat.

The Mistress was a witch. And so was Alice. But what about the first Elizabeth?

I closed my eyes. On the backs of my eyelids, a picture flickered to life, although it was less clear than most of the dreams. I saw the first Elizabeth, her bony arms held up, an earthy green light floating between her hands. Magic fell from her lips like a stream.

And then the voice spoke. *"I was."*

I shot into a sitting position with a gasp, eyes flying open. One of the green paper lanterns, the one hanging right at the locked door of the cage, glowed brighter than the rest. I stood and walked over to it, leaning against the bars to read the thin red script.

Elizabeth. Elizabeth. Elizabeth.

"Elizabeth," I echoed. "It's you talking to me, isn't it?"

"Yes." Her voice sounded quiet. Not distant, exactly, but muffled, kind of like I was hearing her from underwater.

"Did you talk to the others?" I almost felt afraid to hear the answer. *What if this is another part of the Mistress's plot? What if this doesn't mean anything?*

The voice—*she*—mumbled too quietly to hear. What was it that Madame Selene had told me? That my ears weren't equipped to hear her. But there had to be a way. I was *so close* to an answer, something definite, something I could work with. *I can't let this slip away.*

Feeling like I was dreaming, I watched my fingers reach as far through the cage bars as they could. My feathered fingertips didn't quite brush against Elizabeth's lantern, but

145

warmth still glowed against my skin. I closed my eyes, willing myself to focus on nothing but her, and tried again. "Did you talk to the others?"

"*I wanted to.*" She sounded like someone shouting from far away. "*But none of them would have heard me.*"

"Why can I?"

"*Because you have my name, Elizabeth. And names have . . .*"

Her voice faded away. When I opened my eyes, the lantern glowed dimmer than the rest. But I already knew how the sentence ended. The Mistress had told me the same thing when I first woke up in the cage.

Names have power. Elizabeth was a witch. She had the power of magic. And if we share names . . .

A part of my mind tried to reject the idea immediately. I recognized it as the part of my mind that always piped up when I thought of stuff like this. It claimed to be the voice of realism, the one that told me I was unimportant, the one that tried to convince me that mantra was a good thing. It spoke in my voice—not because it sounded the same, like the first Elizabeth, but because it *was* my voice.

You're crazy, it told me. *What, you? Are you serious? Elizabeth, you couldn't even get your teacher to remember your name. And now you're trying to tell me that you think you can tap into some magic power? Maybe use that same voice the Mistress uses, if you just really believe in yourself, like in one of your cartoons?*

I reached up to rub the faded scar on my shoulder. My fingertips met feathers, not skin.

A sort of defiant frustration bubbled up in my chest. I didn't know why I was so easy to miss before. I didn't know why teachers forgot my name or why my advisor kept forgetting my appointment. But the harsh truth was that a person like me probably existed in every school. In classrooms full of prodigies and trouble-makers, of course decent but average students would slip through the cracks.

But those students? They weren't kidnapped and tortured. This wasn't my destiny. I wasn't meant to die here. The Mistress chose this for me, and she was just a person—a very powerful person, yes, but a person nonetheless. And people could be stopped.

She *had* to be stopped.

I didn't want to die. Especially since, if I did, it wouldn't just be me that suffered. Alice, the one with the messy topknot, would come next. She'd never play her violin or learn to play guitar. She'd never doodle in her notebook or pet Smush again.

The thought weighed heavily on me. Maybe it made me a little creepy. After all, I was basically spying on her without her permission. But I liked watching her live her life, and I wanted her to keep it. Dreaming of her and the things she did gave me the only break I had from all the frightening, supernatural things that haunted my waking hours.

Is that really all, though? I have a connection to the first Elizabeth. She has a connection to the first Alice. And they loved each other. What if those feelings are influencing me?

I shook the thought off as ridiculous pretty quickly. I didn't love Alice. What did I even know about her? That she played violin and wanted to learn guitar. That she liked sappy romance and pastel-colored blouses. That she wore thigh-high socks even when she wasn't in her school uniform. That she had piles of soft-looking blankets on the floor at the foot of her bed. I knew a bunch of facts. I didn't know *her*. And I couldn't love someone I didn't know.

But *still*, imagining her in this cage, white feathers covering her skin, made me feel sick to my stomach. Imagining her having to watch me die like I watched Elle die made me hug my blankets to my chest.

I had to fight.

I lay down on my blankets, lack of sleep burning in my eyes. I didn't fight the exhaustion that weighed down my bones. I couldn't hear the voice—the first Elizabeth—anymore, but I could hear her in my dreams. I *was* her in my dreams.

If we really share power, Elizabeth, give me some of it. Give me some power.

I closed my eyes, letting sleep carry me away.

Alice—the present-day Alice—walked through a nice park, carrying a picnic basket. She held a checkered blanket and a book under one arm as she hummed to herself.

I couldn't help but notice that she was alone. Come to think of it, I hadn't ever seen her interact with anyone but her cat. She hadn't quite been able to reach out to her classmates. Was she anything like me? She might have been. If someone like me really did exist in every school, it made sense that the Mistress would pick people who were easy to erase.

Before I could see if the people walking past Alice looked through her like they looked through me, the scene shifted. I stood in a different park—no, a field full of flowers. And I really was standing, not floating like I did in the dreams where I watched the Alice in the present day. I was in the first Elizabeth's body again, with the first Alice.

148

The aromatic aura of lavender and sage enveloped me, glowing warm with the sun's rays. Ahead of me strode Alice, her braid bouncing softly as she skipped along.

I heard the first Elizabeth's thoughts, but I also thought my own, layered on top of them, as I watched the first Alice walk. The effect made me feel the same way I felt in really noisy crowds—overstimulated and a little dizzy.

"I know, and I'm sorry. But I'm trying to get this information to you."

The voice spoke to me. I knew it was the voice because I couldn't feel my—the first Elizabeth's—lips move.

My sister lagged behind both of us, keeping me in the middle. She could have easily caught up to Alice, of course. She was just being difficult, sulking. She always preferred harvesting flowers under the cool and mysterious moon, not the warm sun.

My head spun. I wanted to ask the first Elizabeth what all of this was about, but I couldn't seem to find the words, even in my thoughts. She must have caught on somehow, though, because she answered.

"This is one of . . . dreams. I'm trying to manipulate it."

One of what dreams? I shot the thought at her as the other half of my brain continued musing about the difference between flowers gathered by sunlight and by moonlight.

"I am trying. It may be best for you to sink into it and become me, in the past. Focus."

Although I knew part of it was my sister sulking, I couldn't help but wonder if she remained behind just to watch Alice walk. She had more grace than anyone I'd ever met. My sister danced beautifully, of course, but she had a different sort of grace. More purposeful, almost forceful. Alice's grace was more effortless.

Watching her from this angle was . . .

But of course, it wasn't proper to think like that. She was my *sister's lover, not mine.*

I hurried forward to catch up with Alice, banishing those thoughts from my mind. She favored me with a warm smile, blue eyes twinkling with good cheer.

"Do tell your sister to hurry along, would you please?"

I had never heard Alice speak above a soft tone. Maybe that was why she asked me to call out to my sister in her stead. But truthfully, her reasoning mattered little to me. I would have done anything Alice asked of me . . .

There were those thoughts again, unwelcome and unbidden. They were pointless. I cared about Alice as a friend, so why did I linger on such foolishly romantic thoughts? Dreams of throwing myself at her feet should have been confined to the quiet, dark hours of the morning. They had no place in this sunshine-brightened field. The blooming flowers cared not an ounce for my loneliness.

"If it's a trouble, you don't actually have to do it."

Did my thoughts show on my face? I did not intend for that. And my thoughts were not true, not in the slightest. I did not covet Alice— just the relationship that she had with my *sister, while I remained alone. Yes, that was all.*

"It is no trouble." I kept my voice level, neutral. I turned to call out to my sister . . .

The flowers and sunlight began to fade away. My thoughts became separate from those of the first Elizabeth's again. I started to feel the pillow against my cheek, the blankets against my sleeping body.

"No, Elizabeth. Stay for just a little longer."

I focused all my will on clinging to the dream. The scene grew a little more solid for a moment, and I felt the sun on my—the first Elizabeth's—face once more. I opened my mouth.

Then the scene faded away again, but just before it went completely dark, I heard myself speak.

"Hurry up, Margaret!"

seventeen.

I woke up with my head throbbing like my brain had swollen too big for my skull.

My thoughts buzzed like static on TV, and a sharp, metallic taste flooded my mouth. I sat up and retched, but nothing came out—probably because I hadn't eaten in close to a month. My stomach spasmed and seized, and I felt a little like I had just ridden the world's fastest tilt-a-whirl.

But none of that—not even the fresh clumps of hair on my pillow—could stop the joy that welled up in my chest.

Margaret. The Mistress's name was Margaret. I had her name.

And names have power.

But did this mean I had at least a little bit of power over Margaret? Or just that she had less power over me? I couldn't be sure, but the first Elizabeth had gone through all that to show me the dream. It had to be because it could help me.

I looked down, trying to feel something different inside

of me. I tried to figure out if the dream had left me with a magic that I could identify, something that I could wield the way the Mistress wielded that powerful, commanding voice.

But I felt the same. Or maybe the truth was that I felt too *different*. My body, my mind, my soul—none of it felt the same as it did before I woke up in this cage. The feathers that stole my skin sapped the energy from my bones, leaving me feeling hollowed out like an old tree.

It went beyond the physical, too. My brain swelled full of questions that sent me running around in circles. My emotions themselves felt manipulated by the dreams.

I didn't feel like the high school senior who had once vaguely daydreamed about college without committing to one, who loved to sing but couldn't imagine being in front of a crowd on her own, who watched cartoons and wrote in her journal and made fun of herself without ever stopping to ask why.

The Mistress had stripped all individuality from me. Even singing became something I did just to survive. *How am I supposed to find hope in any of this?*

I drew up my legs, pressing my forehead to my knees. But that made the feathers there pulse warm and feverish, like limbs that had lost their circulation. I shivered into a sitting position, fighting the urge to retch again. My stomach turned uncomfortably again and again, like a toy being worried over by fidgeting hands.

That said, it didn't really hurt or ache the way it should have from nausea alone. It didn't have the hollow, deadly numbness of the feathers, either. Several dotted the area around my belly button, but my stomach felt different from the rest of my body.

Was it the magic that kept me from starving to death? Or was I feeling something more?

I took a deep breath, focusing. I didn't really know what to do. I had never been very good at meditation or mindfulness, even though I'd tried some tutorials online back home. My mind was always too prone to wandering. But now that my life literally depended on it, focusing was a bit easier.

Something in my stomach fluttered. Lightweight but strong, the feeling reminded me of bird wings. *Healthy* bird wings, ready to break free.

It's wishful thinking. The pessimistic thought weighed heavy on my shoulders. Part of me wanted to stop here, to not even try anything else. Because what if I was wrong? How would it feel to have even this tiny shred of hope ripped away from me? I didn't think I would be able to bear it.

But I didn't have a choice. If I wanted to save myself—and save Alice, for that matter—I'd have to try something.

I grabbed one of my blankets.

I set it on the cool metal ground and backed away rapidly, feeling absurdly like I had just pulled the pin on a grenade. I stared at it for a long moment, afraid to start. Afraid it wouldn't work. Afraid it *would* work. I didn't know any of the rules for using magic. I didn't know any of the dangers. I didn't know any of the side effects or consequences or—

No. I wasn't going to let myself do that, wasn't going to talk myself out of acting before I had even begun. *You can't do this to yourself*, I thought. The first Elizabeth stayed silent, maybe saving the power we shared for me to use. *You can't back down, not this time. And hey, what do you have to lose? Your life? You're losing that already if you don't do something soon.*

I took a deep breath, squared my shoulders, and spoke. "Move."

My voice came out in a high squeak that wouldn't have scared a field mouse into scurrying away. It certainly wouldn't bend the laws of the universe to my bidding—which, when I thought of it like that, made it feel all the more impossible.

But the feeling in my stomach stayed. Anticipation and anxiety mixed together into raw longing, growing inside me like a plant reaching toward the sun.

"Move," I said again, louder.

The blanket didn't do anything.

"Move!" I shouted at it, desperation clawing at the inside of my ribs. If I couldn't do this, everything ended. And wasn't it stupid to even try in the first place? I might have been in a supernatural situation, but that didn't make me supernatural, too. It didn't matter whose name I shared. I would never be like the first Elizabeth. I would never be *important*—

"*No!*"

Something inside me *flexed*. Some muscle I hadn't known existed, something that felt like more than flesh and bone. And for a moment, that doubting voice just stopped, like someone hit pause. It went beyond just willfully ignoring my thoughts and into something that left me feeling almost light-headed and dizzy.

It only lasted for a moment. Then the same old doubts crept back in. *You imagined that. You didn't actually do*

155

anything. But the thoughts didn't carry their usual sting, because something *had* happened. I could feel that muscle, near my stomach but not quite inside it. I couldn't explain it any more than I could explain the way the Mistress's voice stole my free will.

My heart thundered in my ears, and my breath shook in my throat. I waited until my hands stopped trembling before I tried again.

"*Move.*" It was unmistakable this time. My voice took on an echoing, ethereal quality—not exactly like the Mistress, but close.

In front of me, the blanket twitched.

The rational part of my brain tried to convince me I imagined it. *But let's be honest. I'm being held captive by an immortal witch who's cursed me to grow feathers and die. Just how much credibility does the rational part of my brain have these days?* A semi-hysterical giggle bubbled up my throat, and I clapped a hand over my mouth.

I steadied myself and tried again.

"*Move. Lift off the ground.*"

The voice became easier to find the more I used it, a little like learning how to whistle. It didn't echo with the same power as Margaret's voice. I couldn't imagine a person with free will doing what I said, but it was enough for a blanket. It lifted off the ground, hovering and trembling in the air. I felt the weight of it—not physically, but in my mind, like a tension headache beginning to form.

"*Come here.*"

The blanket shuddered its way toward me, like a child taking their first steps, before it finally tumbled into my arms.

I held the blanket to my chest, my heart racing and my muscles jittering. Cold sweat covered my skin and dripped down my feathers. The muscle in my stomach ached in the same way my arms and legs sometimes did after gym class.

"*Good job.*"

The first Elizabeth's voice sounded so loud, so clear. *Was she here the whole time?* I wondered if she moved the blanket, not me. Maybe she took over my body without me even noticing it.

"*Don't be ridiculous.*" Her voice sounded a bit farther away but still more clear than I had ever heard it. Maybe figuring out the magic had unlocked something inside of me. "*Of course it was you.*" I couldn't tell for sure, but I thought she sounded a little proud.

But not all the voices in my head were so nice. The usual, self-deprecating voice piped up as if to counter her. *So what? You can move a blanket. What are you going to do? Throw it over the Mistress's head and hope she falls asleep like a parakeet?*

But instead of making me feel discouraged or stupid for trying, the thought made me laugh. Because no matter how much my rational brain tried to pretend otherwise, hope had set up shop in a tiny corner of my heart, glowing brightly and forcing the shadows of doubt to retreat.

eighteen.

Alice—the younger Alice, from my time—stood in the doorway of a kitchen, watching a woman do dishes.

The woman had Alice's brown hair and her button nose. I guessed who she was even before Alice addressed her. "Hey, Mom?" Alice asked, one hand wrapped around the doorframe.

Her mom glanced over her shoulder for a moment, then went back to the dishes. "Yes, hon?"

Alice shifted her weight from one foot to another, then tugged up a stocking. "Can I . . . tell you something?"

"Of course." Her mom kept her back to Alice.

"It's kind of a big deal to me," Alice admitted.

Her mom paused for a moment, sud-covered plate in one hand. "Are you in trouble, hon?"

A nervous, high-pitched laugh bubbled out of Alice's lips. It sent an odd wave of endearment through me. "No."

"Oh." Her mom went back to scrubbing. "What is it, then?"

Alice took a deep breath. The knuckles wrapped around the

doorframe turned white.

"I like girls, Mom."

"I'm sorry?" Her mother's words didn't come out passive-aggressive or threatening. She just sounded genuinely confused.

Silence stretched between them. Alice visibly pulled her nerve back up, squaring her shoulders and lifting her chin a bit. "I'm bisexual."

"Oh! That's all." Her mother glanced over her shoulder with a smile. "Alright then, hon. Thanks for letting me know." She might have been talking about a new hairstyle Alice wanted to try.

Alice's eyes widened, her shoulders relaxing. "Really? You're not . . . surprised or anything?"

Her mother shrugged. "It's not a big deal, hon. Could you get the laundry started?"

"Sure! Sure." Alice walked away, and while there was relief in the deep breath she drew in, her brows were knit together, her blue eyes cloudy with confusion.

I woke up in stages, becoming aware of my feather-covered limbs one by one. *Poor Alice,* I thought, still half-asleep.

She wore her heart on her sleeve just as much as the first Alice did, apparently. I could tell that she didn't want to be disappointed by her mother's reaction, but she had been, anyway. And I could understand why.

Her mom had taken it well, all things considered. She didn't yell at her or get mad or cry. She had smiled and told her it was fine—except she didn't say, *It's okay. I'll love you no matter what.* She said, *It's not a big deal,* right after Alice said, *It's kind of a big deal to me.* No wonder she felt conflicted about it. It was like her mother didn't hear her at all.

Like her mother hardly saw her.

On the backs of my eyelids I saw my mom sitting at the kitchen table and grading papers, not even looking up when I walked in.

Even though I never came out to her or Dad, I could easily imagine them reacting in the exact same way. How would I have felt after the hours I spent imagining telling them, trying to work up the courage to do it? I probably would've felt just like Alice.

A rush of sympathy bordering on fondness ran through me. I wished I could talk to her. I liked to think that if we knew each other in real life, we might have been friends. We liked the same shows; we both liked music. And it seemed like we had even more in common than that.

I sat up, wincing at the feeling of feathers matted flat and uncomfortable against my skin. New feathers lined my spine in twin rows and prickled along my shoulder blades. Too many strands of hair lay on my pillow.

Maybe considering a hypothetical friendship with Alice isn't the best use of your time.

I had to focus on what was really important. If I didn't, we'd have more than just tastes in television or non-heterosexuality in common. We'd both be victims of the Mistress.

Letting out a sigh, I knelt at the door of my cage to examine the lock. I didn't have time to try this last night, because even after the show, I felt exhausted, the new muscle in my stomach aching and trembling. But now it felt rested. I was ready to try again.

"*Unlock,*" I said. My voice echoed with the same power from last night, but nothing happened. I jiggled the door, but it remained as tight as ever. I tried again. "*Break.*"

"*You're making a wonderful effort, but that won't work.*" The first Elizabeth's voice chimed in, loud and clear. Maybe I was getting better at hearing her. "*It will only unlock from the outside, just in case a girl gets ahold of the key. Margaret's charmed it.*"

Her voice warped at the sound of Margaret's name, like the word wanted to twist itself into something else. I remembered the dreams, how the first Alice and Elizabeth only called her "your sister" and "my sister." *She must have made the dreams that way. Names have power, after all.*

"*You catch on fast, Elizabeth.*" The first Elizabeth sounded pleased. I smiled.

I lowered myself to the floor of the cage. The feathers itched uncomfortably under my dress. Honestly, my body was probably covered enough that I didn't even need the dress, but I didn't really want to take it off. Floating blankets or no floating blankets, I already felt vulnerable enough. No need to add nakedness into the mix.

I have so many questions to ask you. I didn't need to speak to have the first Elizabeth hear me. Knowing that she could hear my thoughts made me a little uncomfortable, but I couldn't blame her. Neither of us had much of a choice.

"*I'm sorry.*" The first Elizabeth's tone turned gentle, more like the way she sounded in the dreams. "*I do try to give you all of the privacy I can afford you, though. It's complicated. And answering your questions is complicated, as well. I am not a product of Margaret's magic. Not exactly. But I am still beholden to it to a certain extent. I cannot give much of the information she would wish to conceal from you. Even getting her name to you took a tremendous amount of effort. I wouldn't have been able to do it without you. It's why you had to figure out how to work your magic on your own and why you had to ask that boy about what it all meant."*

Mark. He hadn't come to visit me, except for when he silently pushed my pillow and blanket through the cage bars last night after the show. I couldn't be sure, but I hoped he wasn't avoiding me. *I didn't mean to scare him.*

"You're not the one who frightens him." The first Elizabeth didn't finish her thought, but she didn't have to. I knew who she meant.

I practiced magic on the blanket a few more times but didn't do much outside of that. I couldn't help feeling like doing too much would be wasteful, somehow. I didn't really know what I was saving the magic for. I didn't have a plan. But if I needed it, I wanted to have it.

Eventually, the crew members came to get me. Nerves jittered in the back of my skull as I thought of rolling past Margaret. Part of me was sure that she'd see something different about me, that she'd just *know.* But she had already disappeared into the fabric-covered building by the time I rolled out.

Madame Selene didn't speak when I rolled in. She stared with wide, blank eyes and didn't answer when I called her name.

"I'm not an expert in prophecy," the first Elizabeth said. *"It's more grueling and dangerous than other forms of divination or precognition, so few witches ever tried. But I believe she may just need time to adjust to this timeline. It was an unlikely one, with my sister's meddling."*

I was willing to take the first Elizabeth's word for it. It was amazing how quickly I grew to trust her. But I knew who she was, and I knew how she thought.

"*Besides, I daresay our interests align at the moment. I'd gain nothing from deceiving you.*" I couldn't be positive, but I thought her tone was almost teasing. She was right, though. We both wanted the same thing—freedom from the Mistress.

I watched her when the crew rolled me to the backstage area. Even when talking to Bridget, the Mistress faced me. A cruel light twinkled in her pointed irises. *She likes watching me sit here silently,* I thought. *She thinks she's broken me.*

"*Has she?*" It wasn't the first time the first Elizabeth asked me that, but it sounded different this time. Instead of mere curiosity, I could hear something else in her tone.

Fury.

Fury over what she'd been through, over what Margaret took from her. Fury for every girl she couldn't save. Fury over watching the soul of the woman she loved fall before her eyes again and again and again.

My pulse sped up, matching her mood. When the Mistress looked at me like a toy, like a doll for her to dress up and destroy and toss away, I was furious, too.

"*Has she broken you?*"

No. I bowed my head, not wanting Margaret to read the emotions on my face. *No, she hasn't.*

When I went onstage, I sang a song I heard the Alice from my time play. It felt good to pick a song that reminded me of the girl I wasn't even supposed to know about yet. I sang clear and strong, a new confidence seeming to echo behind my voice, like the first Elizabeth was singing along with me.

Maybe the Mistress sensed something. Or maybe she couldn't stand the idea of me having any sort of hope. Whatever the reason, she followed me back to the storage room after the show, smiling with Bridget in her wake. "You hardly look human anymore, you know."

Unease dripped down my spine, like a drop of chilled rain. I knew she was right. Feathers covered over half of my body at this point. They were starting to pile up on my arms and legs, turning them into shapeless masses. I remembered how Elle looked when I met her, how I hadn't even realized she was a person until she opened her eyes.

"How much time d'you think she's got left? Like, a couple weeks at the most, right?" Bridget tried for cool and casual, matching the Mistress's tone. To me, she sounded like a child trying to mimic her mother, playing at being an adult.

The fury from before returned as I thought about how she had lured me in. Before, she treated me like I was interesting. Now, she talked about my upcoming death like she'd talk about an episode of a show she only half-cared about.

"What do you *want*?" It came out sharper than I intended. I could feel the first Elizabeth's anger behind my own, but it didn't influence my tone. I had plenty of my own anger to fuel that.

The Mistress laughed. "We're not here to answer your questions, little songbird. But Bridget is right, you know: you are growing quickly. We'll have to start moving toward . . . *Well*." She grinned, sharp and wolfish. "You'll figure it out when we get there, won't you? Or maybe not. Maybe you'll die never knowing."

Alice. She was threatening Alice. Margaret didn't even realize that I knew about Alice yet, but she was counting on me remembering this conversation later. I remembered what Elle had sobbed when I first heard her voice in the dark room.

I understand everything now. I'm so sorry.

Something inside me snapped, taking out every rational bone in my body with it. I opened my mouth without thinking, just wanting to hurt her as much as she'd hurt Elle. As much as she hurt *me.*

"I know plenty, *Sister.*"

"*Elizabeth, maybe we shouldn't—*" The first Elizabeth's cautious voice sounded in the back of my mind. I ignored it. I wanted to wipe that grin right off Margaret's face.

Which was exactly what happened. The Mistress's expression dropped, like that of a crouching predator preparing to strike. "What did you call me?" Although she was calm on the surface, I could hear a note of fury in her voice. And a note of surprise. I loved it, and I could tell that the first Elizabeth did, too, even if she didn't want to.

I want this, I thought to her. *I want to make her scared for once. Please, Elizabeth. Please help me.*

"*Very well. If this is your choice.*" The first Elizabeth's voice echoed. And then something shifted.

I opened my mouth, and when I spoke, it was still me. I still picked the words. But the first Elizabeth helped, filling the gaps in my knowledge and influencing my tone.

"Oh, *dear.* Did I figure it out ahead of your schedule?" I threw her own grin back in her face. It felt beyond good to do so. It felt *powerful.* "Wonderful. I'm *done* being on your

165

schedule."

Margaret narrowed her eyes. "I don't recall giving you a choice in the matter." Her tone sat on the edge of fury. Bridget stared back and forth between us with wide eyes.

"There's always a choice." I laughed. It didn't sound like my laugh at all. "You should have known, Sister. You told me at the beginning that names have power. And you can lock me in a cage, you can cover me in feathers, you can force me to sing—but you can't take my name away from me. It frightens you, doesn't it? It's always frightened you. That's why you call me 'little songbird.' You're afraid of the power 'Elizabeth' holds."

"Shut up." Anger weakened her voice instead of strengthening it. No power echoed behind it.

"Or what? You'll kill me, like you did all those years ago?" Even as the first Elizabeth's influence over my words grew, I could have stopped speaking if I wanted to. But I didn't want to. "Did you think I'd forget? That I'd let you get away with what you did to me? To *Alice*? You claimed to love her, but that was all a lie, wasn't it? You loved *owning* her. No wonder she came to me in the end. She was right about you, Sister. Would you like to hear all the things she said about you when she was lying in bed beside me?"

Margaret's eyes were twin infernos, red swallowing brown in her pointed irises. "*Shut up!*" Her command tried to worm its way into my vocal cords, but I wouldn't let it. I flexed that new muscle, screaming right back.

"*No, Margaret!*" The words burned my throat, tingling like an electric shock on my lips. "*You shut up!*"

A million miles away, Bridget gasped.

Margaret rocked back, like I'd slapped her. She opened her mouth to scream at me—and not a sound came out. I had silenced her. An angry sort of joy roared through my chest.

It only lasted for a moment. "You!" She threw herself at the bars of my cage, and I flinched back on instinct. "You *little* . . ." A thousand emotions flickered across her face. For just a moment, I swore that I saw fear.

She spun on her heels and stormed away. Bridget gave me a wide-eyed look before following in her wake, looking like a small child.

"That was probably very foolish," the first Elizabeth said.

I know, I thought. *But I don't regret it.*

"Neither do I."

Even though the laughter that came out of my mouth sounded and felt like mine this time, I was pretty sure it belonged to both of us.

nineteen.

"Alice."

Her eyes fluttered open, blue irises warm with contentment. I almost considered changing my mind. What I had to say would destroy the sleepy calm between us, but I could no longer hold my tongue. What we were doing ate at me, even if I didn't regret a moment of it.

"Dove . . ." I took a breath, steadying myself. "We need to tell Margaret about this."

Even though I expected it, watching Alice's face fall tore at my heart. She clutched at the blankets as if she meant to hide under them like a frightened child. Her voice trembled. "Must we?"

"Alice." I reached out to touch her cheek. She leaned into my touch. "You know this isn't right."

Alice took a deep, shaky breath. She wore her emotions plainly— she always did—but for once I couldn't put a name to the expression on her face. "Elizabeth, you know . . . I would not have done what I did without a good reason."

"Of course. Our love—"

"Is not the only reason I have let things play out the way they have."

I was not used to Alice using such a firm tone, much less using it to interrupt me. It could not have come to her easily. "I am listening, Alice."

For a long moment, she didn't speak. I found myself wanting to fill the silence with something, wanting to finish Alice's thought for her. But I knew that would not be fair. I held my tongue.

When she finally spoke, her voice was smaller than usual. "If it were only a matter of falling for you, I would have done things properly." She shook her head, sighing. "Or as properly as I could have. I would have told Margaret right away, explained that my heart did not belong to her. But I didn't. I stayed with her, even as my heart strayed. And I did that because Margaret—your sister—frightens me."

My breath stopped in my throat. I had to force my voice not to tremble. "Alice, has Margaret harmed you?"

Alice's eyes widened, the truth spreading across her face before she gave voice to it. "No. Nothing like that. However . . ." She reached out and laced her fingers through mine. "In my family, there runs a string of precognition. I do not have it as strong as some of my aunts and uncles, but neither has it passed me up entirely. And as my feelings for your sister began to fade, I noticed a certain . . . anxiety at the thought of leaving her. A sureness, something bone-deep, saying that it would be unwise—dangerous—to anger her."

Silence filled the air between us. I could not for the life of me think of how to break it.

Finally, Alice spoke again, barely a whisper. "There is a darkness in her, Elizabeth. I have seen it in . . . other ways. Heard it in her

169

words, felt it in her actions, however subtle."

I ran a thumb over Alice's knuckles to reassure her, even though I couldn't figure out what to make of her words. My sister had a temper, I knew. I had seen it flare up countless times, sometimes at a perceived slight, sometimes over uncontrollable circumstances. She did not like to lose anything, especially attention.

But dangerous? Margaret was my sister. I could not believe that she would harm me.

A low, throaty chuckle interrupted the dream, dragging me back into the waking world with sharp claws. I sat bolt upright, clutching the blankets to my chest.

Margaret stood in front of my cage, the light from the paper lanterns casting long shadows over her face. She was alone. The feathers around my throat pulsed with the memory of what had happened last time she showed up here, alone, at night. Her face held the same amused contempt it always did, not that dull expression, but that did nothing to steady my jagged nerves.

"*It's different now.*" The first Elizabeth's voice sounded too far away to be reassuring. "*You aren't so helpless anymore.*"

"Sweet dreams, little songbird?" The Mistress circled my cage, dragging the tip of a fingernail from one bar to another. *Click. Click. Click.* A shiver climbed up my spine.

"What do you want, Margaret?" I wanted the words to come out firm, powerful. They didn't. My throat still felt rough and raw from using the voice against her earlier. *I just learned how to do this. She has over a century of practice.* Not even knowing her name could take away the dread that burrowed into me as feverishly as the feathers burrowed beneath my skin.

The Mistress laughed, low and awful. "*Margaret*," she echoed in a high, mocking tone that reminded me a little of Bridget. "Throwing that in my face was a nice touch, I'll admit. How *did* you come across it, little songbird?"

I looked desperately for even a flicker of Margaret's earlier fear, trying to coax the stunned first Elizabeth into action. "It's me, Margaret. You know—"

"Oh, hush." Her voice overpowered mine easily. "I didn't command you to answer, silly thing. Truthfully, it doesn't matter. Your answer is as unimportant as you." She rolled her eyes, lips curving up in a smirk. "And you can stop pretending to be her. I'll admit it, little songbird. You startled me. For a moment, I *almost* entertained the notion that my little sister had outsmarted me for once. That she managed to take that little shard of a soul I put inside you and turn it into a weapon."

"How do you know she didn't?" I realized my mistake as soon as the words fell out of my mouth. "I am here, Margaret. You must—"

"Enough." She waved a hand. "My sister is just as powerless as she's always been. I would never allow for anything more."

"*Pride comes before the fall,*" the first Elizabeth whispered. But Margaret didn't look like she was going to fall. She towered above me, eyes glittering with a cruel light.

"No, little songbird," she said. "You didn't come by that little *parlor trick* on your own. You had help putting it all together." She turned back to the entrance, shouting in a voice that managed to be commanding even without the echoing whisper-shout. "Bring him in."

Bridget appeared, dragging Mark by the arm.

"No!" I wanted to shout, to scream. All I managed was a hoarse croak.

Margaret laughed. "Oh dear, aren't we upset?" She circled Mark in long, predatory strides. He didn't move a muscle—only his eyes rolled around in their sockets. I remembered the painful magic that had locked me in a half-crouch and shuddered. "Do you care for him, little songbird? Did you try to steal his heart, like my sister stole Alice's?"

"It's not like that!" In that moment, I would've said anything to please her. When I had shouted at her earlier, it was because I felt like I had nothing to lose. I didn't feel that way now. "He didn't do anything!"

The Mistress rolled her eyes. "Don't bother lying. Do you really think anything here has changed? That my name—or yours, for that matter—is enough to make any difference? You've had your fleeting moment of glory, but you will *always* lose. You have no choice. I'm going to give you a lasting reminder of that."

She turned to Mark. His eyes darted like those of a trapped, frightened animal.

"*On your knees,*" the Mistress commanded. Mark collapsed awkwardly, the rest of his body still stiff. A wince clouded his eyes as he hit the ground. Margaret smiled. "Now, *speak.*"

Mark heaved in a long, croaking gasp. "Please. Don't hurt me." His voice sounded high and thin, ten years younger. My heart shattered. "Don't hurt me. Don't hurt us. We've done what you wanted. We've gone along with everything—"

"We've?" Margaret laughed. "Please. Violet's thrived here,

it's true. But you? You never quite grew into what you could have been, the way she and Bridget have." Behind Mark, Bridget seemed to puff up in pride. "You still act like a useless, frightened *child.*"

"Honestly, it's super pathetic," Bridget added eagerly.

But Mark didn't seem to hear her or anything else that came after Violet's name. I could almost read his thoughts. *She's not going to hurt Violet. No matter what happens, at least she's safe.* Tears welled up in my eyes, and I pressed a hand to my mouth to stifle a sob.

"As for doing what I wanted," Margaret continued, pacing around him slowly, "you perform, certainly, but for all intents and purposes, *I* am the one doing what *you* wanted. I tolerated your eccentricities, did I not? I let you bring your pillows and your blankets. I let you ask their names and pretend to be their friend. I tolerated all that the same way I tolerated your presence here, because it made no difference to me."

She stopped walking, fixing Mark with her gaze. "But this, Mark?" She knelt until she was eye-to-eye with him. What little peace he managed to find drained from his face as she stepped closer. "This is *more* than I can tolerate."

Mark winced. He said nothing.

"You're going to tell me everything." Margaret spoke in an even, measured tone. "I'm not going to force you, because I don't have to. You know what will happen if you lie."

Bridget flicked her wrist in a familiar gesture. A silver knife appeared in her hand. Mark shuddered.

"Elizabeth—she asked a lot of questions." He shot me a guilty look. "About her dreams, I mean. She was—it really

173

bothered her, not knowing. I felt bad for her, so . . ."

"You told her the story I told you." Relief, or something close enough to it, colored Margaret's tone. "And it was enough for this little fool to think that she stood a chance." Mostly to herself, she murmured, "Of course, there's magic all over this room. It was pure, dumb luck."

The first Elizabeth tried to say something, but I couldn't focus enough to hear her. Terror clutched at my throat, freezing me in place. It felt like one of those nightmares where I sat paralyzed in my own bed, watching shadows writhe their way closer to me.

"I don't—" Mark's voice cut off with a harsh rasp, and he had to take a few seconds before trying again. "I don't know what to say. If I knew she was planning something? I wouldn't have done it. I don't think."

"You don't *think*!" Margaret's scorn dug into my guilty conscience like a sharp knife. "Well, that inspires me with confidence."

Bridget laughed, the sound overloud in the thick air of the storage room.

Mark's voice got even smaller. "It won't happen again."

"No." The Mistress bared her teeth in a grin. "It won't." She advanced on him, bare feet silent against the fabric.

"Please." Mark's breath constricted and locked in his throat. "Please, don't."

"Don't waste your final words on appeals for mercy," Margaret scoffed. "Surely, you know I have none."

Finally, something in me unlocked. I threw myself against the bars. "No!"

This time, both Margaret and Bridget laughed. Mark

looked at me with the most heartbreaking mix of fear and resignation on his face. "It's okay, Elizabeth." I didn't need the tremble in his voice to tell me that it wasn't. It wasn't okay *at all*. "You didn't ask for any of this. None of the girls did. I don't blame you."

"*Stop!*" The magic inside of me trembled with effort, but it didn't carry to my voice. It felt like pressing against a wall with all my might, trying in vain to get it to move.

Mark spoke in a voice that was terribly quiet. "If you see Violet, tell her . . ." He sighed. "Never mind. She already knows."

Bridget grabbed Mark by the collar, hauling him to his feet. "Psh, enough already!" She turned to Margaret and beamed. "He's all yours, Mistress."

In that long second, I imagined a thousand things. I imagined her slicing his throat, bashing his head into the floor until it turned to pulp, commanding him not to breathe and watching him die, like she almost did to me.

She did none of those things. Instead, she did something worse. She snapped her fingers, and she, Mark, and Bridget disappeared, leaving me to my imagination.

"Margaret!" Desperation clawed at my throat more painfully than any magic. "Margaret, what did you do to him? What are you doing to him?"

Margaret didn't answer. But from somewhere, I heard Mark scream.

Then all I heard was my own harsh breathing, on the edge of a sob.

twenty.

"I'm sorry, Elizabeth. Truly, I am."

The first Elizabeth's voice echoed through my head, impossible to ignore no matter how much I wanted to. I didn't want her guilt or pity. I didn't want her dreams. I didn't want anything to do with the ghosts of Margaret's past.

Mark's scream echoed in my ears. Guilt clung to me like a shroud, burrowing beneath my skin with a sting more painful than the feathers.

What had they done to him? Not knowing was the worst kind of torture. It allowed me to imagine Mark dying in a thousand different ways—because he had to be dead. I couldn't think of another reason for that scream to sound the way that it had. I couldn't imagine the Mistress doing anything else.

Mark had to be dead. And his blood was on my hands.

"*I'm sorry*," the first Elizabeth said again.

I pressed my palms against my ears. "Shut up, *shut up!*" Finally, the magic came—too little, too late. The first Elizabeth's voice went silent, like I'd pressed pause.

Being alone with my thoughts didn't give me any relief. I had been stupid. Beyond stupid. Did I really think I stood a chance against Margaret? Even if I had been able to use that voice—even if I hadn't exhausted it in a dumb shouting match—what had I expected to happen? She had me locked in a cage. No voice, no matter how powerful, could keep her from hurting others just so she could hurt me.

It did hurt. And along with the hurt, I felt angry. I couldn't believe that I let the first Elizabeth use me as a pawn in a centuries' old grudge. I got myself emotionally invested in some murder that didn't have anything to do with me, and it cost an innocent man his life.

Mark went through so much. He just wanted to survive. And I managed to take even that away from him.

I curled up on the floor of my cage and sobbed, feeling the cold metal press against my cheek. I cried and cried until my head spun and there was a low, droning buzzing under my skin, exhaustion creeping up on me.

I didn't want to sleep, but sleep—and the dreams that came with it—came for me anyway.

My head spun. Something like seasickness churned in my stomach, perhaps because of the way that my senses seemed to roll away from me like waves. Only dread remained constant, clutching my heart in a vise grip.

What did I have to be afraid of? I couldn't think. A sharp pain spiked at my temples. I winced, and I might have cried out.

I heard someone laugh. I heard someone cry. I heard someone do both of those things at once, a mad sound.

"Open your eyes, little songbird."

I recognized Margaret's voice. It sent a bolt of fear through me, a lightning strike aimed at my heart. What did I have to fear from my own sister? Why didn't I want to open my eyes? I pried them open in spite of the fear and regretted doing so immediately.

My vision doubled, tripled. And so did the nausea. My bedroom looked wrong, off in ways that I could not process, sending a nightmare sort of unease through me. Red ran in drips across the moon outside—or was that just the windowpane . . . ?

"Ah, you're awake. I thought I lost you already."

Something warm puddled beneath me. I couldn't move my head to look. I couldn't move any of my limbs.

"I'm glad that you aren't gone yet."

Memories returned to me in drips as obscene as the ones of blood—blood—on the window. Margaret had done this. The amused tone in her voice proved what my foggy memories could not.

"I wanted you to see."

A huddled mass sat in the corner of the room. Its long black hair hung limp, yanked from its braid with rough and careless hands. Alice. What had happened to Alice? Why couldn't I see her face?

"I wanted you to see what happened."

Understanding struck me, making me wish for ignorance. I couldn't see her face because she didn't have a face. Not anymore.

"I wanted you to see what your betrayal did."

I wanted to scream. I wanted to cry. But I couldn't find my mouth to do it. I couldn't do anything but stare at the space that should have held Alice's lips, her cheeks, her eyes.

"Goodbye, Sister."

I woke up with a scream lodged in my chest. I clutched at

my throat, trembling at the memory of the pain, of Margaret's power ripping me open from the inside. The feathers around my neck pulsed faster and harder, overwarm from my frantic heartbeat.

It isn't real. It isn't real. That happened to the first Elizabeth, not you. I was in one piece. I was still alive, for now.

Unlike the first Elizabeth. Unlike the first Alice. And unlike Mark.

"I'm sorry, Elizabeth."

I couldn't keep the first Elizabeth's voice away forever. I curled in on myself, clutching at my body, trying to convince myself I was still whole—or as whole as I could be, with the feathers turning my insides hollow. "You knew." My voice rasped painfully against my throat. But I still spoke out loud, mostly to prove to myself that I still could. "You knew what she was capable of, and you forced me into this anyways."

"I forced you into nothing!" The first Elizabeth snapped at me, her echoing voice clipped and harsh. *"You knew what she was capable of, too. Look at you! She's killing you as surely as she killed me! Your death is just slower."*

My feathers had never hurt before. They did now. They pulsed like open wounds in the wake of the dream.

It wasn't fair to be mad at the first Elizabeth. I had wanted to make Margaret angry. I wanted to believe I could beat her. Not as revenge for the first Elizabeth or the first Alice. I wanted to beat her for me, for my own safety. And maybe just a little bit for the Alice in my time, to keep her safe.

I wiped my eyes with the back of my hand. "I wouldn't have minded if she just hurt *me*. She's killing me anyways, so it would've been . . . I don't know."

"*I know.*" The anger in the first Elizabeth's voice evaporated. "*I understand. And I am sorry, truly.*"

I held myself, trembling, and thought back at her. *I'm sorry, too.*

I pulled the pile of blankets around myself, wishing I could cocoon in them like the poetry women hanging from the ceiling. I just wanted a break, a rest that was actually restful. My body ached with the phantom memory of the first Elizabeth's death.

"*I'm truly sorry you had to feel that.*" The first Elizabeth's voice trembled slightly. "*Do you want a dream of her? Your Alice?*"

She's not mine. The thought came faster than I would've been able to say it out loud, firm and instinctual.

"*No, no, of course not. I didn't mean it in that sense. I didn't own my Alice, either, it's just—*"

"It's totally different." I cut her off out loud, as if that would make it more effective. Wrapping my arms around myself, I thought, *I don't even know Alice.*

"*No.*" I got the impression that the first Elizabeth was choosing her words carefully. "*But it's as good of a distinction as any. The Alice from your time is your Alice. The Alice from my time is mine.*" She didn't sound finished. Catching on, she continued. "*It's just that . . . I do sense that you care for her on some level. You want to protect her. Your actions are for her, at least in part. Or am I wrong?*"

She wasn't wrong. *I mean, mostly I just want to get out of here. But . . .*

I didn't have to finish. The first Elizabeth knew what I meant. "*It's not unlike the way I felt for my Alice,*" she said. "*I would have done anything to protect her from . . . that."*

I thought of the dream, of the first Alice's body, what remained of her face. My stomach lurched. No, I didn't want that to happen to Alice–my Alice, if the first Elizabeth insisted on calling her that. But I didn't think that meant our feelings were similar. I wouldn't want that to happen to a complete stranger, much less someone I saw in her more private moments.

Which, of course, made me remember the person I *did* let that happen to. That or something similar.

"What more can be said?" The first Elizabeth picked up on my train of thought. *"He is most certainly gone, yes. So are all of the girls who came before you. The dead have surrounded you for a month now, Elizabeth. You'll become one of them if you've truly given up."* It almost sounded like she was snapping at me again, but I knew it wasn't directed at me.

I looked up at the paper lanterns. I thought of Elle and Rochelle, then all the girls who came before them. I thought of the first Elizabeth, glowing in her lantern and watching them die one by one. Exhaustion weighed heavy in my bones, and I knew that the first Elizabeth felt it, too.

Are you telling me you haven't given up? I pulled my knees to my chest, wrapping my arms loosely around my legs. Even doing that felt wrong, warm feathers crinkling in the bends of my knees and elbows. I shuddered. *I can't beat Margaret. Not on my own. And I can't ask anyone else to get hurt for me. I just can't. You can't ask me to do that.*

"I'm not–" Crew members sweeping in interrupted the first Elizabeth.

It almost disgusted me how everything seemed so normal.

Crew members rolled me toward the fabric-covered building as if nothing had changed. Bridget lounged near the entrance, twiddling her fingers at me as they pushed me past her.

Madame Selene didn't look any different, either. I tried to find some sign of grief from her. I wanted to believe that a good person sat beneath that stoic exterior.

She turned her gaze to me. "The cost of freedom is not so easily predicted, little songbird."

I shuddered. "I didn't want this. I didn't want him to die."

"Die?" Madame Selene cocked her head to the side ever so slightly. "Death surrounds you on all sides, little songbird. Do not attribute it to him."

After that, she wouldn't say anything more. She just stared silently ahead until the crew members came to collect me and bring me backstage.

Violet sat huddled in one corner, blonde hair covering her face. I couldn't see her expression, but my heart twisted in my chest when I imagined it. The Mistress and Bridget held their usual, murmured conversation. The crew members set up like they always did.

And facing the stage, as casual as could be, stood a familiar figure in a black leotard.

"Mark!"

A rush of hope rode on a wave of confusion and doubt. Mark didn't look in my direction. He didn't even flinch, like he always did at loud noises. In fact, his expression was totally blank. The usual crease between his eyebrows, the slight downward tilt of his mouth—it was all gone. His eyes, which usually darted around the room, stared unblinkingly forward.

He could have been a statue, but I knew that wasn't it. Standing next to him, staring and wearing identical expressions, were the crew members in charge of moving my cage. What had Mark called them? *Husks. Like dolls.*

He was one of them now.

"No, no no no. Please, *no*."

Anyone walking through the dark room that evening would have heard more than Bridget and the Mistress's whispered conversation. They would have also heard my voice begging for Mark to say something—anything. They would have heard me apologizing again and again to ears that didn't hear it.

twenty-one.

Alice played her violin.

I didn't know the name of the song, but I recognized it as a classical piece. Even though I hadn't asked the first Elizabeth for this dream, I couldn't help feeling glad that she sent it, anyway. Being with her gave me permission to stop thinking about how scared I felt, even for a second.

I wished I could reach out to her somehow. It felt wrong to be watching her without permission—thinking about her without permission, even, and referring to her as "my Alice" when she didn't even know my name. It made me feel creepy.

Alice stopped playing for a moment. A smile played across her lips, crinkling in the corners of her eyes.

Then she started playing a different song. I recognized this one. Someone had written a song about two of my favorite characters a while back, and it became popular among fans of the show. I knew that Alice was a fan—she tried playing the theme song on guitar earlier—but knowing that she liked the same characters I did made me happy. I wondered if she found it romantic, the way they found each other and saw each other for who they were. I wouldn't be surprised—with all her romance books, she seemed the type.

For just a moment, thinking of her as "my Alice" didn't seem so strange. I didn't feel possessive or anything like that. Just fond. I felt fond of her, this girl with her infectious giggle and cute smile. The one who doodled birds and read out loud to her cat.

Maybe it wasn't so weird to call it a crush. Like the kind of crush I'd get on an actress or a singer I liked.

Besides, I couldn't stop watching her even if I wanted to. So instead of focusing on the rest of it, I just floated above her and focused on the sound of her playing.

I didn't know how long I stayed with Alice, listening to her. But eventually the song faded away, and the scene faded with it.

And instead of floating peacefully above Alice, I found myself trapped inside my body again, with its feverish feathers and hollow bones. What remained of my bare skin felt clammy, covered in sweat and stretched to the brink.

For a moment, the idea of curling up in a ball and waiting for everything to be over wasn't totally unappealing.

But Alice, my Alice, lingered on the back of my eyelids. I couldn't let her fall to this, not without a fight.

I opened my eyes, expecting the usual empty storage room. Instead, I watched as Bridget strode in. And she didn't stride in alone.

One of the Mistress's husks followed her in. Her long, silver hair swung lifelessly past her shoulders, her face as expressionless as it was when she pushed my cage forward every night.

Bridget ignored her entirely, striding to my cage with a sunny grin. "Good morning, little songbird!"

I crossed my arms over my chest, more defensive than defiant. "What do you want?" Even as I spoke to Bridget, my eyes kept darting to the silver-haired woman. Her glassy stare was a carbon copy of the one that Mark wore now.

Bridget laughed, shaking her head. "Me? I don't really want anything, little songbird. I'm just doing the Mistress a favor by dropping off your guard." She ran a hand through the woman's hair, twirling the thin, light strands between her fingers. The woman didn't react.

"Guard?" Something like hope skittered across the back of my mind. *Are you still scared of me, Margaret? Is that why you sent Bridget instead of coming yourself?*

Bridget shrugged, either unconcerned or really good at acting that way. "I told her, y'know, I don't think you're smart enough to get up to anything else. But she said she didn't get this far by being careless! And well, she's been around way longer than any of us, so she'd know, right?" She sighed, a fond smile spreading across her lips. It would've been sweet under other circumstances. "She's *so* smart."

"If she's so smart, why did she choose a husk as a guard? Even if I did something bad, she couldn't say anything." I didn't even know if that was true, but if I phrased it as a question, Bridget wouldn't answer. If I phrased it as a statement, I didn't think she'd miss the opportunity to make me feel stupid.

Sure enough, Bridget laughed. "She's five steps ahead of everyone. Haven't you figured that out by now? She's got ways of getting information from them when she needs it."

She tapped on the silver-haired woman's temple, not getting any sort of reaction. "But I even offered to watch you! And you know what the Mistress said? 'I'm sure you have better things to do with your time, my dear.' She's very considerate like that."

I balled my fists in the fabric of my dress. Feathers, pulsing and warm, pressed at odd angles against my palms. "Yes. She was pretty considerate to Mark, too. Until she wasn't."

Bridget's face didn't show even a flicker of doubt or worry. "Well, yeah, because he was *stupid* enough to go against her."

"Is that why you obey her? You're scared of her?"

"I'm not scared of *anything*!" Bridget's eyes flashed, like a spark of fire from flint. "Fear is pointless. People live their whole lives based on fear. Did you know that? They *beg* for an end to it. They think if they do all the right rituals and say all the right things, then the fear will end. But it never does. I don't have time for it. I never have. You, on the other hand . . ."

She lunged for the bars. I cried out in spite of myself, flinching back. Bridget laughed.

"Just what I thought." She stepped away, clasping her hands behind her back. "Anyways, I don't have to be afraid of the Mistress because I respect her. Why wouldn't I? She showed me the truth: that nothing has to limit me, especially fear. I can take whatever I want and not apologize for it."

A shudder climbed up my spine. "And what happens when she decides that you aren't useful?"

Bridget grinned. "Don't you worry your feathery little head about me, little songbird. The Mistress and I have an understanding. Save your worries for yourself."

And then, whistling, she strode out. The silver-haired woman stayed behind.

Bridget's faith in the Mistress was unshakable. I could keep trying, but it would only be an exercise in frustration. I didn't know what happened to her to make her like this. Maybe I never would. But wondering about it wouldn't help get me out of this cage.

Instead, I turned to the silver-haired woman.

I can't even practice magic, now. What am I supposed to do?

I sent the thought toward the first Elizabeth but didn't get an answer. For now, either because the dream exhausted her or something else, she stayed silent.

I sighed, drawing my knees to my chest. The silver-haired woman sat in the chair by the bookcase, hardly moving. Her gaze made me intensely uncomfortable. I couldn't help comparing it to the thousand-yard stare Madame Selene usually wore. But even when she wasn't seeing me, exactly, she was seeing *something*. The husk's gaze reminded me more of a stuffed animal head mounted over a fireplace or maybe one of those creepy porcelain dolls.

I turned away. I didn't like the way her gaze felt like a judgment—or a death sentence.

But nervous energy jittered in my arms and legs, reminding me of simpler, sleepless nights before big tests. I couldn't practice magic, but I couldn't just sit and do nothing, either. So I paced the floor of my cage, doing my best to avoid the silver-haired woman's gaze.

And I did that until the other crew members joined her, preparing for the show.

After I had a brief and mostly one-sided conversation with

Madame Selene, the crew members brought me backstage. Mark stood slack and unchanged, staring off into space. Violet's entire body seemed rigid with anger, her back to me. Bridget sharpened a knife, whistling.

And Margaret smiled at me. "Did you enjoy your day, little songbird?"

Glassy-eyed and lifeless, the consequences of my anger stood less than a foot from me. But I felt it twisting at my chest anyway. "Please, leave me alone." My voice trembled, but it sounded more like fear than suppressed rage, which was probably a good thing. *And also not exactly a lie.* "Haven't you done enough?"

Bridget laughed so loud that it almost felt like overkill. Margaret only smirked.

"Oh, you silly thing." She shook her head. "This was never about you. It was always about my sister. About Alice. I punish you to punish her, as simple as that may be. You . . . You aren't important. Don't take it personally."

Hearing my own catchphrase echoed back at me felt like someone had struck the air from my lungs.

"He was pretty unimportant, too, y'know?" Bridget cocked a thumb toward Mark. "I don't see why you have to act all *wounded* by it."

I pressed my lips together. Nothing good would come out of my mouth if I opened it.

The act started. When my turn came, I almost considered singing for help. I knew it wouldn't do any good, but my inability to practice magic made me desperate to do something—*anything*—different. My voice shook, and what little applause echoed after I finished was subdued.

The Mistress followed me back to the storage room. She grabbed the broad-shouldered man as he finished putting the poetry women back in their fabric cocoons. "*Watch her.*" Her voice echoed with power before she turned to me with a smirk. "Thought you might like some variety." She gave a mocking laugh before sweeping from the room. The broad-shouldered man stayed, along with the silver-haired woman.

"I'm going to sleep," I grumbled. "What sort of trouble could I possibly get into?"

They didn't respond, of course. All they did was stare with glassy eyes, making me wonder if they could even understand me. They could do what Bridget said, I believed that. But what if all they could understand were those echoing commands? Pity rushed over me, plucking at my heart with light fingers.

"Who did you used to be?" Even if they could speak, they wouldn't have had time to answer, because as I spoke, the curtains rustled. And for once it wasn't the Mistress or Bridget who entered. Instead, Violet rushed in.

Rage twisted her face. In one hand, she held a knife.

Strangely, a wave of calm washed over me, turning my thoughts slow and rational. *She's come for me. That's fair.* She had to know that I was the reason Mark had turned into that thing. If she wanted to get revenge by killing me, could I blame her? Could I even bring myself to use the voice to stop her?

Violet darted forward. But not at me.

The broad-shouldered man looked strong, and I'd seen him carry props with ease. But Violet was strong, too, with the element of surprise on her side. The broad-shouldered man didn't even have time to turn all the way around before Violet's knife slashed across his throat.

Something inhuman flickered behind the silver-haired woman's eyes. She turned toward Violet with her hands reaching out, thumbs ready to gouge eyes, hands ready to grab and snap necks, or—

"No!"

I didn't stop to think or plan. I just *acted*, unleashing all the pent-up anxiety and fear inside me. It made the *shut up* I had shouted at the Mistress sound like a transmission on a bad radio. Actually, it made even the *Mistress's* voice pale in comparison. For just a moment, the lanterns around me seemed to glow brighter.

Time stood still. The silver-haired woman's hands froze, her fingertips brushing Violet's cheeks. Violet, the only fluid and moving thing other than my throbbing heart, looked at me with wide eyes. Then she drove the knife into the silver-haired woman's stomach, up to the hilt.

That broke the spell. The silver-haired woman staggered to her knees, then collapsed silently to the floor. In the back of my head, I could hear a high, clear sound—the first Elizabeth's voice. I thought she might have been singing. I opened my mouth, maybe to help her, and retched instead.

My head spun, and I couldn't tell which thoughts came from me and which were the first Elizabeth speaking. I just knew that Violet had to hurry. If she left now, the Mistress wouldn't catch her. She'd be able to leave, and no one else would have to get hurt because of me . . .

The black fabric of the room lurched forward, trying to swallow me whole. The bright lights of the lanterns threatened to blind me.

"Hey! Fucking focus!" Violet's voice echoed from a thousand miles away. I squinted up at her. She pressed three faces against too many bars to count. *When did she . . . ?*

"You know, don't you? What happened to him?"

It took a few tries before I could draw enough of a breath to answer her. "Yes." Then I collapsed forward, into the black.

twenty-two.

A low thunder thrummed beneath me.

The sensation was soothing—I was more comfortable than I could remember being in a long time. I sat on something cushioned but solid, nothing like the thin blankets that barely kept away the chill of the cage floor. For a moment, I just wanted to sink into it the way I'd sink into bed after a long day at school.

But then came the ache in my bones, the throbbing in my head. I found my lips just in time to groan.

"Fucking *finally*. You awake?"

My eyelids felt weighted, filled with sand. It took what felt like an eternity to pry them open and focus. What I saw when I finally did stole the breath from my lungs.

The *sky*. I could see the sky, stars, trees, and steel gray clouds across a dark backdrop, moving steadily past. Instead of fresh air, I smelled the manufactured perfume of a car air freshener.

I sat slumped against the passenger door of a truck. Used napkins and empty energy drink cans littered the floor at my feet. A skull bobblehead wobbled on the dashboard. Several aches in my body competed with the new setting for my attention, but I forced myself to turn and face the driver's side.

Violet sat behind the wheel, still in her leotard. Blood covered her in spatters, bright against her pale skin and blonde hair. She glanced at me for a moment before turning back to the road. "Glad to see you awake. I would've been *really* pissed if you died on me after all that."

Silence stretched between us as I tried to manage my racing memories and thoughts. Finally, I gathered enough of my wits to ask a single question. "Why?"

I didn't mean it as a direct answer to her words, and Violet didn't take it that way. She laughed, loud and shrill. "Why? I don't fucking know. Thinking things through was Mark's job, but now he's not thinking *anything*. I hate it. I fucking *hate* the way he is now, and I just . . . I just wanted to talk to you. That was all I was gonna do, but then backstage they were *joking* about him and I just *couldn't . . . !*" She made an aggravated noise, gesturing wildly with one hand. "I remembered seeing the fucking key to the fucking cage once, thought I might be able to—I don't know—bargain for information with it. Something. I don't know."

Her words hung heavy in the air after she finished. I waited for a moment before speaking. "That's not what I meant." I understood why she lashed out. I saw how gentle she was with Mark, how in sync they were on stage. That much made perfect sense to me. "What I meant was, why did you take me with you?"

Violet slammed on the brakes. The force of the stop flung me into the dashboard.

"Are you *fucking* kidding me right now?"

I eased back into my seat as Violet pulled over. "I mean, I'm grateful! It's just . . . You might've made it if you went alone. She might have let you leave. But she'll probably come looking now." I didn't say who *she* was. Violet had to know. But I didn't see a trace of fear on her face.

"You think I'm leaving for good? Fuck *that*. Fuck *no*." She jabbed her finger against the dashboard twice for emphasis.

My voice rasped against my throat, like sandpaper. "What do you plan on doing when you get back there?"

Violet looked at me with defiance in her eyes, chin tilted up. "I'm going to kill the Mistress."

My heart free-fell down to my stomach like a broken elevator. Mark's glassy look haunted me. *No, not again.* "You can't."

"Who's gonna stop me? You?" Violet's voice shot up an octave as she spoke.

"*She* is! You have to know that you can't beat her."

"I—" Violet cut off with a disgusted noise, scrubbing hard at the bridge of her nose with her fingertips. "*Fuck*, you're probably right. But I have to try. For Mark."

"Mark wouldn't *want* this!" My voice cracked, my breath turning solid in my throat. "He wouldn't want you to get revenge. He'd want you safe!"

"This isn't *about* revenge!" Violet slammed her hands against the wheel. She seemed to force herself to speak softer as she continued. "I asked that creepy fortune teller chick how I could get Mark back to normal! And she said that the Mistress's magic stops if she dies—or something like that, I think. Too hard to know for sure with her bullshit, but whatever. It doesn't matter. I'm not giving Mark up without a fight. I don't know everything that happened, but I don't need to. I know he didn't deserve this."

I curled in on myself at the accusation in her voice. "I know. I'm sorry." I wrapped my arms around my knees, willing myself not to cry. Violet had every right to be furious at me.

But she didn't get angry. Instead, something in Violet's gaze seemed to soften. "Hey, look. I'm . . . I'm *beyond* fucking pissed right now, but I can't be pissed at you. It's not right that you were in that cage. I know I don't . . . You have to know, like, with Mark, too! It's not . . . *Uuuuugh*." She dropped her face into her hands. "I *suck* at this sort of thing."

"No. No, I get it." I sat up a bit straighter, my spine aching in protest. "I don't blame you, either. Or Mark. That's not what happened. I never wanted him to get hurt."

"Well, yeah. I heard you, that first night. You were obviously pretty fucking torn up about it." She looked out the window. "And look, I want to know what happened. I want you to stick around long enough to tell me, but after that? You don't *have* to come with me. You can go live out your life. Try to, at least. Best case scenario, I manage to kill the Mistress and you ditch the feathers. Worst case . . . Well, you don't have to die in a cage."

For a long moment, all I could do was stare at her. Violet knew she was probably going to die. She wore that knowledge like she wore her dark eyeliner. In her face I saw the same acceptance Mark had worn in the end, the same fear I felt when the Mistress strangled me. And she didn't care. The girl who did so much to survive was willing to throw it all away for the person that mattered to her.

I related to it. Even with freedom dangling in front of me, I related to it.

"I'll go with you."

Violet's head whipped around to face me. "Now, don't go pulling some martyr shit. You don't owe me or *anyone* anything. You can't honestly think—"

"I feel guilty." I didn't raise my voice, but Violet stopped when I spoke, anyway. "I'm not going to lie and tell you I don't. But that's not why I want to go back. Not really. It's because I have someone I want to protect, too. I want to stop this cycle, Violet. I want to protect Alice."

Violet nodded, looking thoughtfully at me. "You figured it out, huh? Most of them don't. I guess that's as good of a name to call her as any, huh?"

I frowned, shaking my head. "No, her name *is* Alice. I have dreams about her."

Violet raised her eyebrows. "Uh, no, that chick you're making out with in your dreams isn't—"

"Not *that* Alice." I took a deep breath. "Violet, do you know anything about me? Do you even know what *my* name is?"

Violet's cheeks flushed red. "Well, fucking excuse me. I didn't have time to ask in between saving your ass and, uh, *saving your ass.*"

I raised my hands, palms out. "I'm not offended or

anything! It's just—Elizabeth. My name is Elizabeth, like the Mistress's sister."

Surprise flooded Violet's face. I could practically see the gears spin in her head as she tried to rationalize it. "Okay, whatever, that's a common name. It's—"

"It is," I interrupted. "But Alice isn't. And I've dreamt of the next girl. A girl around my age with a cute laugh and a talent for playing the violin. Her name is Alice, too, and I have . . . I *have* to keep her safe."

I couldn't pretend that Alice was just an afterthought anymore, her safety an added perk to my own. I couldn't pretend that my feelings for her only mattered in the context of the cage, where I had nothing left to lose. Even with freedom dangling in front of me, I still chose her.

For a long moment, Violet only stared at me. Then she said, "You love her."

"I . . ." Part of me wanted to deny it, but considering everything, I didn't know if I could.

Violet took my silence as an answer. A terse laugh fell from her lips. "Awesome." She pinched the bridge of her nose. "Let's use the power of love to kill the immortal witch, then. That's how it always goes in fairy tales, right?"

Hearing the word "love" made me acutely uncomfortable. I did my best to change the subject. "If you think it's hopeless, why even bother?"

Violet deflated, pressing her palms against her eyelids. All at once, the fearless girl who danced through the air looked very small. "I don't *know*." Her voice wavered but didn't quite crack. "I just couldn't give Mark up without a fight. Doing that would've broken something in me, I think. I can't deal with the way I feel when I look at him now. I feel so helpless. I swore I'd never feel that way again. I—" She cut her words off with a quiet sound, like a swallowed sob.

I reached out for her, then thought better of it. I couldn't imagine the feeling of my warm, pulsing feathers being very comforting. I used my words instead. "Violet . . . I think we have a chance." Saying it out loud felt wrong. It was something I'd hardly admitted to myself, but I wanted Violet to believe in us, to have some kind of hope.

She looked at me with eyes that were dry but unconvinced. "Don't sugarcoat shit for my sake. I'm aware of how thoroughly fucked this whole thing is. If I had stopped to think for more than five seconds back there, I wouldn't have done any of it."

"I get that." I paused, forcing myself to breathe and gather my thoughts. "But what happened to Mark happened because I challenged her—scared her, for a second. And if I could just have time away from her, to figure out everything, I think I could do more than scare her. I'm not sugarcoating things—our chances are . . . are not great. I'm terrified. I'm already dying, but I'm scared of her using someone else against me, like she used Mark."

I met Violet's gaze. Her eyes were blue, darker than Alice's. I wondered if Mark thought about them as much as I thought about hers.

"If we go after her, she might try to use you the same way."

All the exhausted despair drained out of Violet's face as she laughed. "Listen to you. Whose idea was all this, anyways?"

She had a point. I just wasn't used to having someone like

her on my side. Mark only helped me out of guilt, and he had plenty of reservations. The first Elizabeth didn't have a body or a way to actually be with me. And I could hardly be sure of Madame Selene's motives, much less her cryptic words.

But Violet's motives were obvious. She was here, and she was ready to act.

"Right." I nodded, letting out a short breath. "You're right. I'm with you, then. And I will tell you everything, including the stuff about Mark." I leaned against the door. "But for now, um, we should probably keep moving. Find someplace safe?" I still felt lightheaded, and I definitely didn't have the energy to prove my magic to her.

"Someplace safe doesn't exist." Violet clipped her words. "But we can hit the road."

She started the truck up again. I rolled down the window. The chilly air rushed through the cabin, but Violet didn't complain as I held out my hand to feel the wind against my feverish, feather-covered palm.

twenty-three.

Alice doodled in her notebook.

For once, her long hair was down, covering the page. I wished I could see what she drew. Wanting to know everything about her, right down to what she doodled in her notebook, was silly. But I did want to. Maybe if I knew more about her, I could justify the way I felt.

Here in her room, I struggled to deny what Violet said. Watching her made my troubles feel more distant, if only for a moment. My heart felt lighter, my bones less weary and hollow. I liked the way she smiled, her nervous giggle, the way she loved music and doted on Smush.

I felt something for Alice. I didn't know if it was love, but I didn't have a better word for it.

It wasn't fair. What I felt for her was the echo of a love shared by two murdered witches, brought on by stress and the constant threat of death. But even knowing all that, I couldn't regret or feel bitter about it. Dreaming of Alice made me feel happy. It made me feel hopeful that there was a future for me, past the Mistress. At the very least, I could save that future for her.

I'd be okay with that, I decided. I'd be okay with not making it out alive if it meant Alice would be safe.

Alice looked up at the ceiling and smiled. She pushed her hair away from her face, throwing it into a messy bun. Something in my chest warmed as I pretended that she did it so I could see what she drew. Birds flapped across the top of the page, happy little music notes floating above them.

As the dream faded, I heard her hum, slightly off-key. I recognized it as the fan-made song she played on violin before.

I woke up, foggy and confused. After spending so many nights curled up on the floor of my cage, sleeping leaned against the passenger door of Violet's truck immediately sent off warning bells. My heart rate spiked for a moment, just on instinct.

But then my rational brain kicked in. Rubbing at my shoulder, I looked around the truck.

I fell asleep shortly after Violet started driving again, my head spinning too much to do anything else. It looked like she had stopped at some point—a fast food bag lay crumpled on the floor, a few stray fries spilling out. My stomach lurched at the thought of food.

We weren't moving. The car sat off to the side of an abandoned-looking road. And Violet was gone.

I looked in the cramped back seat, wondering if she had fallen asleep back there. But it was empty. Worry started to squeeze at my chest.

Then, out the back window, I saw straight blonde hair. Violet sat in the truck bed, facing away from me with her head tilted up toward the sky.

I opened the door and eased myself out of the car. The gravel bit painfully at my bare feet, and the chilled air turned the sweat that dripped between my feathers cold and uncomfortable, not quite stinging what remained of my skin.

But the air was so *fresh*. I never really had a chance to appreciate that before shows. And the stars that sparkled above me were brighter than any paper lantern.

I used the side of the truck to support myself as I made my way to the end. Violet didn't look at me as I clumsily pulled myself into the truck bed. She must have cleaned up and changed somewhere—I couldn't see a trace of blood anywhere, and she'd replaced her leotard with a pair of ripped jeans and a graphic T-shirt under a leather jacket. She sat on a blanket, staring up at the sky. With a pang, I recognized it as the same kind of blanket Mark gave me. Several more sat folded near her.

Silence stretched out between us like a tightrope that I didn't dare cross. I pulled one of the blankets around my shoulders and waited for her to say something, maybe a comment on how long I'd slept.

Instead, she said, "Mark and me used to stargaze a lot."

I watched her expression, but I didn't see any anger in her features. I didn't see much of anything, actually. But it seemed like she was waiting for a response. "Oh?"

"Yeah." She sighed. Her words came out more slowly than earlier, like she had to force them. "Back when we were . . . Before the show. Did he tell you about any of that?" She finally dropped her gaze to look at me.

Would she be mad at Mark for telling me? I wasn't sure, but I didn't want to lie to her. "He told me a bit. Enough for me to, um, put things together." An apology danced on the tip of my tongue, but I held it in. I didn't think Violet would appreciate it.

She looked back up at the sky, heaving out a breath that was almost a sigh. "Yeah, well, we used to sneak out at night all the time. Sometimes we got caught, which sucked, obviously, but it always felt worth it. Being out of the house always felt better than being in it, no matter what happened when I got back."

I didn't know what to say. Not to her, not to her words, not to her slow tone or her eyes that wouldn't leave the sky. I said nothing, waiting for her to fill the silence if she wanted to. Eventually, she did.

"We'd lie out on the grass for hours," she continued. "Mark used to tell me about all these constellations. I don't think all of 'em were real—he probably made some of them up so he'd have an excuse to tell me stuff. He liked doing that. And I liked listening, so I never called him out or anything."

I swallowed hard. My throat ached, the backs of my eyes prickling. "He loved you. I know he did." *He loved you until the end*, I almost said, but the air already hung over us, heavy like a shroud. I didn't want to add to that any more than my death-reeking presence already did.

Violet let out a long, hollow breath. She looked at me with dry eyes. "Tell me everything."

"Are you sure?" She didn't look like she was ready for this discussion. She didn't look like she was ready for anything.

I could relate.

But I could relate to what she said next, too. "I'm pretty sure I have to be."

I took a deep breath and let it out slowly. Then I nodded. "Alright. Well . . . you know how he'd come and talk to us, right? The girls like me?"

Violet nodded, a spark of impatience flickering in her tone. "*Duh.*"

"Right. So." How did I even begin to tell her everything? "He wasn't the only one who talked to me. Madame Selene talked, too, before shows. She said . . . Well, you know how she is. It's hard to tell for sure. But she said enough to make me think that maybe . . . maybe I could do something with more information. So I asked Mark. And he didn't want to tell me, but I guilted him into it." I looked down at my lap, clenching my feathered fingers together. "I didn't think anything I did would hurt him. I didn't think at all."

Violet shook her head briskly. "What did he tell you?"

I swallowed the urge to beg for forgiveness. "He told me the truth. About the Mistress's sister, the first Elizabeth, and her Alice. What happened to them and why the Mistress kidnapped me."

Violet looked at me, mouth hanging open slightly in disbelief. "That's all? You were going to figure that shit out on your own, anyways. Why punish him for that?"

"Because . . . that information got me thinking. I had *time* to think about it, when none of the other girls did. Plus, there's the whole name thing." I paused. I knew it became more unbelievable from here, and nerves danced against the walls of my stomach. "The first time I woke up in the cage, the Mistress told me that names have power. I have the first Elizabeth's name. And the first Elizabeth . . . she was a witch."

"Lot of fucking good *that* did her in the end," Violet said dryly.

"*I got caught by surprise.*" The first Elizabeth's voice, distant but unmistakably her, echoed in the back of my head.

Violet hurried on. "Look, not trying to be the asshole here, but—"

"You didn't offend me," I interjected. "I was listening to the first Elizabeth . . . telling me that the Mistress had caught her by surprise. And it makes sense. They were sisters. She never would have guessed that the Mistress would hurt her." I wrapped my arms around my knees. "We know better now."

Violet stared at me like I had suggested stealing her skin to wear as a coat. "You *hear* her?"

It was time. If I could hear the first Elizabeth again, some of her power must have returned. I looked around. Either Violet or I had tracked a small stone into the truck bed. It sat out of reach, just at the edge. I focused on it and felt that now-familiar muscle in my gut tensing.

"*Rise.*" The pebble trembled and rose, wobbling in the air. "*Come to me.*"

The pebble hovered toward me, slow and jerky. I could feel the weight of it pressed against the inside of my skull. It wobbled in front of me until I held my palm under it, and then it dropped.

I turned to look at Violet. She stared at me, mouth hanging open. "Holy shit." Shock dulled the edges of her usually sharp tone.

"Names have power." I forced my voice to stay even and strong. I wanted her to believe in me, wanted her to believe we had a chance. I thought our odds would be better if she did. "And I have more than the first Elizabeth's name. Like I said, I hear her. She's inside of me. And she wants revenge."

"*What do you want, Elizabeth?*" When I answered, I spoke to Violet as much as I did the first Elizabeth.

"I want to protect Alice. That's what's really important to me."

Violet bared her teeth in an uncheerful smile. "Well, how fucking convenient. I want to protect Mark, and if that doesn't work, I want revenge for him. Glad I'll have something in common with at least one of you." She looked up at the sky, her fists clenched. "Hell." She seemed like she was going to say something else for a moment, but then she turned back to me. "What are we gonna do? No fucking offense here, but I don't think tossing pebbles at the Mistress is gonna cut it."

Relief washed over me like a wave. Maybe it was silly, but half of me had been expecting Violet to run, to leave me at the side of the road. But she wanted to act with me. She wanted to trust me.

And I had absolutely no idea how to answer her.

I rubbed at the back of my neck, shivering as the feathers shifted. "Um . . ." I waited to see if the first Elizabeth had anything to say, but she stayed silent. This was all on me. "I need more rest." I spoke slowly, putting the plan together as I went. "I used too much power too fast when you took me,

207

trying to keep us safe."

Violet raised an eyebrow. "When that chick came at me, trying to gouge my eyes out, I thought I was for sure a goner, but then she froze. That was you?"

I nodded. "Me and the first Elizabeth together, I'm pretty sure. But yeah, she'll show me more once we get our strength back. Then I'll practice magic—for as long as I can." I looked down at my body. Even if the Mistress wasn't searching for me, I didn't think I had longer than a month. Two weeks, maybe.

"And then?" Violet didn't take her gaze off me. The stars glittered above us like broken pieces of glass catching the light.

"We're going to fight the Mistress," I said. "When I'm strong enough, when the time is right . . . We're going to end this."

twenty-four.

Snow dusted the ground, dull and brown in the moonlight.

Violet told me that it was the middle of November now. I'd gone over a month without eating, drinking, or using the bathroom, not even getting my period. Over a month without going to class or seeing my parents or spending more than a handful of moments outside.

I got to do that now, if nothing else.

I glanced over my shoulder. Violet stood feet from me, thumbs hooked into the pockets of her jeans as she stretched her legs. I stayed near the truck, ready to duck inside if someone drove toward us, but I didn't think that was going to be an issue. Violet seemed to have a knack for finding abandoned country roads. Besides, it was dark enough that no one would see how strangely my borrowed sweatpants and hoodie bulged. No one would see the feathers covering my face.

It had been less than a week since Violet broke me out, but already I was getting stronger. Moving smaller items like pebbles and the empty cans in Violet's truck took way less effort. I could hold them up higher, for longer, with less shaking and wobbling.

Now, I stood by the truck bed and stared at it, balling my hands into fists.

"*Lift.*" The back tires shifted slightly. I flexed harder. My skull strained against the skin of my temples, my teeth clenching. The back tires began to hover, trembling less than an inch from the ground. Sweat ran down my feathered skin in shivery lines.

"Ay, easy there. That's the only transportation we've got."

Violet had come up behind me while I worked. I eased the car down before turning to face her, panting. "I just wanted to see if I could." I itched at a few new feathers dotting the tip of my nose.

"Well, consider that mystery fucking solved." Violet's light tone didn't make it to her face. She stared at my feathers like she wanted to tear her eyes away but couldn't. "Do those things hurt?"

I stared at my hands. Except for a few small spots on my palms, they were completely covered. If I stared hard enough, I could see the feathers pulsing in time with my heartbeat. "They itch, mostly. They don't hurt, but they do make me feel uncomfortable. It's like . . . I've never donated blood, but I think it must feel something like this. Not quite lightheaded, but not right. Like something's being taken."

I looked up at Violet. She was frowning in this small, tight way that she did. "That sounds like it fucking sucks."

"Everything about this . . . sucks." I shoved my hands into my hoodie pocket. "I just want to get it over with, which is why I keep practicing, I guess."

Something in my stomach coiled at the thought of going back and facing Margaret. I couldn't tell if it had to do with the magic or not. Was that muscle cowering in fear or preparing to strike?

Violet opened the back of the truck bed and hopped inside, feet dangling off the edge. "Is the other Elizabeth helping you at all? She's still camped out in your head, right?"

"*I'm trying.*" An edge of exhaustion tinged the first Elizabeth's voice.

"She's trying." I pulled myself into the trunk next to Violet. "But it's complicated. She needs to work around the Mistress's magic, and there are things the Mistress did to keep me from finding out things. So a lot of things I have to figure out on my own."

Violet raised an eyebrow. "That makes no fucking sense. You know that, right?"

I sighed, rubbing at my temple as best as I could through the feathers. "I'm trying to kill an immortal witch that used to be my sister in a past life."

"*I'm not a past life,*" the first Elizabeth said. "*You have a piece of my soul, and you share my name, but you aren't me. You're your own person.*"

"She's saying something, isn't she? You get this spaced-out look on your face." Violet let her face go slack, trying to mimic me. Despite everything, it made me laugh a bit.

"Yeah." I looked up at the sky. "She was correcting me—

211

she's not a past life. It's a bit more complicated than that. But still? None of this makes sense. I'm just trying to put the pieces together."

Violet nodded, staring up at the sky. A few stars blinked to life against the gray night. "Want to know what I've been thinking?"

I looked at her. I couldn't read her expression. "What?"

"You've been spending a lot of time moving shit around, but that's not what the Mistress does." She gestured with quick, decisive motions as she spoke. "She moves *people* around. Like chess pieces."

I scratched at one of the feathers on the back of my hand. "Yeah . . . and?"

"Can you do that?" Violet leaned forward, starlight glinting cold in her dark blue eyes. "It just makes sense. If you want to beat the Mistress, it's gotta be at her own game, right?"

Something in my chest seemed to expand, leaving less room for my lungs to draw breath. "I don't know. There was that thing with the husk, and I made the Mistress stay quiet for, like, a second. But both of those things were in the heat of the moment. I don't know if I could do it on purpose."

"Why?"

I shrugged. "I don't know. It just feels wrong."

Violet looked at me like I'd admitted to lighting the truck on fire. "Well no fucking shit, Sherlock! All of this is wrong!"

"No, no, I get that. It's just . . . It's not the sort of thing you can take back." I sighed, curling my arms around my knees. "I remember the first time, you know. The first time the Mistress cast a spell on me, when she put me to sleep. I haven't felt right since. It's like . . . she got inside my head and left dirty fingerprints on the inside of my skull."

Talking about it brought it to my attention all over again, the way talking about breathing forced you to do it consciously. Just the reminder of it made the magic that lived inside me feel shriveled and weak.

"Having that happen," I said slowly, "knowing that she could control me, that I had no choice about anything—there's nothing I can compare it to. I felt . . . violated. I don't want to make anyone else feel like that."

Violet stared at her lap, clenching her fists tight enough to turn her knuckles white. Silence sat heavy between us, and I tried to figure out how to break it.

Before I could, she looked up at me. Her eyes seemed to almost drill into mine. "I want you to try it on me."

"Are you . . . *What?*" Spoken words were never exactly my strong suit, but they failed me entirely in that moment. "You—"

"Look," Violet cut me off, her tone tense. "You're going to have to be able to do this if you're going to fight the Mistress. We can't go into this without knowing what we're doing. And I al—I'm the only one around. So try it on me."

I fidgeted with the too-long sleeves of my borrowed hoodie, then stopped when I remembered Mark doing the same thing. "I . . . I don't want to make you feel—"

Violet let out an annoyed grunt, almost a growl. "Yeah, yeah, you're a fucking saint. I get it!"

I didn't know what to do with her outburst or the way she glared at me. I held up both my hands, palms out. "I'm not a saint," I murmured. "But you helped me. I don't want to hurt you, not if I can help it."

Violet leaned back and let out a long sigh. "I want to see the Mistress dead, and right now that seems like a long fucking shot. So whatever we can do to improve our odds, we gotta do it." She looked at me, dark eyes solid and sure. "I'll be fine, okay? Just do something simple."

"*She has a point,*" the first Elizabeth said softly. "*The fact that you worry is admirable, and I love that you're trying to be responsible about this, but . . .*"

She didn't finish her sentence. She didn't need to. "You can tell me to stop at any point, and I will."

Violet's lips twitched into an expression that didn't even come close to a smile. She curled her fists along the edges of her sleeves. "Sure. Go for it."

"Alright. Here we go." I took a deep breath, willing my trembling nerves to steady. Then I flexed. "*Lift your arm.*"

My voice echoed. It sounded different than before—more solid, somehow. Violet's arm spasmed a little bit but stayed dangling in her lap. She looked at it, eyebrows curling up into the blonde swoop of her bangs. "Huh. Well, that's different."

"How do you feel?"

Violet rolled her eyes. "Oh, would you relax already? It's not like you're telling me to go streaking down the street or anything. It feels like I want to, but I don't have to. I don't know. It's fucking weird but I'm not traumatized or whatever you're worried about." She breathed out. "Try it again."

I clenched my fists, speaking with more certainty this time. "*Lift your arm.*"

Violet's arm jerked into the air hard enough that she had

to brace herself with the other to keep from toppling over. She looked up at it with wide, startled eyes.

"Sorry! I'm sorry. Did it—"

Violet cut me off with a snorting little laugh. "Dude. Fucking weird." She looked at me, eyes sparkling. "Keep going! Do something else."

"Oh! Uh . . . Wave it around? *Wave it around!*"

Giggling, Violet watched her arm flail above her head. I'd heard her scoff before, or chuckle, but I'd never heard her make such a happy sound. I started to giggle along with her.

"Do something else! Something harder!"

Grinning, I said the first thing that came to mind. *"Take off your jacket."*

The humor fell from Violet's expression in a rush. "Wai—" But by the time I registered the horror in her face, it was too late. She had shrugged her jacket off, letting it drop to the floor of the truck bed. Then I realized that I had never seen her bare arms before. Even her leotard, which showed off a lot of skin, kept them covered.

For a second, I thought she had a rash. Then I realized that the little circles dotting her arms were actually small indents too uniform to be natural. Then Violet was hastily shoving her jacket on, and I was looking away, trying not to compare the marks to the burns on the old rug in the living room—the ones Mom said were from her grandfather's cigarettes.

Mark's voice echoed in my head. *Whatever you're thinking, they probably did worse.*

"So it works." Tension lined Violet's voice, but it didn't tremble.

I couldn't work up the nerve to look up at her. "Violet, I'm so sorry. I didn't know."

"Save it." Her harsh, snapping tone made me wince. She must have seen, because her voice softened when she spoke next. "I'm not pissed at you. I just . . . Save it, okay?" She said it softer this time, almost pleading.

"Okay." I chanced a glance at her out of the corner of my eye. She wore her jacket again. She looked pointedly away from me, her entire body tense. I fidgeted with my overlong sleeves. "So before that . . . It didn't hurt you, did it?"

Violet shook her head, curling a knee to her chest and stretching the other leg out. "No. It felt weird, for sure, but not anything like you described it."

I leaned against the side of the truck bed, curling my arms around myself. "Good."

"Don't know why you're so fucking happy about that." Violet let out a little huff. "You know, it's not going to be anything like this when you face the Mistress. Are you going to be ready to hurt her?"

Anxiety fluttered against my ribs, like birds in a cramped cage. I didn't think all of them came from fear of failure, either. What would it feel like to use that power against someone who hadn't asked for it? What would it unlock inside of me?

I took a deep breath, trying to quell those thoughts. It would be okay, as long as I remembered why I was doing all of this—who I was doing it *for*.

"*Alice*," the first Elizabeth whispered.

Alice, I thought.

"I'll be ready," I said. "When the time is right, I won't hesitate."

twenty-five.

The sound of Alice's violin soared, high and sweet. I sang
loud and clear to match.

"If I were the sky
Dear, you'd be my star
People would admire you from afar
But you'd stay near me
And I'd hold so tight
No one could take me away from your light."

I sang Margaret's lyrics with as much sincerity as I could muster,
but in truth, they perturbed me. Then again, everything about my
sister perturbed me lately. Alice's words echoed in my ears, a
maddening refrain. There is a darkness in her. I jumped at every
shadow, seeing that darkness everywhere.

But when I watched Margaret dance, she looked like the same
sister I had always known. A bit arrogant, forceful perhaps—but
never a danger.

"If I were a god

Dear, you'd be my muse
All mine to cherish and love and subdue
For you I would make
A world oh so fine
Making sure all you'd want is to be mine."

I couldn't help but read into her lyrics further. She didn't speak of love as I knew it—as something between two equals. She sang of a lover that was subordinate, someone to show off as a prize and nothing more. Did she truly view Alice that way? Wonderful, creative, softhearted, free Alice? It seemed impossible to me that anyone could look upon Alice and see her as something to own.

As childish and undoubtedly foolish as it was, I found myself changing the lyrics. I replaced them with my own, letting love as I knew it swell in my throat.

"If I were a bird
You'd be the ground
Where I could touch down, safe and sound
I'd give up my wings
And I'd give up my flight
Because, love, you're the one
Who sets me alight . . ."

Margaret glared at me, slowing and then stopping her dance. The utterly put-out look on her face almost made me laugh. She looked like a child denied dessert. Alice hid her face in her hair, and I got the sense that she smiled. She changed the tempo of her violin to match me.

"Because flying alone is not really free
Not if I can't choose who flies beside me."

I woke up gasping for air, my head throbbing.

This dream had been different from the others. It actually

felt like a dream, fuzzy and indistinct. Right before I woke up, that final note seemed to stretch for minutes without giving me time to catch my breath.

Outside the car window, the landscape rolled past. When I turned, Violet glanced at me out of the corner of her eye, hands still on the wheel. "You good there?" Beneath her laid-back tone, I could hear a small note of concern that I didn't think I would've heard the night she rescued me.

"Yeah." It wasn't really a lie, but I felt myself frowning anyway.

Violet turned her attention back to the road. "Oookay then."

She didn't press further. She might have realized that I needed to think things through in silence. When I tried to talk them out, my words became jumbled and unsure. Before, I'd write out all my thoughts in my journal, but that had been when I was alone. And my worries then had much lower stakes. I'd wonder whether I did badly on a test or what I should get my parents for their birthdays. Thinking of that other life made my heart ache, but I didn't have time to mourn it.

I had far more pressing concerns.

Elizabeth, what was that about? The dreams of the first Elizabeth's life were from the Mistress, I knew. But the first Elizabeth could've had something to do with the weird quality. Maybe she'd know something, at least. I listened, but she stayed silent.

Are you there? I tried again, but I didn't even get a whisper of a response.

Had she exhausted herself to bring that dream to me?

Why?

I rubbed my forehead, wincing. A thick layer of warm feathers seemed to vibrate beneath my fingers. Margaret's lyrics echoed in my mind. I had to agree with the first Elizabeth—they were creepy. I had a bit of a bias, of course. I knew Margaret as the Mistress, and she was capable of unspeakable evil. But the way the lyrics talked about love came across as possessive, controlling. It made me wonder how she had treated the first Alice.

Even though a lot of the dream had been hazy, the look on Margaret's face when the first Elizabeth changed up the lyrics was crystal clear. She hadn't been expecting that. But who could? Making up lyrics on the spot was impressive.

Something about that nagged at me. I knew that the first Elizabeth was smart, but that smart? And something about her voice seemed off, too. Her speaking voice sounded and felt like mine, but her singing voice didn't. It sounded similar, but it had an ethereal quality to it. The first Alice's violin seemed to resonate more than my Alice's, too. And then there was Margaret's dancing, but I already knew how magnetic that could be. It was practically magic.

Wait.

Margaret's dancing *was* magic.

It all clicked into place then, a neat puzzle.

When the Mistress danced, she captivated everyone. She manipulated lights and colors, making the world itself sway in time with her. She could do far, far more with her dancing than with her words alone.

And the first Elizabeth must have been able to do the same thing, with singing.

They were doing magic together in the dream. That was why it was so hazy. The Mistress wouldn't have wanted me to see that, wouldn't have wanted me to know anything about how magic worked in her world.

But it made sense. Even if you weren't a witch, getting lost in the thing you loved to do could be magical.

It also explained why the Mistress forced the girls she kidnapped to perform. She wanted to humiliate the souls of the first Elizabeth and Alice, so she twisted their talents. She turned what should have been magical and empowering into something that hurt and degraded them. My stomach turned as I thought about the power she must have felt while watching us perform, watching us humiliate ourselves as we did something that used to be fun.

Rage replaced nausea as I thought of all the girls who came before me, the hundreds of paper lanterns with their names. They all had normal lives, just like me. They liked to paint or write poetry or sew. Elle liked telling stories, and she died with her final story tasting like ash on her tongue while she sobbed.

For the first time, it occurred to me that I'd be getting revenge for the girl who died in my arms.

"Violet." My voice grated in my throat. How long had I been sitting silently? It felt like coming out of a trance.

Violet glanced over at me, brow furrowed. "Yo?"

"I think I know how to beat her."

If I'd been one of the protagonists in the cartoons I used to watch, I would've said that confidently. But I didn't *feel* confident. Anxiety sat heavy on my chest and filled my throat. But even with all that, I didn't want to turn back or say that I made a mistake, that I changed my mind.

Violet huffed out a breath. "Wow. Okay. Good to see that you had a productive meditation session, then." For a second, I thought she was making fun of me. But then she gave me a strained smile, her knuckles even paler than usual against the wheel. *She's just as stressed as I am.*

"You should, um, probably pull over for this one." I brushed back the remaining hair around my face, sick to my stomach at the feeling of the feathers on my cheeks.

Violet pulled into an empty lot near an abandoned building. The sunlight, thin and without warmth, glittered against the concrete. She killed the ignition and turned to me. "Alright, let's hear it."

"I . . ." The words caught in my throat. Violet didn't hurry me along or snap at me. I wondered if being friends with Mark had taught her patience or if she was just kinder and more considerate than her harsh exterior let on. From what I knew of her, it felt like a mix of both.

Focus, Elizabeth. The first Elizabeth wasn't around to put me back on track, but imagining her voice helped anyway. I swallowed hard and tried again. "You've watched the Mistress dance before, right? Like, *really* watched?"

Violet nodded. "Yeah, of course. Hell, the first time I saw her, I watched her dance during the show. It was—" She coughed, shifting in her seat a bit. Pink dusted across her pale cheeks. "Well, you know. Attractive doesn't even begin to fucking cover it. Magnetic?"

I nodded, even though I hadn't felt quite the same way. "When she uses the voice, she can control one person." I had to pause for a moment before continuing, just to pull

223

up my courage. "But the dance is more powerful. She controls the whole room."

"The whole world, it seems like." Violet's soft voice sounded almost wistful—or maybe jealous. Even though it made me uncomfortable, I couldn't really blame her for wanting that sort of power after everything she'd been through.

I looked out at the parking lot as I spoke, afraid of seeing disbelief on Violet's face. "The first Elizabeth and Alice were witches. So they had that same power, except they didn't dance. The first Alice played violin, instead." I took a deep breath, mostly to delay my words. "And the first Elizabeth sang."

Violet gasped. "Seriously? You think you can do that?"

"I think I can try." I turned to face her. Her face was a mix of shock and hope, but not the disbelief I had feared. Something in my chest seemed to shrink, leaving more room for my lungs.

She flapped her hands at me. "Well, go on! Try then!"

I opened my mouth, but then the first Elizabeth's voice came through, faint and unmistakable. "*Wait.*"

"The first Elizabeth is telling me we should wait."

Violet rolled her eyes. "Of course she is. Any reason why, or is it just for fun?"

I shook my head. "You're, um, going to have to give me a minute on that."

I closed my eyes, doing my best to clear my mind. I pictured the first Elizabeth's lantern glowing bright and warm beneath my fingertips. That seemed to help, at least a little. When the first Elizabeth spoke next, she sounded a little closer. *"That specific sort of magic takes a lot of energy. Far more than anything you've done before. It's taken my sister centuries of practice to use it once a day as she does now. And you're so new . . ."*

Her voice faded out. I turned back to Violet and was impressed all over again with her patience.

"The magic's too powerful. If I tried to test it, I might not be able to do it again for a while." I looked down at myself. Staring at the feathers made them feel worse, made it feel like I had poison dripping down the insides of my bones. Shuddering, I looked back up. "I don't have that kind of time."

Violet's dark blue eyes turned flat. "So, we're going up against an immortal, vengeful witch armed with a weapon we're not going to learn how to use?"

What little confidence I had swirled away from me like water down a drain. When I spoke, my voice squeaked. "Uh, yes."

Silence stretched between us. Seconds passed with only the pounding of my heart against my ribs. Then Violet laughed. And in spite of everything, I laughed along with her.

"Fuck," she said. "Still beats my original plan, yeah? When are we going to do it? I only know the travel schedule for another week, so it's gonna have to be before that."

I paused, waiting for the first Elizabeth. And when she answered, faintly but there, I felt her weariness. I felt a century of anguish over getting torn to pieces and killed bit by bit. I closed my eyes, half of me wishing we could wait and the other half of me knowing that we couldn't.

"Tomorrow night. Tomorrow night, we end all of this."

twenty-six.

"You're sure about this?"

Violet tapped her foot repeatedly against the pavement. I peered around the corner of the building we hid behind, watching as the line of people in front of the black-draped building steadily diminished.

"I'm sure." I didn't *sound* sure. I leaned against the wall, sighing, and tried to be slightly more honest. "It's the only way." My legs ached with a feverish warmth. The feathers around my calves pulsed like the effort of standing was too much for them to handle.

I slid down into a crouch. Then I peered around the corner again, entertaining visions of the black fabric and paper lanterns disappearing with the echo of Margaret's laugh. Or maybe Margaret herself would stride out and finish all this before it started.

None of that happened, of course. The line dwindled to ten people, then five, then two. I could feel Violet's anxiety next to me. She paced, stuffing her hands into her pockets repeatedly.

Finally, after what seemed like an eternity of waiting, the line ended. The two husks went in to prepare for the main act. I took a deep breath, sending a silent question to the first Elizabeth. *Are you with me?*

"*I'm here.*" Her voice felt stronger, surer than I'd ever heard it. "*I'm here. Let's end this.*"

"It's time." I stood, my sore muscles protesting. Even that left me feeling winded.

Violet raised an eyebrow, the corners of her mouth quirking down. "Are you sure about this? You can hardly walk."

"I'll make it to the end." I rubbed at my shoulder, shivery discomfort crawling up my spine as I pushed the feathers against the grain. "I have to. I have to finish this. I have to try."

Violet opened her mouth for a moment, but closed it without saying anything. I had some idea of what she had to be thinking, though. Neither of us would turn back. She had to go in for Mark, and I had to go in for Alice, so we'd go in together.

Violet offered me an arm. I took it and tried not to lean too heavily against her. Together, we made our way up the black-draped steps and through the fabric.

Madame Selene's room looked exactly the same. The small, circular table still sat in the same position, covered in the same midnight blue fabric, and Madame Selene still sat behind it. It almost looked exactly the same as the first night I walked in.

Only the shock on Madame Selene's face was different.

It was slight, and it only lasted for a moment. Her eyes widened, and her grip against the edges of the table tightened. Then it faded, leaving only the vague, stoic face she often wore. "So, the songbird flies willingly back into her cage."

The words could have been cruel, but I thought the slight curve of her mouth showed more pity than anything. I sat in the seat across from her, mostly because I didn't know if my legs would hold me for much longer. I reached my hands across the table and felt a rush of comfort when Madame Selene took them in her own. They felt solid and warm. I tried to make my voice come out the same.

"I'm breaking the lock. I'm making sure no one else is ever trapped here again."

Violet leaned against the table, palms flat. "You can see the future, right? Tell us if this is a good plan!"

Madame Selene let out a slow sigh almost too quiet to hear. "Good in the sense that it is admirable. I'm afraid that is the only answer I can give to you."

Violet groaned. "Of fucking course it is!"

The annoyance in Violet's voice made sense, I guessed, but I still didn't like it. "It's not her fault. Things are more complicated than that, I think. The future isn't, um, always set in stone." I glanced to Madame Selene, who nodded slowly. "Anything can change it. And that makes it hard to predict."

Madame Selene squeezed my hands. "The outcome you desire . . . is possible, but it is not guaranteed. The strings of fate have frayed into more paths than I thought possible.

Sometimes, I fear they might strangle me."

Dark patches of purple stood out against the tan skin beneath her eyes. In spite of everything, my heart broke for her a little. "I'm sorry."

Violet made an odd noise in the back of her throat, almost a scoff. "Let's keep moving."

Madame Selene released my hands. "She is right, songbird. Walk the path that you will."

For a moment, I had a childish urge to curl up there, like how I used to hide under my blankets when I was a kid. I wanted to stay here with Madame Selene, with Violet, with the two women I felt at least relatively safe with. But if I did that, I wouldn't be safe for long.

Neither would Alice.

"Alright. Let's go." I leaned against Violet, and we made our way into the next room.

I knew that the red feather would still be there in the painting room, but I still flinched a little when I saw it. The white and green feathers scattered around it didn't help. It was all too easy to imagine my own added to the mix, the only thing left of me getting trampled.

"I don't get it," Violet said.

I had a hand pressed hard to my shoulder, and she probably felt the way I jerked back. "Red birds freak me out. I was attacked—"

"What? No, not that." Violet flapped a dismissive hand at the feathers. "I mean the way you just . . . the way you were with her. With Mark. With me. Like you want to be friends with us, even though none of us did a damn thing about you being in that cage for over a fucking month."

230

"Oh." I looked down at the crumpled feathers beneath our feet. "Well, I guess I can't get mad at you guys for that. If I were in your situation, I would've probably done the same." I echoed something Mark told me. "You were just surviving. You all were. Besides, you're helping me now."

Violet looked like she wanted to argue some more, but then she sighed. "Whatever."

We had to keep going. I knew that. Yet I couldn't help but pause for just a moment to look at the paintings. I recognized the scenes they showed now. Against the canvas sat the first Alice's pink lips, the first Elizabeth's hand curled to her chest. Their hands intertwined, dark skin and light meeting against a red backdrop.

These had come from one of the girls before me, one who had dreamt of the first Elizabeth and Alice, just like me. Why had the Mistress kept them? I didn't have the answer to that.

"She told you she was bored, once," the first Elizabeth murmured. *"I think she told the truth. It's probably why she allowed people to join by choice, as well. She's bored, and she's acting on whims. Other than the cycle of girls like you, of course."*

I shuddered, not wanting to speculate about Margaret's motives any more than I absolutely had to. Imaging the way she looked at people like toys, or tools, made me feel sick. I glanced over at Violet instead. "Did you know the girl who painted these?"

"Huh? No, they were here before me." Violet's dark brows drew together. "Why?"

I didn't know how to answer that. I wanted to know if it was a hazel-eyed girl or a blue-eyed one who painted them, but why? Why did it matter to me? I couldn't give a good answer to myself, much less Violet.

"Never mind." I sighed, ignoring the weary ache in my body. I could make it through a few more rooms. I had to. "Let's keep moving."

Violet offered me an arm. I took it. We made our way across the gallery, to the entrance of the next room.

"I see—"

The poetry woman's voice stopped the second that we walked through the curtains. In unison, both turned to us, still gripping each other. The gauzy fabric around them made it hard to see their expressions, but I could feel the weight of their gaze as they stared.

Violet stared right back, a disturbed expression on her face. "Um . . . they don't usually do that."

I frowned, shaking my head. "No. But a girl like me wrote these poems. Mark told me her name was Rochelle."

"I remember her, I guess." Violet shifted her weight, stuffing her hands into her pockets. "Still, this is creepy."

They continued to stare, silent. I agreed with Violet a little, but I didn't see the poetry women as a threat. The Mistress kept them locked up when they weren't reciting poetry, unlike the rest of the husks. Besides, they spoke Rochelle's words. "I don't think they want us hurt."

Violet shot me an annoyed look. "There, you're doing it again! Assume everyone in this place wants you hurt, alright? Or that they're at least okay with seeing you die."

I met her gaze. "And you?"

Violet looked away. "I would've been just fucking fine with seeing you die before. Don't make me out to be something I'm not." The gentle way she helped me to the other side of the room didn't match her words.

The video room came next, countless screens glowing beneath their flaps. I went to one and opened it. It showed a video of a woman standing onstage and talking silently to the audience. Telling stories like Elle, maybe. Even through the fuzzy video, I could see that she struggled, taking long pauses and fidgeting.

I remembered not understanding the women's weird outfits before. I understood them now. They were feathers. The Mistress captured all of them at their worst, maybe at their first performance. I remembered how blindsided I was then. It was a final humiliation, one that would live far longer than them.

None of them had the opportunity to fight back. None of them even had a chance.

"Is now really the time for that?" Violet spoke in a dry voice.

I knew she was right. We had to keep moving, had to finish this. But I didn't regret pausing or the reminder it gave me. *I won't just be protecting Alice. I'll be avenging all of these girls, too.*

"Let's go." We made our way into the last room before the stage. *The dark room.*

The darkness was no less disorienting when I knew it was coming. In fact, it was *more* disorienting than last time, because now there were no whispers—only a silence so complete that it felt like it might swallow me. I felt suddenly very grateful for Violet's arm supporting me. It made the dark less lonely.

Muffled music began to play. Then Bridget's voice rang

out, calling to the crowd.

I tugged on Violet's sleeve, urging her to stop walking. I didn't speak. I couldn't risk the Mistress hearing me. We needed to wait until the exact right moment to strike.

Violet seemed to understand. She eased me to the floor, keeping one hand on my arm. I wasn't sure if it was for her benefit or mine. When she did things like this, I could almost see the relationship she must have had with Mark.

I closed my eyes to the disorienting dark and listened as the act continued. The audience clapped, and the music that accompanied Mark and Violet's dance started. I imagined Mark dancing out there, silent and alone, and felt a small pang. Violet stiffened next to me and stayed stiff until the music faded into silence.

Finally, a new song started—the one Margaret danced to—and when it did, I recognized it as the same tune the first Elizabeth sang in my dream.

twenty-seven.

"It's time."

Determination steeled the first Elizabeth's voice. I squeezed Violet's hand, using it to push myself to my feet. *Alright, Elizabeth. I trust you. I'll help you. End this.*

For a moment, nothing happened. But then, slowly, something shifted. As Violet stood, it felt as though she did so from miles away. Everything felt muffled except for the blood rushing through my veins. My heart pounded in my ears like a drum.

An electric current started at my stomach and spread outward. It hit my throat with a heat that energized rather than hurt. Bridget must have felt something similar when she put her lips to the flames and roared.

It felt like power—the first Elizabeth's power, everything she was, given freely and shared with me.

The ache of Margaret's magic no longer sapped my

energy. I walked forward on legs that felt firmer and surer than I ever remembered them being. Was I the one who moved them? It was difficult to say. The first Elizabeth flavored my thoughts until I stopped thinking of her as being separate from me at all. As the magic coursed through my veins, it became mine and hers at once, because we were one.

I reached out, and my fingertips met thick velvet. I pushed it aside to reveal Margaret twirling upon her stage. The entire audience stared—captivated, of course. Energy pulsed from her in waves, crashing over them. It clutched at their eyes and stole the breath from their throats with greedy hands. Margaret's magic had always been more demanding. It surged forth with all the aggression and boldness of the red she so loved to wear.

Her magic curled at my feet like tendrils that I felt rather than saw. They tried to slip beneath my skin and command me, but they couldn't. Not with the first Elizabeth's magic buzzing within me, alive and cleansing.

Together, we opened my mouth. The first Elizabeth's words fell from my lips.

"*If I were a bird . . .*"

Margaret stopped dancing. Time seemed to slow, stretching seconds into eternities. Her eyes widened in shock, but she made no further movement. For a moment, fear prickled the back of my neck like broken violin strings. Then I felt *our* magic beneath my feet, tickling like a grassy meadow on a sunny day. It pulsed, forcing Margaret's tendrils to retreat.

"*You'd be the ground . . .*"

Our magic pooled and spread. Margaret's magic clutched

in vain for a foothold, but it was pure reflex rather than a defensive maneuver. We caught her by surprise, and we had been waiting *so long* for this moment.

"*Where I could touch down, safe and sound . . .*"

Something like heartburn clawed against the inside of my ribs. The taste of copper flooded my mouth as though Margaret's magic were an alive, bleeding thing that we tore through with my teeth. But I didn't stop. I didn't *want* to stop.

The heads of the audience turned to face me.

"*I'd give up my wings . . .*"

Our magic crawled up the sides of the stage, then advanced. Soon, only a small circle within Margaret's spotlight remained under her power. Danger glinted red and angry in her eyes. Pulsing tendrils started to cut through our spell, spidering out.

No. I wouldn't let that happen. I *couldn't* let that happen. I thought of Alice—my Alice. I thought of her playing her violin, riding the bus to school, cooing at her cat. I thought about her being happy and free and how, maybe one day, I'd get to meet her for real. Or maybe I wouldn't. It didn't matter as long as she was safe.

Something in me that even the first Elizabeth didn't recognize flexed. My magic abruptly spread over Margaret, extinguishing her spell completely.

"*And I'd give up my flight . . .*"

Margaret's arms rose into the air, a shaking and ungraceful contrast to her dance. I felt her fighting me, a pressure like fingernails pressing against the inside of my temples. But she couldn't break free. There was something almost terrifying about how good it felt to hold her under my power. It was all too easy to compare it to how Margaret must have felt whenever she claimed a new victim.

My thoughts returned to Alice instead. She was my reason for doing this, and that made me and Margaret different. She had love, but she acted in anger. I had anger, but I acted in love.

"*Because, love, you're the one who sets me alight . . .*"

Margaret's hands found her own throat. They squeezed.

"*Because flying alone is not really free*

Not if I can't choose who flies beside me."

"Holy shit." Violet's voice came from beside me, but it sounded a million miles away. "Holy *fuck*, you're doing it."

I couldn't afford to answer her or even glance her way. Margaret commanded all my attention. The *song* commanded all my attention. I shifted from lyrics to a wordless *aaaah* sound, never running out of breath.

And with that wordless song, I took the last thing that belonged to Margaret—the tune of the music. I changed it to a soft, sweet melody I'd heard my Alice play in my dreams. The instrumental music changed to match me, just as the first Alice's violin—and her heart—had changed all those years ago.

Margaret fell to her knees, thrashing against the hands that remained locked and steady against her throat. But soon that thrashing slowed and became muted.

For a brief moment, I swore I heard the echo of a sweet violin playing along with my voice.

Then Bridget barreled into me with all her strength.

A loud crack seemed to come from inside of me and

outside of me at the same time, and pain ripped through my side. For one confused moment, I flew through the air like a bird—but when I hit the floor, I was more like a fish, gasping but unable to draw air into my lungs.

The music stopped. But the room didn't go silent.

Bridget screamed, the noises too angry to become full words. She came toward me like a storm, arms outstretched. But then Violet dove at her, pulling at her hair, clawing and even biting when she could.

"Finish it! Goddammit, finish it!"

I opened my mouth—to sing, to scream, to do *something*—but only a hoarse wheeze came out. My breath caught on the ragged edges of what felt like broken ribs. I could still feel the first Elizabeth with me, but instead of her power, her panic and fear amplified my own.

"*Elizabeth, get up, please. This can't be the end . . .*" Even with me clinging to her with all my strength, her voice sounded distant. Something like a sob caught in my throat. I didn't want it to be over. It *couldn't* be over. We had to keep going; we had to finish this for Alice. For Alice. The first Alice, with her thick black braid, or my Alice, with her messy brown topknot? It didn't matter. The first Elizabeth's thoughts and my thoughts muddled together, but somehow one of us managed to push my body to its feet.

The audience shifted and started to stand. They realized that this wasn't part of the act. On the verge of running, those closest started shuffling to the exit.

"*Stop!*"

Even with a hoarse voice, Margaret's power blasted across the room like an icy gust in a blizzard, and it had about the same effect. The audience, Violet, Bridget, me—we all froze.

She pulled herself to her feet, stumbling in a way that was particularly unsettling compared to her usual grace. Her auburn hair lay in snarls around her face, and the skin around her neck looked roughened and red. I felt hollowed out. *So close.* I couldn't tell if the thought came from the first Elizabeth or me. *We were so close.*

Margaret's eyes cut through the audience and landed on me. Her lips drew back in a feral snarl, pointed irises glinting red. *She doesn't even look human anymore.* Horror flooded through me like a tidal wave, and all I wanted to do was flee. But her gaze rooted me to the spot.

"So it is you, little *sister*." She spat the word like a curse.

The first Elizabeth made a hesitant sound in my head. We felt like two distinct people again, but I could still tell what she wanted without her having to put it into words. She wanted to speak, but not without my permission. *Go ahead.*

"It's time to end this, Margaret." I could have pressed my lips together to keep the first Elizabeth's words from coming out, but I didn't. "You've done enough."

Margaret made a contemptuous noise, more of an exhalation than a laugh. "And what of the other girl?" She didn't leave the stage, but her voice carried easily, even though it was hoarse from her own hands wrapped around her throat. "The one who owns this little body, the one who shares your name. Is she there, too, or have you blown her out of her own brain like dust off a windowsill?"

A bolt of anger struck my chest, the first Elizabeth's indignation mixed with my own. "I'm here, too," I said.

Margaret sneered, every bit the enigmatic Mistress in spite

of her ragged appearance. "How *altruistic*. You're lucky, you know. My sister never knew how not to take what didn't belong to her."

"Alice did not *belong* to you!" I shouted, the fury in my chest belonging half to the first Elizabeth and half to me. "That's exactly why she—"

"*Silence*." Her magic wrapped around my vocal cords like ice. "That's enough of that, little songbird. You always were a nuisance. I don't know what Alice saw in you when she could have had me—when she *did* have me." Her expression darkened for a moment. Then she composed herself, her voice coming out smooth. "Well, I suppose it was my own fault for thinking that she could possibly match up to me— for thinking that *anyone* could."

She's insane. That thought rose above all the rest as Margaret chuckled, low and deep and slow. It sounded exactly like the laugh she gave over Elle's corpse.

"I learned my lesson, little songbird," she said. "But you *never did*."

She paced the edge of the stage. The heads of the spellbound audience didn't move an inch. I couldn't even look to Violet and Bridget to see what was happening to them. I couldn't do anything but stare at the Mistress as the first Elizabeth frantically tried to figure out how to fix this, how to end it.

"Well, little sister," Margaret continued. "I have no idea how you managed to convince this insignificant thing to go along with your schemes. How you managed to convince her that she was worthwhile when I have spent her entire life convincing her of the exact opposite."

241

I gasped, a flair of pain shooting up my side. The noise was hardly audible, but of course the Mistress heard it anyway.

"Ah, yes." She grinned, teeth glinting white under the stage lights. "Surely, you've thought about it. The way no one ever noticed you. I marked you from a very young age, little songbird—with my sister's soul and with your pathetic insignificance. You've been preparing to die in that cage for a long, long time. The fact that my sister managed to convince you otherwise . . . I don't know if that makes you brave or just stupid. Perhaps a mixture of both."

I opened my mouth, then closed it. Even the first Elizabeth had gone silent.

Margaret stopped pacing, fixing me with her gaze. "Do you want to know where it started, little songbird? When you were marked? I can show you easily." She raised her arms above her head, slow and graceful. "You'll remember me, I think. I tend to leave an impression."

Silence stretched between us like the crumbling edge of a cliff. Then, in a single graceful movement, she leaped into the air. It looked like she was beginning to dance.

Instead, red feathers sprouted along her raised arms. In front of my eyes, she morphed, her arms into wings, her bare feet into talons, her lips elongating into a beak.

My voice finally unlocked. I screamed as the bird from my nightmares, somehow even larger than I remembered, swooped and descended on me in a flurry of feathers. The bird screamed with me. Margaret's voice, distorted but unmistakable, laughed at me through the bird's beak as it dove.

She knocked me to the ground, wings powerful and impossible to escape, talons and beak searching and finding their target. They tore into my face, my neck, my shoulders. All thoughts of winning, of Mark and Violet, of the girls who came before me, and even of Alice flew from my mind.

There was nothing but pain.

twenty-eight.

Noises, distorted and distant, swam out at me from the dark. Bridget's mad laughter. Too many screams to count. The harsh caw of the Mistress, the red bird.

"*We could leave her . . . let her die here.*"

"*No. She deserves far worse . . .*"

I didn't want to hear what they had planned for me next. I sank in on myself, and the outside noises faded completely.

It was over. I had failed. And now I'd be forced to die slowly, covered in feathers. I knew what I would see right before I went. I knew *who* I would see.

Alice . . . I'm sorry. I couldn't protect you.

I heard harsh, jagged sobs. My chest heaved, and I realized that they were coming from me. *Were* they coming from me?

Something was off. My skin felt smooth and unbroken instead of torn and lumped with feathers, but it also felt separate from me. I flexed the fingers and they moved, but the action had the odd, distant quality of a dream. I curled in on myself. Whatever this was, I didn't want to see it.

"Elizabeth, it's alright. Well, it's not really, but it is *safe* here. I can promise you that."

The first Elizabeth's voice murmured at my ear. It sounded strange to hear her voice coming from outside of me. But was it *really* outside of me? It echoed, a whisper along the inside of my skull. The sensation was just strange enough to tug at my curiosity.

I opened my eyes to an old-fashioned living room bathed in moonlight.

A violin sat in the corner. An old chair—the same one that sat across from my cage—sat in another. I recognized this room, although I'd only ever seen it as hazy and indistinct. The first Elizabeth, the first Alice, and Margaret had practiced magic together here in my dream—the dream that showed me how to use the first Elizabeth's power.

"Yes. And that was my mistake."

I blinked, and the first Elizabeth appeared, kneeling right in front of me. Her curls hung limp and lifeless around her face. Her dark skin lacked its usual rich, warm undertones, seeming ashy and gray instead. But it *was* her.

She held out a hand to help me up. I had gotten so used to being in her body, to seeing glances of it in mirrors and windows while I dreamed. Watching her move separately from me was as strange as seeing my reflection suddenly take on a life of its own.

She gave me a small smile. She looked fond and understanding but not at all happy. "This *is* strange, Elizabeth. For me as well as for you. But I'm still very sorry that you have to go through it."

I curled away from her, ignoring her offered hand. "Could you *stop* reading my mind?"

The first Elizabeth's smile faded. "I can't, Elizabeth. We're *in* your mind. This is the part of your mind where I reside." She gestured all around us. "I spent a long time trying to make it look like this so I could send you the dream about my magic. It was so hard to give us a fighting chance."

I shook my head. "We didn't have a chance, though. We failed. It's over."

The first Elizabeth knelt by me again, almost close enough for her knees to brush against me. But it didn't feel that way. Her body didn't radiate warmth the way bodies were supposed to. If I closed my eyes, I never would have known she was there. It felt like sitting next to a projection—a ghost.

"I have much I'd like to tell you." The first Elizabeth sighed, brushing a hand against her curls. "I can speak freely here. Elizabeth, please . . . You owe me nothing, I know. But will you at least hear me out?"

Part of me wanted to say no. Whatever she wanted to say, whatever she wanted to convince me of, I didn't want to hear it. But denying her felt cruel. She watched so many girls die. She never even had the chance to say anything to them.

I stood, wobbling a little on feet that didn't feel real. "Alright." I sighed, exhaustion weighing down my chest. "I'll listen."

The first Elizabeth's face relaxed. I remembered how often she thought about Alice wearing her heart on her sleeve, how she couldn't do that. *She's not hiding anything right now.*

"No, Elizabeth." The first Elizabeth led me to a couch

made of plush, velvety fabric. "I don't want to hide anything from you. You've had to fight for every scrap of information you got. I want to give you everything—as much of the truth as I am able."

Now that I was sitting next to her, it felt a little awkward to have her answering my thoughts. I scrubbed my hands over my eyes, half-surprised at how easy it was to do without palms full of feathers. Had I already forgotten? "Just . . . tell me what you need to tell me."

The first Elizabeth probably caught all my thoughts, but she only responded to my words. "Elizabeth, I . . . I was wrong. I spent centuries waiting, planning, hoping for someone like you to come around. But even with all that time to think, I made a critical error. I thought that, in order to defeat Margaret, you'd have to use my power. My song. My intentions and my hopes. But I should have known better. Between the two of us, Margaret was always the stronger witch. She should have been able to overpower you instantly."

I felt a surge of almost childish annoyance. "Is this supposed to make me feel better?"

The first Elizabeth surprised me by smiling. "Yes, Elizabeth, it is! Because she *didn't* overpower you instantly. In fact, if it wasn't for Bridget, you might have won. You *would* have won. And do you know why?"

I shook my head.

"When we began," she continued, "we were one. You were the channel that I used to direct my thoughts. My feelings. My love. But that alone wasn't enough. We almost didn't reach Margaret at all. And you . . . You thought of

247

your Alice. *Your* love. And it was your power that allowed us to get as far as we did. Not mine."

I stayed silent for a long moment. A thousand thoughts tried to fight their way to my tongue but died at the back of my throat instead. When I finally found my voice, it wavered. "I don't understand. This whole time I thought the only reason I could fight was because I shared your name and names have power. So I shared your power, and that's it."

"I thought so, too." The first Elizabeth frowned thoughtfully. "It made sense. Magic doesn't even *exist* in your world. That's why Margaret chose it, I imagine, so she could lord over everyone like a god. But somehow, something about you . . . You were able to tap into it. I don't know how. But you did."

It felt like something out of one of my favorite television shows—and about as believable. "So, what? I'm the chosen one?" *I hope sarcasm existed back where she came from.*

The first Elizabeth shrugged, politely ignoring my thoughts. "In a sense. Chosen by Margaret, chosen by me. But you weren't destined to beat her. You didn't have to be successful, but you were anyways."

"Except I *wasn't*." I shook my head, disgust coating the back of my throat like bile. "Who cares whose power got us as far as we did? It didn't matter. Margaret still won."

For a long moment, the first Elizabeth stayed silent. She looked down, clutching her hands in her lap. I felt a sort of ridiculous urge to mimic her.

Finally, she spoke, her voice almost too quiet to hear. "You have a choice to make, Elizabeth."

I opened my mouth, then closed it. What could she possibly say? What choice did I possibly have left to make?

"I think that, if we continue, we have a chance to win." The first Elizabeth caught my gaze, her pointed irises solemn. "No, *you* have a chance to win, with me supporting *your* power rather than the other way around. It won't be like before. Now that we've shared magic so intimately, not even Margaret can deafen your ears to me."

Silence stretched between us. I kept waiting for the rest of the choice, but the first Elizabeth didn't seem to want to give it. I prompted her. "Or?"

The first Elizabeth sighed. "I'm not offering you a definite victory, Elizabeth. Or an easy one. Going back will be hard—and frightening. You'll have to face Margaret again, and she will be *very* angry. So, if you would like, this could be the end of your fight. You could succumb to your injuries, here and now. I would not blame you for choosing that. Truly, I wouldn't, because . . ."

She paused, taking a deep breath like she needed to steel herself for what she had to say next. The silence between us seemed to have weight.

"If it ends for you here," she finally continued, slowly, "you can move on to whatever comes next. You will not be granted that choice if you go back and fail. It is not just my soul that's trapped here. Or my Alice's soul. Margaret keeps the souls of all the girls before you, because they were bound to us. She keeps them trapped in those lanterns. They aren't conscious like you and I are, but they are aware of the passing of time. They know they are imprisoned. I can unbind you from me, while we are both here, and save you from that

249

fate. I will not be able to do so again."

It took me several moments to digest that. It took several more for me to find my voice. The first Elizabeth didn't say anything else. She just waited for me to speak.

"Leaving now seems like the easier choice," I finally admitted. "But it also doesn't feel like a choice at all."

The first Elizabeth leaned forward slightly. "In what way?"

"Well, there's Alice to think about." I sighed. "My Alice."

"Oh." She nodded, understanding creasing her brow. "Yes. There's that. But there's *always* a choice, Elizabeth."

I leaned back, pressing my hands to my face. My palms met skin instead of the feathers they'd feel if I went back. "You're wrong. It's *not* a choice. We're soulmates or whatever." I shook my head. "I don't have any choice in loving her."

"Is that really what you think?" The first Elizabeth's tone, soft and almost hurt, caught me off-guard.

I lowered my hands to look at her. "What am I supposed to think? Why else would you have sent me those dreams of her?"

The first Elizabeth shook her head. "I wanted you to understand what was happening to you. I tried sending them to all the girls who came before you, and not all of them would have loved who they saw. After all, every girl was different. Not all of them desired women as you do, and in some the age difference would have been too vast. And that isn't even taking into account compatibility in personality, ideals . . ."

"But . . . our souls?"

"Elizabeth." The first Elizabeth reached out, taking both

250

of my hands in hers gently. "You have a piece of my soul, it is true. She has a piece of Alice's. And you share our names. But your hearts are your own. If you do love her—and you very well may, although I know you've been unsure—you aren't forced. No one is ever forced to love anyone. Not even Alice and I. Our love was a conscious choice—one that we weren't necessarily proud of, given the circumstances. But we never regretted it."

I pressed a palm to my shoulder. "Even now?"

"Of course. Because it was of our own making." The first Elizabeth gave a soft smile. "'I don't want to be a bird if I cannot choose who flies beside me.' That is what we told each other. And that is what we truly believed. Love is a choice. If you love Alice, that is a choice, too. And you don't *have* to choose her. You can choose to secure your freedom and go on."

"You don't want that," I said. "You want me to stay and fight."

"What I want doesn't matter." The first Elizabeth looked down at our clasped hands. "You never asked for any of this, Elizabeth. I will not ask you to risk an eternity's freedom. If you do it, you must make the choice for yourself."

I thought for a moment. "Why did you choose to love Alice, then?"

"Are you stalling?" Despite everything, the first Elizabeth's voice turned almost teasing.

And despite everything, I smiled back. "It's an honest question. You said you never regretted it. If you could have chosen not to love her, to have never crossed Margaret, why didn't you?"

"I would have." The first Elizabeth's eyes were deadly serious. "If Alice could have been happy that way. But then she chose me, too. After that, nothing else mattered to me."

I didn't say anything else. The first Elizabeth didn't break the silence. She simply sat beside me, holding my hands and letting me think.

I could go, I decided. Alice didn't deserve her fate, but neither did I. And I couldn't guarantee that going back and fighting would save her at all. In fact, it felt pretty unlikely. There was no supernatural force compelling me, telling me that I *had* to take the chance to save her.

And still, I wanted to go back. I wanted to help Mark and Madame Selene and even the poetry women if I could. I wanted to protect Violet, if she hadn't managed to escape on her own. I even wanted to help the girls in the lanterns.

And I wanted to protect Alice. Was it because I loved her? I thought so.

But in the end, it didn't really matter what motivated my choice. What mattered was that the choice was mine to make.

"I'll go back," I said. "I'll fight. I'll try."

The room around us started to glow, warm and green, reminding me of the feeling of the first Elizabeth's magic. She smiled and placed her hands on my cheeks. The sensation lingered, even when the glow became too bright for me to see her.

"I'm proud of you, Elizabeth," she said. "No matter what happens, I'm proud to share your name."

The glow faded slowly into darkness, and the first Elizabeth was gone. I could still feel the warmth of her hands on my cheeks. After a moment, I realized they weren't her hands at all. They were my own. I was no longer sitting but lying down with my eyes closed.

I opened them. I was back in the birdcage.

twenty-nine.

A thousand thoughts swirled through my mind as I sat up. I looked around, hoping for a sign of Violet and fearing a sign of the Mistress or Bridget. But I couldn't see anyone—just the poetry women wrapped in their gauzy cocoons.

The storage room seemed colder than before. I looked down to see my borrowed clothing gone, save for a few scraps of fabric stuck between the feathers that, admittedly, covered everything that needed to be covered. Still, nausea rolled in waves through my stomach as I plucked out one of the scraps to examine it. The memory of the Mistress's talons haunted me, but I couldn't see any wounds. And even when I shook out my limbs, I didn't feel any pain.

"*That's me.*" The first Elizabeth's voice echoed clear in my mind. "*Margaret made your wounds invisible so you could perform without eliciting sympathy. But they would hurt without my help. You should still act hurt when she comes.*"

It took a conscious effort not to speak out loud to her now. *You're really with me for good?*

"Yes," she said. "*It's hard to explain, but when we were together, it bonded us in a way that's more powerful than even Margaret's magic. It's useless when it comes to fighting, but this much I can give you.*"

Comfort bloomed in my chest, like warm tea with honey. I'd never been more scared in my life. I didn't know what would happen to me or Alice, to Mark or Violet or Madame Selene, but at least I wouldn't have to face whatever came next alone.

As if summoned by my thoughts, the Mistress strode in.

Her eyes widened when she saw me, red-painted lips curving up. "So, you lived." She shook her head, smile spreading like a rash. "Tell me, little songbird, does that make you lucky or unlucky?"

Remembering what the first Elizabeth said about acting hurt, I curled in on myself. "Leave me alone." I let my voice come out trembling and frightened. I didn't want her to think of me as a threat, yes, but I was also genuinely frightened. The fact that I had chosen to come back and face her didn't make the actual act of doing it any less terrifying.

Margaret barked a laugh, like a crack of thunder in a graveyard. "Where's that bravado from before?" She tapped her fingernails against the cage bars. "Come now, little sister! Give your puppet some courage! Help her make another ill-fated attempt on my life, why don't you?"

My eyes stung, the cheerful lilt of her voice shivering down my spine. I shot a quick thought at the first Elizabeth. *Should she know that you're there?*

255

"*The decision is yours, but I'd suggest not,*" she replied. "*The element of surprise can't hurt our case.*"

I agreed. "Your sister's gone." I didn't look up at Margaret to see her expression. I didn't want to chance her catching the lie in my eyes. "You ripped her out of me, didn't you? That's why it hurts."

Margaret made a noise of contempt in the back of her throat. "I'm not surprised, I suppose. She never *did* know how to face the consequences of her actions."

"*You miserable, evil–*" The first Elizabeth's anger was so potent I had to grit my teeth to keep the words from spilling out of my lips. I did my best to disguise it as a wince. The first Elizabeth's tone turned contrite, barely masking the rage beneath. "*I'm sorry, Elizabeth.*"

Margaret didn't seem to notice anything amiss. She simply continued smiling her cold Mistress smile. "Well, it doesn't matter. You surviving makes one of my decisions easier, at least. Wait here, little songbird." Laughing, she strode from the room.

Fear and anger and disgust shuddered through me in waves. *What do you think she's doing?*

"*Nothing good, surely,*" the first Elizabeth replied. "*Have courage.*"

I stood, meaning to pace away the nervous energy that tugged at me like marionette strings. But I didn't have time. Just as I found my feet, the Mistress strode back in, wearing a triumphant grin. And she didn't come alone.

"Violet!"

Watching Bridget drag Violet in sent a cold shock through me. Locked in place by magic, she looked so much like Mark had, other than her expression. Instead of fear or resignation, Violet's face was full of rage. If she didn't have magic binding her, I thought she'd be throwing punches.

"Don't hurt her!"

Bridget laughed. *"Don't hurt her,"* she mocked in a nasally voice. She turned to Margaret, like an eager child begging for dessert before dinner. "Mistress, can *I* do it? *Please?*"

Margaret put a hand on top of Bridget's head, her smile fond but chilling. "Patience, my dear. A punishment is not truly effective unless one takes the time to explain it."

Bridget grinned, leaning back with disturbing casualness. "Of course! Take your time."

The Mistress turned to me, smiling. "You see, I was quite at a loss for what to do with this one." She gestured at Violet behind her. "I knew I'd have to punish her, of course, but would turning her into one of my crew be sufficient? If you had died, perhaps it would have been. But you're still here. And since turning that little boyfriend of hers didn't seem to get through to you, I believe that more *drastic* measures need to be taken."

Bridget made a gesture, and an overlong, lethal knife appeared out of thin air.

"No." My heart sank like a stone in water. I still had a chance to save Mark, if what Madame Selene told Violet was true. But I didn't think that the most powerful magic in the world could reverse death.

The Mistress laughed. "Silly little songbird. Even if you used the voice you managed to get ahold of, your words would have no power here."

She spun. Bridget seemed to almost vibrate with

257

excitement.

Margaret leaned forward until she was at eye-level with Violet, her smile cold and unforgiving. "Alright then. *Any final words?*"

Violet's eyes rolled as far as they could to the side, just barely catching mine. She opened her mouth, then closed it and looked down instead. Her throat worked, her features tightening. For a moment, I thought she was going to burst into tears.

Instead, she spat in the Mistress's face. "Fuck. You."

The Mistress smiled, wiping the spit off her cheek with a finger and flicking it away. "Oh, but I *will* miss you. Your attitude was entertaining, at the very least." She stood, waving a hand airily. "Alright, Bridget. Finish it however you like."

Bridget spun her knife with the flashy sort of bravado that would have been perfectly at home onstage. But she didn't toss it at a target this time. Instead, she gripped the hilt and drove it forward.

If this were a television show or a movie, time would have slowed down. The camera would have lingered on the arc of the knife, would have taken the time to catch every expression in the room. That didn't happen. If anything, time seemed to speed up. I didn't have time to try the magic voice or even to scream. In the time it took me to draw a breath, Bridget had lodged her knife in Violet's heart.

I stared, mouth hanging open but unable to make a sound. Violet didn't scream or cry. I wondered if she did it to be brave or if she felt as shocked and trapped as I did.

Bridget pulled the knife out and stood, watching with a

wide grin as Violet collapsed face-down on the ground. And then it was over, and I kept staring, feeling like I did when I watched Elle die, feeling like I had missed something, that I should have done more.

From a million miles away, I heard Bridget laugh. "Ha! That's better than any target practice!" I tore my eyes away from Violet to face her. She winked at me. "I hardly ever get to play with my knives for real. I mean, sometimes I pick off people on the road, but not a lot. Who has the time to find someone who won't be missed? Not everyone's as easy to erase as you. Gosh, poor Mistress had enough trouble with all those witnesses!"

Something cold settled at the base of my spine. I felt the words pass from my lips before I really decided to say them. "What are you talking about?"

Bridget rolled her eyes. "The *witnesses!* From that show you tried to ruin. We had to get rid of *all* of them." She sighed. "Fire's not as fun as knives, y'know, but it's still pretty fun."

A thousand words clogged my throat, trembling down my spine. Fear and sadness and anger wracked my body, but none made it through the stunned numbness in my skull yet. Every time I looked to Violet, it felt a little harder to breathe.

When I finally did speak, my voice cracked. "You're evil."

Something more genuine and infinitely more chilling than I'd ever seen in Bridget flickered behind her eyes. "Everyone's evil, idiot. I just went ahead and embraced it." She spun to face Margaret, her voice turning cheerful again. "Are we done here?"

The Mistress smiled. Even as she addressed Bridget, she kept her gaze on me, as though she was savoring my expression. "We are. Clean up your mess, my dear, and we can go."

Bridget gave a little salute. She hefted Violet's body over her shoulder as though it were just another prop, and then she skipped out, humming to herself.

The Mistress stayed long enough to give me a cool, contemptuous look. "Little sister, if you can still hear me, remember this. Remember this the next time you think you can win." She swept from the room. The silence in her wake seemed filled with voices, echoes of the dead.

That weighted silence finally broke through. I pressed my hands to my face and screamed.

"*I'm sorry, Elizabeth.*" The first Elizabeth's voice echoed through my head. "*Truly.*"

My eyes burned, but tears wouldn't come. The thought of all those innocent people who died hurt, of course, but Violet's death weighed on me the heaviest. This felt a thousand times worse than Mark, and not just because Violet had been killed right in front of my eyes. The Mistress's words haunted me. Violet might have lived if I hadn't chosen to come back. The knowledge clung to me like the aura of death clung to Elle.

"*Being turned into one of Margaret's puppets is hardly a life,*" the first Elizabeth said. "*There's nothing you could have done to help her. Now, the best course of action is to make sure she didn't die in vain.*"

She was right. If I couldn't do anything for Violet, I could at least do my best to save Mark for her. I could make sure the Mistress never hurt anyone again. I needed to be strong.

But I didn't *feel* strong. I felt sick and shuddery, and every time I so much as blinked, I saw Violet crumple, saw her blood freckling Bridget's face. I saw the Mistress grinning and sprouting red feathers as she dove for me.

"*It is okay to be frightened.*" The first Elizabeth's voice came through, gentle and kind. "*You can be frightened and still be strong.*"

I sighed, curling in on myself. *Maybe I should be used to feeling this way. The Mistress has been haunting my dreams since I was a kid.* The thought ran through me like a cold shock. *Could you turn into a bird, too? Is that why she called you little songbird?*

The first Elizabeth began to reply before I had even fully finished my thought. "*No, no. That nickname came from my looks and voice. But I couldn't become an animal. And neither could Margaret. I'd only ever heard of witches turning into animals in stories. They were always the most evil ones, too. Witches who had completely forsaken any shred of their humanity. That only happened to Margaret after my death.*"

I looked down at my feather-covered body. The first Elizabeth sensed my question before I asked it.

"*Forcing you to grow feathers humiliates you in a few ways. It uses my nickname against you. And I referred to Alice as a dove, which is where the white feathers come from. But in addition to that, making the girls like her, stripping them of their humanity . . . It's the ultimate way to break them.*"

I remembered the question the first Elizabeth had asked me before I even knew it was her. "*Has she broken you?*" And in spite of everything, somehow, the answer to that question was still *no*.

But that didn't mean I felt triumphant.

"*Rest,*" the first Elizabeth said. "*I'll do my best to help you.*"

My blankets and pillow were gone, and I didn't really think I would get any sleep, considering what just happened. But I still lay down, pillowing my head in my arms.

The first Elizabeth began to sing, something sweet and gentle like a lullaby. The warmth of her magic drifted through my veins, soothing my worried and racing thoughts.

I knew I wouldn't be able to rest for long. I'd have to face what came next. But for the time being, I took refuge in the only place I could—my dreams.

thirty.

"Do you trust me?"

I trusted Alice with every ounce of life inside of me, and she knew it. But although she didn't have to, I understood why she asked. She required my affirmation, freely given again and again, for something this intimate.

I slipped my hands into hers without a single reservation. "Of course."

She smiled, gentle and almost shy. "This may feel a bit odd, since it is your first time. I'll admit I'm a little nervous. I've . . . only ever been on the receiving end of this in the past."

Something danced along the edge of her words—an unspoken reminder that she never did this with my sister. It didn't surprise me. Margaret would never let herself become this vulnerable in front of anyone, not even a lover.

I could only hope that Alice didn't think I wanted to do this for that reason. I was merely curious, and . . . "This is how people in your region show that they love each other." I squeezed her hands.

"And I love you, Alice. Unconditionally. But if you do not wish to, for whatever reason, we do not have to go through with this."

"I do wish to." She gripped my hands a bit tighter. "But the same goes for you. We can stop at any point, if you so decide. You need only tell me."

I nodded solemnly. Although I highly doubted I would ask her to stop, I did not want her to think that I took this lightly. I did not ask her to share this part of herself with me on a whim. "And the same goes for you." It felt important to remind her. Too often, I had to rely on her body language to tell me she was uncomfortable. It worried me.

But I didn't think that would be an issue this time. Her culture stressed the importance of being completely sure and honest when it came to this.

Her eyelids fluttered shut. My pulse throbbed, shuddering through my entire body like an earthquake. Surely, Alice could hear my heartbeat. Would she lose her nerve? Had she lost her nerve? I would not blame her for changing her mind.

But then I felt it.

It started at the base of my neck. I couldn't compare the sensation to anything I had experienced before. I felt a little like a stubborn but fragile door, something that required a persistent but gentle touch to open. I closed my eyes to better focus on it. Something warm and soft ghosted across my spine and fluttered in my temples.

Alice did not say a single word. She certainly didn't speak in the voice my sister and I used, the one that demanded absolute obedience. It was my choice whether I allowed this magic to affect me.

"Yes." I spoke out loud so there could be no doubt between us. "Yes."

Alice—every part of her—flooded me at once.

Her hands remained in mine, but tactile sensation didn't come close to how intimate it felt to be together with her like this. Her love for me beat warm in my chest, filling me up. And I knew she could feel mine as well. Everything unspoken between us, every worry and hope and dream and fear I had—I felt her echo it. Our souls entwined, perfectly in sync.

Her lips were on mine. Her fingers tangled in my hair. How long had we been that way? I couldn't say. We no longer needed to part for air. We breathed in from each other's lungs, and we melted into each other.

I woke up feeling weightless and warm—and also like I intruded on something very private. But somehow, I knew the Mistress hadn't been the one to send me that dream.

Elizabeth, why did you show me that? I sat up. Already, my worries and fears were setting in. It made me want to cling to the gentle feeling the dream had left me with.

The first Elizabeth paused for a moment before answering. "*It was . . . a gift, I suppose. A thanks for coming back when you didn't have to. And a way to show you what magic could be like when not used under duress.*"

I wrapped my arms around myself. My feathers pressed at odd angles against my palms. *The way you two melted into each other . . . sort of reminds me of what we did when we fought Margaret. The way we stopped being two people and started being one.*

"*I based what we did off of what I learned from Alice,*" the first Elizabeth said. "*But it was different.*"

Of course it was different. The first Elizabeth and I came together to fight, to defeat Margaret. She and Alice had done it in a safe setting. They *loved* each other. The first Elizabeth and I didn't have that. I felt glad to have her with me, of course. The fact that I could hear her at any time, the fact that she supported me, all of that was wonderful in a way I couldn't even begin to put into words. But . . .

"*It's different.*" The first Elizabeth's voice sounded almost amused. "*Trust me, I understand.*"

I smiled a little. The expression felt thin but not forced. *I'm glad you showed it to me, though. Really. And I do care about you. I'd be happy to consider you a friend.*

The warmth in the first Elizabeth's voice wrapped around me like a thick, homemade quilt. "*I'm honored to be your friend. And so would anyone else, after all this is over.*"

I tried to think about it—of a life after the cage, after the feathers. I wanted to believe it would happen, but I had my doubts. Even if I beat Margaret, I couldn't be sure that the feathers would disappear. Violet seemed to think so, but who knew for sure?

"*Magic is very complicated.*" The first Elizabeth spoke gently. "*Some of it lives after a witch dies and some of it doesn't. This sort of magic . . . isn't the sort of magic I'm familiar with. I can't give you a definite answer. I'm sorry.*"

I sighed, pushing myself to my feet. *It's alright. I mean . . . It's not, really, but it is what it is.* I thought of my Alice smiling and playing her violin. *I didn't just come back for me.*

"*I know.*" The first Elizabeth paused, then added gently, "*For what it's worth, I sincerely hope it ends up in your favor.*"

I couldn't think of a response to that, so I paced around the cage instead. I needed to do *something*. A hopeless sort of energy sat heavy on my shoulders, smelling of the same scent that hung around Elle. The same aura of death had to be hanging around me by now.

But it *wasn't* just me. It smelled stronger at the edges of the cage.

I paused. The smell—if it was a smell—seemed to be coming from over my head. I looked up to see the paper lanterns glowing there softly. The first Alice and Elizabeth hung on either side of the door, with Elizabeth starting the string. More names followed—an Anne, a Rebecca, an Abigail. They curled all around the room and looped back until the string ended right next to the first Elizabeth's. The final lantern had *Elle* written on it, the red ink looking just a shade more vibrant.

It goes in order, I noted to the first Elizabeth, mostly to say *something.*

"*It does,*" she replied. "*You're thinking something, aren't you?*"

I don't know. I closed my eyes, a headache forming at my temples. *They're important to me. They were just girls, like me. They didn't deserve this.* I reached up until my fingertips brushed the outside of Elle's lantern. Something jolted, and I jerked away more quickly than when I'd brushed against a frayed lamp wire as a kid. It didn't hurt, but the reaction to move away was instinctual.

What was that? I reached up and touched it again.

It *did* feel a little like a live wire, if live wires just felt unsettling instead of painful. It thrummed against my fingertips with something that my brain wanted to categorize but couldn't. I kept throwing adjectives at it, like *warm* and *vibrating*, but none of them quite worked.

I remembered what the first Elizabeth told me about how

Margaret trapped the other girls in here. *It's her soul.* The thought came slow, almost dreamlike. *I'm feeling whatever makes up a soul, I guess. Which . . . has got to be really intimate.* I jerked my hand away, flushing.

"*She can't feel it,*" the first Elizabeth assured me.

That made me feel a little better, but not great. I remembered the first Elizabeth telling me about life in the lanterns. *They are aware of the passing of time. They know they are imprisoned.* Thinking about living in one of those felt like swallowing ice. I looked at the lanterns closest to the first Elizabeth and Alice. They'd been in there for over a century.

I could be the next to join them. I had a chance to avoid that, and I didn't take it.

"*Do you regret it?*" Worry colored the first Elizabeth's tone. "*I did my best not to sway your decision.*"

No, I thought at her, stepping away from the bars. *If you asked me to make it again, I'd choose the same thing. It's just . . . It's not fair. For them, for me, for you. For anyone.*

"*I know.*" The first Elizabeth sighed. I sighed with her and sat down, my tired legs aching from pacing even for that short amount of time. My feathers, warm and noxious and reminding me of what little time I had, folded at odd angles against my skin.

Why was I wasting time thinking about the girls in the lanterns? I had to figure out a way to keep myself from becoming one of them.

"*It's not a waste of time,*" the first Elizabeth said firmly. "*You're right—they were important. You're all important. And it's not fair that you spent your entire lives telling yourselves otherwise.*"

I swallowed hard against the lump in the back of my

throat. Even with a literal voice in my head telling me I was important, it felt hard to deny the metaphorical one that had told me otherwise for so many years.

Well, at least now I have someone to blame. I shifted, trying to find a more comfortable angle to sit. *How many people get to blame their social ineptitude on a literal curse?*

Even by my standards, it was a pretty weak joke. The first Elizabeth laughed a little anyway.

The crew members swept in, preparing for the show.

Madame Selene wouldn't talk to me when they left me in her area. Or she *couldn't* talk to me. The bags under her eyes seemed to have tripled overnight. Beneath her dark tan skin hid a note of something sickly and pale. I thought I saw sweat beading right where her forehead met her straight black hair.

I clutched at the bars of my cage. "Do I still have a chance? Can you tell me that much?"

She inclined her head toward me just slightly. I thought that, maybe, she nodded. That was all she managed to give me.

The cramped backstage area felt too large when the crew members finally rolled me in. I tried not to notice the conspicuous empty space where Violet should have been. I also tried not to notice how utterly unfazed Mark was by her absence. I turned to face Margaret instead.

She smirked when she caught me looking. Fear and anger warred in my chest. I hung my head so she wouldn't see any sense of the latter on my face.

Bridget laughed. "Look at that! You've trained the little songbird at last!"

Margaret didn't laugh. She didn't need to. There was

enough contempt in her voice to make my stomach crawl. "Of course. My fool of a sister should have warned her—I always win."

I curled up and pressed my face to my knees, hoping she wouldn't realize just how hard I was trying to prove her wrong.

thirty-one.

I stared at the last of my hair, which littered the cage floor.

It should have stopped horrifying me at some point, the way the feathers took over every part of my body. But even under the feathers, I didn't think I really looked like myself anymore. The hairstyle I chose, the bangs I never let grow into my eyes—all of that was gone. A shudder worked its way up my body to clamp at my throat.

Even ignoring the hair, I doubted that I really looked like a person anymore. I looked like a creature, something that shambled and shuddered to life. A mass of feathers that could've been mistaken as lifeless, if not for my eyes.

I was exactly like Elle.

We had a matter of days left. A week at the very most. I kept turning the pieces over in my mind, trying to fit them together, trying to figure out how to beat the Mistress at her own game. I thought of the voice she used. I thought of the way the first Elizabeth and I had joined together, the way we sang. I thought of the way she had melted together with the first Alice. I thought of the Mistress's red feathers, so strong and full of life. I thought of the girls in the lanterns.

I would have welcomed even one of Madame Selene's cryptic clues to put everything together.

The rustle of fabric at the entrance interrupted my thoughts. I tensed just in time to see Margaret striding in. No one followed her.

Immediately, my heart felt too large for my chest, straining against my ribcage. The Mistress never brought anything good, but coming alone always meant something exceptionally terrible.

"Good afternoon, little songbird!" Her cheery, light tone seemed to echo through the room. My stomach sank.

I curled away from the cage bars, even though she didn't have to reach through them to hurt me. "What do you want?"

She smiled at me, a glint of white behind red-painted lips. "I know that my sister's left you to fend for yourself, but she is still there. Her soul is bound to yours. So she's listening, in some way."

What is she doing? I directed the thought to the first Elizabeth.

"*I have no idea,*" she responded. "*This speech has never happened before.*"

Margaret smiled, exuding that Mistress-esque pride so thick I could almost see it. Her confidence had a magic all of its own. "So, little sister. I've been watching you fall for centuries. I tore you to shreds just so I could experience the pleasure of killing you a thousand times over. But all of that pales in comparison to the joy I will derive from this."

"Oh . . . Oh, no." The first Elizabeth's voice trembled with panic. "*Elizabeth, you have to—*"

"*Sleep,*" the Mistress interjected, her voice echoing with magic. And then, just like on that first night, I was falling. The gleaming metal floor of the cage came rushing up to meet me. It faded to black just before I hit.

I floated above a city street.

Skyscrapers reached to the sky—no match for the mountains in the distance, but still impressive. Even in this state, I could feel the chill in the air as small snowflakes floated down, glittering in the hard sun. Still, plenty of people walked down the streets instead of driving.

It didn't take me long to find Alice. Her long brown hair was down for once, maybe because the knit hat she wore wouldn't fit her topknot. She buried her flushed cheeks in a soft-looking pink scarf as she walked, blue eyes wandering idly. But after a few seconds, she stopped. Those bright blue eyes widened like she had seen a ghost.

Or, maybe, like she had realized she was *a ghost.*

Terror gripped at my heart. If I had a mouth in this dream, I would have screamed. No. Oh, no . . .

I followed her line of sight to see the flier tacked up on a cement wall. It wasn't the same one I had seen. Instead of a blue eye, a hazel eye dominated the page, framed by short dark lashes instead of thin blonde ones.

It was my eye.

I turned back to Alice. Her face looked like a phantom hand had gripped at her lungs and squeezed the air out of them. She stumbled toward the flier, eyes wide and riveted. I wondered if I had looked like that. Probably I did. Margaret marked Alice just like she marked me, after all. She'd been isolated and ignored for most of her life, too. She probably felt just as unimportant as I did.

I wished, more than anything, that I could tell her how important she was to me.

Bridget appeared from around the corner, striding toward Alice with a wide smirk. Seeing her made my skin crawl. Before, I would have definitely seen that smirk as charming or attractive. I didn't see it that way anymore. Watching her lean forward to murmur at Alice's ear made nausea roll in my stomach.

"Curious?"

Alice spun around, gasping. But the gasp quickly melted into a nervous little giggle. She tucked a lock of hair behind her ear. "Sorry! You startled me!"

"Well then, I'm sorry." Bridget pressed a hand to her chest, all friendly mock-sympathy. Her tone suggested that the two would be laughing about it together later. "I just noticed you staring at our flier."

"The eye looked familiar to me, maybe." Alice's cheeks were already flushed from the cold, but I thought I saw them darken a shade or two. "That sounds sort of silly, doesn't it?"

Bridget grinned. "Maybe. But I like silly." She leaned against the wall, flexing, and Alice gave her nervous giggle again. I felt sick, and not from jealousy. Bridget had flirted just as blatantly with me. How had I not realized how weird it was for some random twenty-something to flirt with a teenager? I felt gross and used and ridiculously naive.

Alice opened her mouth to say something—to ask what the show was about, of course. I didn't want to hear Bridget purr about how *the Mistress found things to suit all tastes. I had seen enough.*

I forced myself awake, clawing back to consciousness through sheer force of will. The Mistress's magic still coursed through me. It laced my thoughts with grogginess, trying to force me down into a dreamless sleep that wouldn't leave me with any time to plan.

I couldn't shake her off alone. *Elizabeth, help me!*

Cool air rushed along the inside of my skull, clearing my head. And then I was back, sprawled where I had dropped on the cage floor. I scanned the room, making sure it was empty before sitting up. My muscles ached in protest.

"*I'm sorry,*" the first Elizabeth said. "*I had hoped we'd have more time.*"

I sighed. *Me too.* I shook my head, doing my best to rid myself of the last of Margaret's magic. *But we have to try, anyways. Try . . . something. We'll figure it out.*

I could feel the fondness in the first Elizabeth's voice; it warmed me from the inside out like a fresh cup of tea. "*I believe in you.*"

Optimism wasn't exactly my strong suit. Before all this, I would have said that I couldn't fight for anything. But that was before I had something to fight for—before I had *someone* to fight for.

Now I did. I wasn't letting Alice into this cage without a fight. If I had to spend an eternity trapped in a paper lantern, I'd do it with the knowledge that I tried everything I could.

The curtains at the entrance shifted. "*Get down!*" I dropped to the floor of my cage before the first Elizabeth even finished her sentence. A bolt of pain shot up my arm as I banged my elbow on the cold metal floor, and I lay face-down so it wouldn't show.

"Left to your dreaming still?"

I almost sat up at the sound of Madame Selene's voice, but taking any risk this close to the end felt like a bad idea. I didn't move, forcing myself to take long, even breaths.

"So you know the end has come." She sounded exhausted, her voice even older than usual. "But in this case, that is quite the blessing. It means that the fate planned for you has a chance of coming undone. But . . ." She almost choked on the words, like she had to force them out. "I only hope . . . that you do not . . . hurry. To do so might be your undoing."

Did she know I was listening? I wanted so badly to sit up, to look into her eyes, to try and read the minuscule changes in her expression.

But then the curtains shifted. Bridget's husky voice barked across the room.

"What are you doing here?"

I knew Margaret had come with her. The Mistress's presence wasn't something I had to see or hear to notice. She exuded power, even when she wasn't using that voice or casting spells.

Madame Selene's voice remained as calm as when she gave me my fortune that first night. "It is comforting to be in the presence of such a sure fate. It is a welcome break from the cacophony of the everyday."

It took every ounce of concentration I had to keep my breathing deep and even. Madame Selene *lied* right to the Mistress's face. I tensed, sure she would notice.

Instead, she scoffed. "I would not care about your

276

reasoning even if your tattered mind could string the words together. Leave, now."

There was a whispering rustle of fabric as Madame Selene left. Any lingering doubts I had about her loyalties fled, like birds from a broken cage.

The first Elizabeth sounded as surprised as I felt when she spoke. "*My sister . . . She's on edge. Not as attentive. That's good for us, I suppose.*"

"Are you *sure* you just don't want me to watch her?" Bridget's voice sounded right next to my cage. "It's not like she's gonna get up to anything."

"I have nowhere else to be, my dear." Something like humor clung to the Mistress's tone. "This one's caused me enough trouble. I want to watch every second of her fall. But if you'd rather be elsewhere . . ."

"I have nowhere else to be," Bridget echoed cheerfully. "I'll stick with you."

"Very well." I thought I heard a note of fondness in the Mistress's voice. I supposed if the Mistress could be fond of anyone, it would have to be someone like Bridget. I still didn't really understand what went on between them, but I didn't have the time to dwell on that.

I could practically feel Margaret waiting for me—the only person in a century to challenge her—to die. I could feel her certainty that I would do so tonight.

"*She's not as sure as she pretends to be,*" the first Elizabeth said. "*She's prideful. She won't admit to anyone—even herself—that she doubts, that she's frightened. But she is. We frightened her.*"

I couldn't miss the triumph in the first Elizabeth's voice. And I couldn't say I blamed her after she had watched countless girls fall without being able to stop it. I just hoped that the Mistress's pride overpowered self-preservation, that it would keep her from realizing I still had fight in me until it was too late.

That was, of course, assuming "too late" ever came.

I don't know how long I lay there, pretending to be asleep and reviewing everything I knew about magic and names and power. It was long enough for the crew members to start setting up for the show, for the Mistress and Bridget to accompany me, even through Madame Selene's room and to the backstage area. Every second that ticked by filled me with unease. Madame Selene had told me to wait, but did she really think I should wait *this* long?

The first Elizabeth encouraged me as best as she could, but she didn't try to offer advice. *"It's your power that will win this, Elizabeth. I support you, but I don't want to influence you."*

But what was my power? What did I have that was entirely my own?

"I don't know, but I can feel Margaret's magic. She's compelling you." The first Elizabeth spoke in a soft, gentle voice. *"It's time to wake up."*

I opened my eyes to see Margaret staring at me and grinning. She pressed a finger to her lips. "Shhh!"

Even without Violet's and Mark's voices to silence, the voice had an effect. Everything went silent. And then, I heard Alice's voice, disembodied but achingly close.

"Hello?"

Hearing her in a dream was so different than hearing her in person. Tears welled up in my eyes, and I didn't even try to fight them off. "Alice . . ."

She laughed—the sweet, nervous giggle I'd grown so fond of. "Who . . . Where are you? How do you know my name?"

My power . . . every ounce of my resolve came from her, from my desire to protect her. The first Elizabeth was right: my feelings for her were my own. The circumstances that led to me feeling this way, all of the girls who came before us—that was something the first Elizabeth and Alice had never experienced. That was something *Margaret* had never experienced.

What could be more powerful than a love born from *centuries* of pain and fear and death?

I didn't stop crying. I had an idea, but I wasn't sure enough. It didn't guarantee Alice's safety, but it was all I had.

When I started sobbing audibly, Alice gave a quiet gasp. "What's wrong? Are you okay?"

I wanted to tell her to leave and to run far away so I wouldn't have to risk her. I wanted to tell her sorry, sorry that the only thing standing between her and an eternity of suffering was a scared teenager. But I couldn't get the words past my sobs.

Alice's voice came through, soft and kind. "Hey, don't cry. You . . ."

And then it faded away. She was gone, through the curtain. Margaret grinned at me.

As I wiped the tears from my eyes, the final pieces of my plan fell into place.

thirty-two.

"How can I help?"

The first Elizabeth's voice sounded calm to me. Maybe it just felt that way because I could feel my heart hammering against my ribs, like a bird throwing itself against the bars of its cage. I took a deep breath, listening as Bridget gave her usual speech to the audience.

I need you to put your magic behind my voice. Not exactly like before, but . . . I couldn't quite think of what I wanted in words, but she understood what I meant anyway.

"*I'll help you,*" she said. "*I trust you.*"

For a moment, I felt just a bit calmer.

Bridget skipped off the stage to thunderous applause. I sat as Mark, more of a prop to aid the Mistress's entrance than anything else, went through the motions of his act alone. Suppressing a shudder, I turned to Margaret.

She was already looking at me, of course. Her red-painted

lips curled up in a final grin before she disappeared. The audience gasped. I knew how she must have looked as she appeared in a flurry of fabric: powerful and invulnerable.

They all went silent as she danced. I wondered what Alice thought of her. I knew it was pointless to wonder that, but I did anyway. After all, I carried a piece of Margaret's sister's soul, so it made sense that I wasn't attracted to her. But Alice carried a piece of her ex-lover's soul. And Alice must have found her beautiful, at least at first.

Margaret's dance came to an end. I watched from the wings as she turned, speaking to the audience in her low, seductive voice. "I have a very special act to show you before we part ways. She does not require an introduction—but indulge me for a moment, anyways."

The twin crew members stood on either side of my cage, clinging to the metal bars, but they didn't move. They were waiting for a cue from the Mistress that didn't come.

"You're about to listen to our little songbird. I'm often asked why she's introduced as such, why she doesn't give her name." She smiled, her tone warm and familiar, sickeningly fake to my ears. She spoke with the ease of someone introducing an old friend, not a captive. "The answer to that is simple. I don't introduce her by name because her name doesn't matter. It isn't important." She grinned, and even though she didn't turn in my direction, I knew she meant it for me. *You aren't important.*

Anger pulsed at my temples and curled in my fists.

"The only thing that's important is her song," the Mistress finished. "I do hope you enjoy it." She gestured imperiously with one hand, and my cage rolled forward. The stage lights felt as bright and blinding as they had on that first night. For a moment, I felt horribly sure that my voice would lock up in my throat, just like before.

But I wasn't that girl anymore. And I wasn't alone.

"*I'm with you,*" the first Elizabeth whispered in the back of my mind, and I felt her power coiling warm and sure in the hollow of my throat.

The audience sat, a mass of barely shifting shadows. I squinted into the darkness, hoping for just a little bit of clarity. I knew that somewhere in the front row, Alice would be watching.

I opened my mouth, and I sang for her.

"*If I were a bird*
You'd be the ground
Where I could touch down, safe and sound . . ."

The lyrics didn't carry the same intent as last time. I didn't direct the magic against Margaret at all. Instead, I sent it forward, letting it settle over the audience like a warm quilt. I didn't want to capture their attention and control them like the Mistress did. I just wanted to send a message.

"*I'd give up my wings*
And I'd give up my flight
Because, love, you're the one who sets me alight . . ."

Slowly, my eyes adjusted. I started making out the features of the audience members in the front row.

And I saw her.

Alice sat in the middle of the front row, just as I had an eternity ago. Even in the dim light, I found myself grasping at every detail. Wisps of brown hair sprung out from her messy bun. She wore a soft pink sweater and clutched at the sleeves. Her glossy lips hung open and her shoulders sat tight and tense, but the most captivating thing about her was her eyes. She had those trained on me with a bright blue intensity so great that mine almost watered.

I felt all too aware that this could be the only moment we had together, even if I succeeded. The harder the feathers pulsed along my skin, the slower and more sluggish my heartbeat felt. I wanted to stretch out this moment to make it last an eternity.

But all too quickly, the end of the song came.

"Because flying alone is not really free

Not if I can't choose who flies beside me."

Silence seemed to swallow the echoes of my voice whole. It stretched for one second, two, three. Then fabric rushed down. Everything went breathless and black.

Stiff, ancient velvet rushed against my skin, scooping me up from the metal floor of the cage in a tight cocoon. It stole the breath from my lungs and the pulse from my veins, leaving only my racing thoughts and throbbing feathers. My head started to swim, my thoughts turning hazy.

"Are you proud of yourself?" I couldn't even tell if the Mistress's voice was real or not. The fabric finally loosened, and I drew in a long, shuddering breath. I grasped at the velvety fabric beneath me and struggled to blink away the black dots threatening to overtake my vision.

I'm not going to pass out. I'm not going to pass out. I felt something gentle brush against my cheek, and my head cleared a little. The spots didn't disappear, but they got a little smaller.

The golden cage was nowhere to be seen. Instead, I sat on

283

the floor of a wide, empty room draped in black fabric. I recognized it instantly—I would have even without the smell of death hanging in the air. This was the room where I found Elle.

The room where she died.

With a loud *pop*, the Mistress appeared before me. She stood tall and proud, angry but not afraid. It wasn't enough for her to have power over me, to have power over the audience for the time she stood onstage. She had to have *all* the power. She couldn't stand me taking it for even a second.

She had to have the final word.

"Do you think you're clever?" The Mistress towered over me, hissing. "Was that little song worth it? Your final stand before you die?"

My body ached. I thought of every girl who had died in this room before me. I spoke the names I remembered from lanterns, forcing my tired voice on. "Elle. Rochelle. Martha." I made myself sit up straight, staring into Margaret's diamond-shaped eyes. "Katherine. Ariel. Margot." As I called out the names of the dead girls, the air in the room changed. The air in my lungs felt a bit cooler, energizing.

Margaret didn't feel it. She spoke with a voice full of contempt. "What—"

"You don't even remember their names," I interrupted. "You only ever bothered to learn them because names have power, and you wanted all of it. But you *can't* take all of it, no matter how hard you try."

Something rang high and anxious in my ears, something that tried and failed to be a voice. It didn't sound anything like the first Elizabeth.

"My final song was worth it, Margaret." A shiver ghosted up my spine. I forced myself to my feet, forced myself to meet Margaret's cold gaze. "It was worth it because I knew it would get you in this room with me."

For a second, I felt cold fingertips against my back—a request for consent.

Something that might have been understanding flickered across Margaret's face. I didn't give her time to act on it. Instead, I closed my eyes, braced myself, and answered that silent request. "*Yes.*"

It felt nothing like the dream. It wasn't just one person who flooded me with soft, loving intentions. Instead, hundreds of girls tore at my body with ghostly hands. They filled my veins with the heat of their anger, stole my breath with the force of their fear, tugged at my chest with the weight of their sorrow. It should have been enough to send me to my knees.

But I didn't fall. The ghost of bony arms around my waist kept me upright. Curls tickled the back of my neck, and a warm cheek pressed between my shoulder blades. The first Elizabeth's voice echoed. "*I'm with you.*"

I closed my eyes. All around me I heard shouts, falling fabric, and rushing night air. But I didn't focus on that. Instead, I focused on the girls flooding through me. I could see them on the backs of my eyelids—first a little girl with pigtails, then a woman with a crooked nose, then a girl a few years older than me with clear, dark skin. They flickered one after the other, all of them mouthing the same words. *Finish it. End her.* Their intentions built up in my chest, bubbled up my throat with the white-hot intensity of a volcano. I opened my mouth and screamed something wordless and primal and ancient. A rocket of pure energy streamed from me and met its target.

Margaret answered with a scream of her own, loud enough to knock me off my feet.

I landed hard, as hollow and empty as an old log. The girls vanished, their job finished. I spread my fingers, feeling something hard and rough instead of fabric-covered beneath me. Struggling to draw breath, I opened my eyes to see a cracked, dirty cement floor.

I looked around with my remaining strength. Items from the show were strewn about an old, abandoned-looking building. I saw the paintings, the television screens, and the paper lanterns, which now seemed dim and exhausted. The crew members and the performers stood among them. Madame Selene looked remarkably alert. And there, in the corner, Alice stared with wide eyes at the scene. She opened her mouth to speak.

Margaret beat her to it, yowling like a dying animal. "What did you *do?*"

Crumpled in front of me, Margaret no longer looked powerful. She seemed shocked, staring at her body as red feathers sprouted from her skin. They weren't the feathers from my nightmares—they weren't strong and healthy, able to carry her across the room to end me.

They were the sickly, pulsing feathers she had given countless others, including me. But they were growing far, far faster.

"Mistress!" Bridget ran across the room, eyes wide and horrified. Margaret looked up at her and began to grin in a way that turned my stomach.

"Bridget," she said. "My dear, it's time. Remember our arrangement."

Bridget leaned down, clasping Margaret's hands. Fear and confusion coiled around my wasted chest and squeezed. I opened my mouth to stop this or maybe just to tell Alice, still glassy and frozen with fear, to run. But I couldn't bring in the breath necessary to do it.

An ominous red light began to glow between Bridget and Margaret's clasped hands. Bridget nodded, almost babbling. "Of course. Of course, I'll bring you back. I'll do whatever it takes. I'll—"

"No."

Madame Selene, armed with one of Bridget's knives, leaped forward. She struck like Violet, so quick and sudden that Bridget had no time to dodge or muscle her away. The knife slashed at her throat in a great, sweeping arc. Bridget died clawing at the wound, making horrible gurgling sounds that made me feel sick to my stomach, despite all that she'd done. In the brief moment of silence that followed, I thought I heard Alice gasp.

A moment was all it took for reality to set in. Margaret didn't just scream this time. She *roared*. Madame Selene went flying.

She turned to face me, grin wide and terrible. Red feathers grew from her gums, hanging over her teeth obscenely. "This is the end then, is it, little sister? Well then. I'm taking your prize with me before I go." With awful, horror-movie slowness, she turned to face Alice.

I could still feel the first Elizabeth pulling on me with all of her strength, but she wasn't strong enough to bring me to my feet. I moaned, wanting to do something—anything—as Margaret stood. But I didn't have the strength to fight her.

Margaret advanced, limping but determined. I expected Alice to scream or try to run. But she did neither of those things. Instead, she dove toward the paper lanterns piled haphazardly on the ground. She grabbed the end of the string and tore open the first blue one.

It happened too quickly for shock or confusion to register. I could only watch, dumbfounded, as a cool white mist seeped out of it and coalesced into a familiar human shape—a shape with a braid hanging over one shoulder.

"*Margaret . . .*"

The Mistress went still. "Alice." She held out her arms. Feathers sprouted across them, dangling limp and sickly. "Of course. You've finally come crawling back to me. You've finally realized."

The first Alice's shape stepped toward her. No one moved or even spoke. We were all just as transfixed by the shape as Margaret was. Feathers continued to sprout, turning her dress lumpy and crude.

"*Margaret.*" Almost within Margaret's grasp, the shape paused. "*What I did may have been wrong, but what you have done is far, far worse. The punishment does not fit the crime.*"

The shape took a single step forward, finally close enough for Margaret to touch. But her clutching hands went right through it. Her arms wrapped around only air. All around us, the first Alice's voice echoed louder and more firmly than I had ever heard it.

"*You will not keep me chained here anymore!*"

Alice disappeared, leaving Margaret staring with a dumb, glassy confusion at her empty arms. She fell to her knees, still staring. "Alice . . ." she whispered. Feathers poured from her mouth, covering her lips, her cheeks. Then they covered *everything*. They continued until she no longer looked like a human at all. Just a pile of sickly red feathers. Nothing more.

They heaved with the force of one labored breath. Another. And then they went still.

I stared, half-expecting Margaret to burst from the feathers alive and whole. It didn't seem possible that Margaret had died with a whisper on her lips instead of an angry shout. I simply couldn't wrap my head around it.

I couldn't wrap my head around *anything*. Static swallowed my thoughts like it obscured the picture on a television screen. Gray hovered in the corners of my vision.

Things were happening around me. There might have been someone grabbing my arm. People were making noises. They didn't matter. It seemed like nothing mattered anymore, except . . .

I saw her: my Alice, her blue eyes full of fear and confusion. *How did she know to rip open that lantern?* The thought faded into dust. The answer wasn't important. Alice was safe, and that was the only thing that mattered to me.

I opened my mouth to tell her that everything was okay, but the gray covered my vision and obscured everything. I was gone.

thirty-three.

Floating in the gray was peaceful.

Particles of glowing dust lazily swirled past my field of vision. I didn't feel any need to look around, to try and figure out where I was. There were no more mysteries to unravel or problems to solve. I didn't have to do anything here but exist.

A familiar voice echoed. "Elizabeth . . . Thank you."

The first Elizabeth appeared in front of me, sudden but not startling. Her skin glowed warm and brown, and her curls made a lively halo around her face. She took both of my hands in hers and beamed, looking like a proud mother. I opened my mouth to speak, but no sound came out.

"It's okay." Soft kindness colored her tone, fondness in her eyes. "You can't say anything here. This isn't for you yet. But I wanted to thank you . . . and to tell you how proud I am of you."

She leaned forward, pressing her lips to my forehead.

Warmth spread through me, making me feel sleepy and safe.

She stepped back, smiling. "Take care, won't you?"

The gray started to fade, and I faded with it. But before I did, I saw the first Alice appear in the distance. She looked over her shoulder as the first Elizabeth approached, her dark braid swinging, and she smiled.

Just before I faded completely, I saw them embrace.

I didn't know how long I slept, but when I finally regained consciousness, my limbs felt heavy and real in a way they hadn't in the gray. I shifted, testing them, and heard a whimper. *Was that me?*

"Elizabeth. Are you awake?"

My eyes fluttered open. An older woman with wrinkles around her eyes and thick threads of gray running through her straight black hair gazed down at me with concern. "Elizabeth, can you hear me? Do you understand me?"

The aged voice made me recognize her even though she looked different. "Madame Selene?" I winced as my voice grated against my throat. I tried to look around, but the movement made my head spin. I lay on a comfortable mattress in an unfamiliar room with faux wooden walls.

"Slow down. You're safe here." Her concerned tone stood at odds with the smile on her face, the brightest expression that I had ever seen her make. Even with the lines on her face, she looked much younger than I remembered. "My name is Belinda, actually. It's . . . very good to see you awake, Elizabeth."

"I—" A coughing fit stopped me before I could say more. I sat up in inelegant, jerking motions. My entire body felt strange, but not in a bad way. I felt the silky fabric of a robe against my skin. It didn't occur to me at first why that should be strange, but—I could actually *feel* it. My heart slammed against my ribs, and I peeled away the fabric to confirm.

All my feathers had vanished. Little bloodless pinpricks covered my skin, but that was all. I patted my head and felt strands of fine hair grown to chin-length like they'd never fallen out in the first place.

"I gave you one of my robes to borrow for now," Madame . . . *Belinda* said. "I hope you don't mind."

I hastily wrapped myself back up, feeling heat rush to my cheeks. "What happened?"

"I wanted to ask the same thing, actually." A soft voice sounded from the corner of the room.

I spun hard enough to start a headache thundering in my temples. Alice sat at a small table, looking small and confused with her legs crossed and her hands wrapped around a mug. She stared at me, brows drawn together over her clear blue eyes.

"Oh." Of all the times I'd thought about meeting her, I never stopped to consider what I'd say if I did. *Should I apologize for flashing her?* My face managed to get even warmer. "Um . . . Hi."

"Here." Belinda passed me a bottle of water.

I tried a small sip. I *was* thirsty, I realized. That part of the Mistress's spell was gone, too. I drank most of the bottle all at once. While I did, Belinda spoke.

"I don't know how much you saw," she said. "After the Mistress died, there was chaos. Her magic stopped working on all of us, and that included the magic that kept us from aging. Most of the people in the show . . . Well, the Mistress took them a long time ago. They crumbled into dust."

My chest constricted at the thought of more death. Maybe something showed on my face, because Belinda reached out and squeezed my arm. "They would have died already if not for the Mistress's magic. It was the natural order of things, Elizabeth. That's all. The two women who recited poetry are still alive. And so is Mark. They're gathering their things, right now, in the next room."

"Um . . . room?"

"Right." Belinda let out a long breath. "This is the trailer that we traveled in. This is my room. And the others are in Mark and Violet's room next door." She frowned a little, then added gently, "The storage room—it's at the end of the hall. Still there, somehow, even though the Mistress enhanced it magically to hold everything."

"Magic is . . . complicated," I said, feeling a bit lame. "Some spells survive after the witch. Some don't."

Belinda paused for a moment, then shrugged like it didn't matter. And it probably didn't. "You can talk to Mark and the women in a moment," she said. "I'm sure they'll want to wait for you. But first, maybe . . ." She nodded to Alice, who startled a little.

"I have so many questions." Alice gave her nervous little giggle, then clapped a hand over her mouth. "Sorry. I didn't mean . . ."

"It's okay." *Should I tell her that I know it's a nervous tick?* I decided that would be creepy. "Um, has Belinda told you anything, or . . . ?"

Alice shook her head. "She said I should wait for you to tell me."

"I thought you might prefer that," Belinda said kindly. "Besides, there are things I can't explain. Everything I knew when I was . . ." She paused, and for a moment she looked fifty years older. "Well. I don't know how much of it I can make sense of or if I even want to try."

"I understand." I didn't want to ask anything more of Belinda. She'd been through enough. "Well . . . I'm sorry. I just have no idea where to start." I shifted, curling the sheets beneath my fingers.

"Well, to start . . . Who *are* you?" Alice's eyes were wide and expressive. "When all of those feathers fell off of you, I felt like I had seen a ghost."

Her words managed to catch me by surprise. "I'm . . . Elizabeth." It felt like a ridiculous answer, but I didn't know what else to say. "What do you mean?"

"I've dreamed about you," Alice said. "Ever since I could remember."

Shock turned my thoughts to static for a moment. I found myself scrambling for the right words to say. "What, um . . ." I coughed, then finished off my water bottle while I tried to regain my composure. "What kinds of dreams?"

Alice shrugged. "In most of them, you were doing normal things. Writing in a journal or watching TV or . . . or singing." She wrapped her arms around herself. "I thought your voice was familiar when I heard it tonight, but I didn't realize who you were until I saw your face."

She began to pick up speed, gesturing with her hands as she continued.

"And then—and then! For the past month or so, I didn't dream of you at all, but I'd think of you. A lot. And I *did* have dreams—the same dream, over and over, where I'd hear that *woman's* voice laughing. And I'd feel more and more scared until . . . until I saw a blue paper lantern with my name on it and ripped it open. And doing that made me feel safe." She shivered. "When she came for me tonight, I saw the lantern and I didn't even think. I just reacted."

She paused for a moment, like she couldn't think of the right questions to ask. That was fair, because I couldn't think of the right answers to give.

Finally, she shook her head and spoke. "What is all of this about? Who was that woman? Who are you? What is this place? Who was that woman who came out of the lantern?"

I took a deep breath. Her last question felt like the easiest to answer. "Out of the lantern . . . That was Alice. The dreams might have had something to do with her. She had precognition, so she might have tried to share that with you. Maybe she wanted you to know me a little. I don't know."

My throat felt tight. I'd spent so much time wondering and worrying. I'd imagined facing Alice with all this knowledge about her while she knew nothing about me. But that wasn't true. She knew *something*.

Something obviously wasn't enough, though. "I don't know what you're talking about! *I'm* Alice."

I had to tell her everything. It would be a relief, actually, to let her know.

"You're Alice," I started. "But centuries ago, in a different world, there lived another woman named Alice. A witch." I waited to see if she'd call me crazy, but she only looked at me. She seemed confused but not in disbelief. Considering what had happened, I didn't blame her. "One day, she visited another very powerful witch named Margaret, who lived with her sister. She was named Elizabeth, like me."

It felt like it took hours to finish the story, to explain. I managed to drink two bottles of water and eat a sleeve of crackers Belinda found when my stomach started to growl. When I finally finished, I felt drained and exhausted, but in a good way—for once.

"So I did it. And it's over. Margaret's gone. And the first Elizabeth . . . She's gone, too." Tears prickled along the backs of my eyes, and I bowed my head. I felt the strangest sort of loneliness.

Alice's voice trembled just slightly when she spoke. "So you're telling me I was always supposed to come here? It was my destiny to die, and you just stopped that in its tracks?"

My face heated up. "Well, Margaret's will wasn't exactly destiny, but it was about as powerful, I guess. For over a century of girls it was, anyways."

Alice stood. "I'm sorry. I want to talk more, but I just— you—I—I need a minute." She rushed from the room. I held my breath, half-expecting to hear a door slam and footsteps rushing away outside. I wouldn't have blamed her, wouldn't have even tried to chase her down. But something in me would have died.

Belinda put a hand on my shoulder. It felt very warm. "She'll be okay. You should probably check on Mark and the women now. Maybe after, she'll be able to talk."

"And then?" I looked up at her, putting my hand over hers. "What am I supposed to do then?"

"You live, Elizabeth." Belinda squeezed my shoulder and brushed my bangs a little straighter. "You deserve it."

It should have been comforting, but instead, my stomach twisted itself into knots. "Live where? Margaret erased me from my old life, from my parents, and . . . and what if it's like the storage room? What if it's just like that now, forever?"

The second the words left my lips, I felt sure they were true. My parents would never remember who I was. I would never hear Mom sing along with the car radio again or Dad quote ridiculous poetry or . . . or . . .

I sniffled, swiping at my eyes and willing myself not to sob.

Belinda stroked the top of my head. "You can't know for sure that it's true. But would it make you feel better to have a plan in place?"

"What do you mean?" I looked up at her. Her eyes were full of emotion and very kind.

"I may be a bit out of practice, being in society," she said. "But I think I can pass as your mother. Adopted, surely, but we can work out the specifics later. You don't have to worry about that right now. Just know . . . You won't be left alone. Not anymore."

For a moment, I could only stare at her. Then I reached out, slowly. She opened her arms in response, and I wrapped mine around her. I buried my face in her shoulder and she held me, patting my back and promising that everything would be okay.

Even though I knew I had things to do, I lingered there for a moment.

thirty-four.

Disorientation hit the moment I left Belinda's room. The hallway looked so ordinary. Only the black curtains draped at the end looked out of place. Seeing them sent a shiver up my spine, and I had to turn away. I wasn't ready to go near them yet.

Instead, I went to the next room over. It was only slightly more furnished than Madame Selene's room, with a small TV and a gaming console. Some dirty clothes sat in the corner.

Mark stood in the center, along with the poetry women. They had their heads together and were talking quietly, but they looked up when I came in. The silence that sat between us seemed very loud. I realized that, although I wanted to talk to them, I had no idea what to say. It just felt like the right thing to do.

Mark finally broke the silence. "Violet . . . She's dead, isn't she?"

Tears prickled the backs of my eyes. "I'm sorry, Mark. She

wanted to protect you. But she wouldn't have had to if it wasn't for me, so . . . I'm sorry."

The anguish on Mark's face was almost too much to bear, but I had to bear it. He deserved that much from me, at least.

"I don't blame you," he said. "But I don't think we can talk. Not anymore. I don't . . ." He sighed, bowing his head. He shuffled toward me—then past me and out the door. "Take care of yourself, Elizabeth, okay?"

I opened my mouth to call him back, then closed it. If he stayed, it would be because he still felt guilty, like he had to make something up to me. I didn't want that.

"Don't worry. We will take care of him."

I spun around. One of the poetry women released her partner's hand to shuffle forward. She gripped my shoulders gently. I once thought she looked like my mom. Now, with her eyes trained on me, the similarities were less obvious.

"Lucia and I will take care of him," she said, her tone serious. "We'll make sure he stays safe."

The memory of Violet taking her coat off, revealing her old burns, flashed across my mind. At the very least, they could make sure he didn't return to that. He said that his parents weren't as bad, but they were bad enough to make *this* feel like a valid option.

"Thank you," I said, my voice hoarse.

"Thank *you*," the other poetry woman—Lucia—said. "Kim and I . . . We're so grateful." She clasped Kim's hands again, and they shuffled after Mark.

I stood in the empty room for a moment. I waited until the trembling in my chest calmed down, until my eyes ached a little less. Then I went back to the hallway.

Shuffling came from the curtained entrance to the storage room. Someone had clipped them open, and a shadow moved inside. My heart trembled against my ribs as I went to investigate.

Lit only by the dim light from the open curtain, Alice stood by the birdcage. One hand reached toward the open door. Panic squeezed at my chest as I had a vivid mental image of a ghostly hand pushing her forward and locking the door.

"Get away from there," I said more sharply than I meant to. When Alice startled, my face flushed. I forced myself to speak softer. "Please. I'm sorry. It's just . . . I fought so hard to keep you out of there. It . . ."

Alice tucked a lock of hair behind her ear, giving that small, nervous laugh. "Right. Sorry." She walked over to me and squeezed my arm. "I'm sorry about before. It's just . . . I needed a second to process, and I figured you didn't need to see me freaking out."

She didn't let go of my arm. *Is she doing it for my comfort or hers?* I wasn't sure, but I leaned into it anyway. "No problem. It's, um . . . It's a lot to take in. I get it."

"I'm ready to talk. Do you want to go outside?"

"That sounds great." The thought of leaving this room for the last time made my chest flutter happily. But still, I paused. "Wait a minute, though."

The paper lanterns had somehow found their way back in here. They lay in a dark heap on the floor. I found the end of the string with Elle's lantern on it and picked it up. The ink was more faded than it should have been, and the blue surface had small tears. I peered through one of them but couldn't see any source of light.

I hugged the lantern to my chest, fighting back tears for what felt like the thousandth time. A little noise crawled out of my throat and died in the air. *Free. You're free.*

A small hand squeezed my shoulder—Alice, again. I wondered if she was normally a physical person or if she could just see the way I leaned into her touch.

She shifted her weight from one foot to the other. "Is there anything I can do?"

I thought about telling her that she had already done so much just by existing—that watching her, hoping I could meet her, kept me from giving up.

What had Mark said about Violet?

Alice was my one good thing. *But that's a lot to dump on someone you just met, mutual dreams or not.*

"Let's go outside." My voice came out hoarse. I set Elle's paper lantern down gently on the ground.

Outside, the sky was just starting to lighten. Hard silver stars still twinkled over the distant mountains from my dreams. When I breathed, the chilled air went all the way down to my stomach.

I shivered a little, and Alice was close enough to notice. "Oh! Do you need a coat or something?"

"I don't mind." I breathed deep again. "I'm just glad to be outside."

"Alright." Silence stretched between us, and I didn't know how to break it. I just wanted to stare at her, honestly. But every time I turned to look at her, I caught her glancing away, too.

Finally, she spoke. "Can I ask you a question?"

I didn't even hesitate. "Anything."

It was hard to tell in the gray winter dawn light, but I thought Alice's cheeks turned a little pink. "When I thought of you these past few months," she began, "in class or in my room, do you think that was when you were watching me?"

I shuffled my feet, feeling the gravel under my toes. "Maybe." I chanced a glance at her. I resisted the urge to apologize or justify watching her—after all, she'd been doing the same to me. If I apologized, she might have felt the need to. Instead, I said, "I liked listening to you play."

"Oh! Thank you." Now Alice's cheeks were for *sure* pink. "So, we dreamed about each other. And I could sense you, or something, and I guess we're connected to those girls who were in love all those years ago. Does all that make us . . . soulmates, or something?"

"No," I said. Then I amended. "I mean, um, not exactly. I wondered that, too, but . . ." I took a deep breath. I had skimmed over this part earlier, not wanting to make her uncomfortable. But Alice deserved to know. "When I failed, the first time, I was almost dead. And the first Elizabeth gave me a choice: to die then and be free or to come back, try to fight, and risk the Mistress keeping me trapped forever."

Alice spoke so quietly I almost missed it. "And you chose to come back?"

I nodded. "I told her it wasn't a choice at all. That I had her soul, and you had the first Alice's, so I didn't have any choice in wanting to protect you, in . . . in loving you." It was my first time saying that word out loud. I glanced at her out of the corner of my eye. She seemed surprised but not upset. "And Elizabeth told me that soulmates don't exist,

302

basically. Our hearts are our own. I made my own choices."

"And you chose . . . me?" Alice looked even more confused.

"I came back for, um, a lot of reasons." I shuffled my feet, looking down. "But yes, you're the main reason I came back. I didn't want to see you get hurt. I didn't want you to have to go through what I did. I couldn't stand the thought of you in pain like that, because I want you to be happy."

Alice stayed quiet for a minute. I worried this was finally too much, too fast, too soon. But when she spoke, her voice trembled a little. "I can't believe it. No one's ever . . . I can't believe anyone would care that much about me."

My heart broke a little. "That's Margaret's fault, too. Part of what I told you about earlier. When she came to you as the red bird, she made it so that no one noticed you, so that it would be easier to erase you from your life when she needed to." I shuddered. "I don't think she did it yet, though. Your parents will probably remember you fine."

"My mom," Alice corrected me absently. "But that's the part that really freaked me out before." She sighed, a small crease appearing between her brows. "Everything in my life has been building up to this thing, right? This thing that's never going to happen." A sharp, almost hysterical giggle bubbled up from her lips. I put my hand on her shoulder, ready to pull away if she seemed uncomfortable. But she leaned into it, patting the back of my hand. "Sorry, but like . . . What do we do now?"

"I don't know." I sighed. "I spent so much time imagining this. But to be honest, I didn't really think I would live to see it." Seeing the stricken look on her face, I hurried on. "I

303

was okay with it, though! I mean, I was going to die either way, so I thought at least it could end with me. I'm, um, much happier to *not* be dead, though. I'm just saying, I don't know what comes next."

Alice looked thoughtful. "Well. What did you want to do before all of this?"

My breath caught in my throat. What had I been planning to do? Go to college for music? For singing? Singing was pretty much ruined for me now. My life was never going back to the way it was. And it had never really been a life, anyway—just a build-up to this, like Alice said.

My vision blurred and doubled as tears began to roll down my cheeks.

"Oh. Oh, no, I'm sorry—" Alice wrapped her arms around me, pulling me to her. I didn't want to make her feel bad, but I couldn't stop the sobs that forced their way out of my throat. I could only cling to Alice and hope that by letting her hold me, I could let her know I didn't blame her.

Alice rocked us, making quiet little shushing sounds and patting my back. Her arms were warm, and I could feel her heartbeat against my ear. I counted the beats until my breathing calmed, until the space between my heart and my ribs grew a little wider.

When I could talk again, I tried to lighten the mood. "You know, you'd think an evil witch kidnapping me would put my higher education woes into perspective, but . . ."

Alice gave a little laugh, but she didn't let go of me. "It's going to be okay," she said in a soft, sure voice.

I wiped the tears from my eyes. "Is *this* okay?" I asked. "All of this hugging, and stuff like that. It isn't uncomfortable?"

She drew away. "No. I'm sorry. Does it hurt? Your . . ." She trailed off, gesturing awkwardly at my needle-marked skin.

"No! No, I guess it's just . . . I know this is a lot: a total stranger saving your life and telling you that she lo—" I cut myself off and tried again. "She has these feelings for you, and I don't want you to feel—"

"Obligated?" Alice finished. I nodded. "I get it. I mean, I think I do. And it's sweet. But I don't want you to think that I'm just . . . I mean, I'm grateful, obviously! You saved my life. But that's not why I hugged you. I hugged you because I wanted to." She giggled again, nervous and a little embarrassed. "Besides, if it makes you feel any better, I did my fair share of romanticizing about you, too."

"Oh. Um, really?" My heart did an awkward little skip.

Alice looked down, a nervous smile playing across her lips. "Of course! A cute girl showing up in my dreams over and over? I'm going to draw conclusions." She tucked a lock of hair behind her ear. I wondered if she could feel the heat radiating off my face. *Did she just call me cute?*

"I like what you said, though," she continued, "about our hearts being our own to do whatever we want with them. If we decide to do anything else, that will be our choice, too, right?"

She glanced at me out of the corner of her eye. Impulsively, I reached out and took her hand. Her body visibly relaxed, and she squeezed it back.

I smiled a little. The nerves coiling all through my body suddenly felt a little less intense. "Yeah. I guess I just worry about making choices for the right reasons."

Alice cocked her head to the side. "Isn't both of us wanting it the right reason?"

I liked her philosophy, I decided. And I liked the way she looked at me.

I was almost afraid I was reading into it too much, that I was putting my own thoughts and desires on her. But when I drew closer to her, she didn't pull away. And when I moved a little closer still, she shifted to the balls of her feet, closing the gap between us even more. I reached out to her face with my free hand, and she grabbed it and pressed it to her cheek. We both leaned forward.

"Is this okay?" I asked when I was close enough to feel her breath on my face, to smell her citrusy-sweet shampoo. Everything in her body language pointed to one answer, but I wanted to hear her say it out loud.

"Yes," Alice said, exhaling a laugh. We moved at the same time, pressing our lips together.

It felt nothing like the dream of the first Elizabeth and Alice, when they surrendered to their emotions. Our kiss was soft and gentle, a little clumsy but not in the messy, desperate way theirs had been. This wasn't *about* them. This was about me and Alice. This was about us choosing each other.

And for a moment, the first Elizabeth's voice, happy and teasing, echoed in my head: "*After all, would you really want to be a bird if you could not choose who flew beside you?*" I couldn't be sure if it was just my imagination or if it was her final message to me. It didn't matter.

I didn't know what the coming months or years would

bring. We had plenty of choices ahead of us. But today, I chose Alice. And from the way that she smiled as she pulled me in again, I knew she chose me, too.

Consider dropping a review on Amazon or Goodreads today! Reviews help authors reach readers like you.

Acknowledgments

I came up with the concept for the story that would become *The Songbird's Refrain* in 2015. A lot of love went into bringing it to where it is today, and not all of that love came from me.

To everyone who loved this concept in its earliest form, thank you. I would especially like to thank Lynn—if you hadn't loved that tale of flowers and fate as fiercely as you did, I likely wouldn't have finished it, and this book certainly wouldn't exist. Thank you for seeing the best in my writing for so many years.

To Audrey, Bryn, Christina, Amanda, Erin, Rachel, Abi, Dylan, Elizabeth, Kate and every other critique partner and beta reader who took time out of their busy schedules to help me—this book is what it is because of your diligence, intelligence and honesty. I'm so grateful to you for helping me make this the best version of this story that I could possibly write. Thank you.

To Bodie, who among many other things, deleted each and every unnecessary "s" from my manuscript (I may never type "anyways" again). Your editing is what brought this book from good to great.

To Dane and the team at Ebook Launch, who looked at my rambling mess of a cover design request and still managed to nail it on the first try. I still can't get over how amazing this book looks, thanks to you.

To all of the friends who supported me, thank you. I've known a lot of lovely people in my time, and without them, I wouldn't be the person I am today, writing for the person

I was yesterday. You could have turned away when I began to discover myself, but instead you met me with acceptance and even joy. I don't think I can adequately express how much that means to me.

To all of my writing friends especially—you are all so talented, and I'm so lucky to know you. Special mention goes to the Avosquado (*please imagine avocado emojis here*). Whenever I felt too much, whether it was joy or terror, you were always there to listen and encourage. Thank you for being the best writer's support group (and friends) I could ask for on this journey.

To my family, especially my mom—my love for you cannot be put into words. Thank you for making me the woman I am today.

To Machigerita-P and kokuto_yu-ki, who will certainly never read this—thank you for creating the song and music video, respectively, that would go on to inspire this work. I like to think that the spirit of your creativity is lurking between the lines, like a red-cloaked figure in the back of a circus tent.

To anyone who encouraged me, to the ones who made gifts of aesthetics and fanart, to everyone who sent a nice message or reblogged a post with encouraging tags—thank you. You kept me going on days where I wasn't sure I'd be able to.

And, finally, to you. You've listened to my story, and all 500+ words of sappy acknowledgments. Thank you. Thank you for letting me tell the stories I want to tell. No matter who you are, you *are* important. Know your own power, and surround yourself with the people who make you feel extraordinary.

Thank you for letting me be a part of your life, for a little while.

 **Jillian Maria** enjoys tea, pretty dresses, and ripping out pieces of herself to put in her novels. She writes the books she wants to read, prominently featuring women who are like her in some way or another. A great lover of horror, thriller and mystery novels, most of her stories have some of her own fears lurking in the margins. When she isn't willing imaginary people into existence, she's pursuing a career in public relations and content marketing. A Michigan native, Jillian spends what little free time she has hanging out with her friends, reading too much, singing along to musical numbers, and doting on her cat.

NOV 0 4 2019

CPSIA information can be obtained
at www.ICGtesting.com
Printed in the USA
LVHW111625170919
631360LV00003B/616/P

9 781733 863506